Elephant with
Wooden Leg

I couldn't hear him.

"Can't hear you, Blenheim. The line must be bad."

"Or mad, Hank. I wonder what that would take?"

"What what?"

"What would it take to drive a telephone system out of its mind, eh? So that it wasn't just giving wrong numbers, but madly right ones. Let's see: content-addressable computer memories to shift the conversations . . ."

I stopped listening. A bug was crawling up the window frame across the room. It moved like a cockroach, but I couldn't be sure.

"Look, Blenheim, I'm pretty busy today. Is there something on your mind?"

He plowed right on. ". . . so if you're trying to reserve a seat on the plane to Seville, you'd get a seat at the opera instead. While the person who wants the opera seat is really making an appointment with a barber whose customer is just then talking maybe making a l

GW00771347

Books by John Sladek

The Best of John Sladek
Mechasm

Published by POCKET BOOKS

THE BEST OF JOHN SLADEK

PUBLISHED BY POCKET BOOKS NEW YORK

All stories contained in this collection have previously appeared in *Keep the Giraffe Burning* and *The Steam-Driven Boy,* published in Great Britain by Granada Publishing Limited.

Another *Original* publication of POCKET BOOKS

POCKET BOOKS, a Simon & Schuster division of
GULF & WESTERN CORPORATION
1230 Avenue of the Americas, New York, N.Y. 10020

ISBN: 0-671-83131-3

First Pocket Books printing January, 1981

10 9 8 7 6 5 4 3 2 1

POCKET and colophon are trademarks of Simon & Schuster.

Printed in the U.S.A.

Contents

6   CONTENTS

The Secret
of the Old Custard

Agnes had been wishing for a baby all day, so it was no surprise to her when she peeked through the glass door of the oven and found one. Bundled in clean flannel, it slept on the wire rack while she scrubbed out dusty bottles, fixed formula and dragged down the crib from the attic. By the time Glen came home from work, she was giving the baby its first bottle.

"Look!" she exclaimed. "A baby!"

"O my God, where did you get that?" he said, his healthy pink face going white. "You know it's illegal to have babies."

"I found it. Why illegal?"

"Everything is illegal," he whispered, parting the curtains cautiously to peer out. "Damn near." The face upon Glen's big, pink, cubical head looked somewhat drawn.

"What's the matter?"

"Oh, nothing," he said testily. "We're going to have a gas war, that's all."

Glen was a pathetic figure as he moved so as not to cast a shadow on the curtains. His bright, skin-tight plastic suit was far from skin-tight, and even his cape looked baggy.

"Is it? Is that all?"

"No. Say, that neighbor of ours has been raking leaves an awfully long time."

"Answer me. What's wrong? Something at the office?"

"Everything. The carbon paper and stamps and paper

clips have begun to disappear. I'm afraid they'll blame me. The boss is going to buy a computer to keep track of the loss. Someone stole my ration book on the train, and I found I had last week's newspaper. I.B.M. stock is falling, faintly falling. I have a cold, or something. And— and they're doing away with the Dewey Decimal System."

"You're just overwrought. Why don't you just sit down and dandle our new baby on your knee, while I rustle up some supper."

"Stealing food! It's indecent!"

"Everyone does it, dear. Did you know I found the baby in the oven?"

"No!"

"Yes, the queerest thing. I had just been wishing for a baby and there it was."

"How are the other appliances doing?"

"The automatic washer tried to devour me. The dish-washer is fading away; we must have missed a payment."

"Yes, and we're overdrawn," he said, sighing.

"The garbage disposal is hulking."

"Hulking?"

"Over there."

He did not look where she was pointing. He continued to peer out the window, where the weather situation was building up. A Welcome Wagon moved slowly down the street. He could not read the sign, but he recognized the armor plating and the blue snouts of machine-guns.

"Yes, it just sits there hulking in the sink, and it won't eat anything. It ate its guarantee, though."

The neighbor, a "Mr. Green," paused in his raking to note down the Welcome Wagon's license number.

"Not hulking, darling. *Sulking*." Glen said.

"You have such a big vocabulary. And you don't even read 'How to Build Big Words.' "

"I read *Existential Digest*, when I find the time," he confessed. "But last week I took their test and learned that I'm not alienated enough. That's why I'm so damned proud of our kids."

"Jenny and Peter?"

"The same."

Agnes sighed. "I'd like to read a copy of the *Irish Mail* some time. By the way, the potatoes had poison again. Every eye." She went into the bedroom and laid the baby in its crib.

"I'm going down and turn something on the lathe," Glen announced. "Something good."

"Take off your cape first. You remember the safety laws we learned at P.T.A."

"Lord, how could I forget? Snuff out all candles. Never stand in a canoe or bathtub. Give name, rank and serial number only. Accept checks only if endorsed in your presence. Do not allow rats to chew on matches, should they so desire."

He disappeared, and at the same time, Jenny and Peter came home from school, demanding a "snack." Agnes gave them Hungarian goulash, bread and butter, coffee and apple pie. They paid 95¢ each, and each tipped her 15¢. They were gruff, dour eight-year-olds who talked little while they ate. Agnes was a little afraid of them. After their snack, they belted on guns and went out to hunt other children, before it grew too dark to see them.

Agnes sighed and sat down to her secret transmitter.

"AUNT ROSE EXPECTED BY NOON TRAIN," she sent. "HAVE MADE ARRGTS FOR HER GLADIOLI. SEE THAT FUDGE MEETS 0400 PARIS PLANE WITH CANDLES. THE GARDNER NEEDS TROWEL XPRESS."

In a moment, the reply came. "TROWEL ARRGD. FUDGE HAS NO REPEAT NO CANDLES. WILL USE DDT. HOLD ROSE TILL VIOLET HEARD FROM."

Always the same, tired, meaningless messages. Agnes hid her transmitter in the cookie jar as Glen came up the stairs. He had his own transmitter in the basement, she was sure of that. For all she could tell, it was him she was calling each evening.

"Look at this!" he said proudly, and displayed a newel post.

Outside, a plane dropped leaflets. The neighbor rushed about, raking them up and burning them.

"Every night, the same damned thing," said Glen, grinding his teeth. "Every night they drop leaflets telling us to give up, and every night that bastard burns them all. At this rate, we'll never even learn who 'they' are."

"Is it really so important?" she asked. He would not answer. "Come on, quit hulking. I'll tell you what I want to do. I want to ride on a realway train."

"Railway," he corrected. "You can't, the Public Health Department says that going more than thirty miles an hour contributes significantly to cancer."

"A lot you care what happens to me!"

Glen bowed his great cube of a head resignedly over the television set. "You'll notice," he said, "that it looks like an innocent Army–Navy football game. And so it may be. Perhaps the ball won't blow up when he kicks it. Perhaps that series of plays is only a coincidence."

"Number twenty-seven fades back to pass," she murmured. "What would that mean, I wonder?"

Glen felt her hand reach out to touch his. He held hands with his wife in the darkened living-room, after making sure she was not wearing her poison ring.

"The common cold," he muttered. "*They* call it the 'common cold.' By the way, have I told you we're overdrawn?"

"Yes. It's that damned car. You would have to order all those special features."

"The bazooka in the trunk? The direction-finder radio? The gun turret? Everyone else had had them for years, Agnes. What am I supposed to do if the police start chasing me? Try to outrun them, me with all that armor plate weighing me down?"

"I just don't see what we're going to live on," she said.

"We can eat green stamps until——"

"No, they confiscated them this morning. I forgot to tell you."

The children trooped in, smelling of mud and cordite. Jenny had scratched her knee on a barbed-wire barrier. Agnes applied a Band-Aid to it, and gave them coffee and doughnuts, 15¢. Then she sent them upstairs to brush their teeth.

"And don't, for God's sake, use the tap water," Glen shouted. "There's something in it." He walked into the room where the baby slept and returned in a minute, shaking his head. "Could have sworn I heard him ticking."

"Oh, Glen, let's get away for a few days. Let's go to the country."

"Oh sure. Travel twenty miles over mined roads to look at a couple of cowpies. You wouldn't dare get out of the car, for fear of the deadly snakes. And they've sowed the ground with poison ivy and giant viruses."

"I wouldn't care! Just a breath of fresh air——"

"Sure. Nerve gas. Mustard gas. Tear gas. *Pollen.* Even if we survived, we'd be arrested. No one ever goes into the country any more but dope peddlers, looking for wild tobacco."

Agnes began to cry. Everyone was someone else. No one was who they were. The garbageman scrutinized her messages to the milkman. In the park, the pigeons all wore metal capsules taped to their legs. There were cowpies in the country, but no cows. Even at the supermarket you had to be careful. If you picked out items that seemed to form any sort of pattern . . .

"Are there any Popsicles left?" Glen asked.

"No. There's nothing in the icebox but some leftover custard. We can't eat that, it has a map in it. Glen, what *are* we going to eat?"

"I don't know. How about . . . the baby? Well, don't look at me like that! You found him in the oven, didn't you? Suppose you'd just lit the oven without looking inside?"

"No! I will not give up my baby for a—casserole!"

"All right, all right! I was merely making a suggestion, that's all."

It was dark now, throughout the lead-walled house, except in the kitchen. Out the quartz picture window, dusk was falling on the lawn, on the lifeless body of "Mr. Green." The television showed a panel discussion of eminent doctors, who wondered if eating were not the major cause of insanity.

Agnes went to answer the front door, while Glen went back to the kitchen.

"Excuse me," the priest said to Agnes. "I'm on a sick call. Someone was good enough to loan me his Diaper Service truck, but I'm afraid it has broken down. I wonder if I might use your phone?"

"Certainly, Father. It's bugged, of course."

"Of course."

She stood aside to let him pass, and just then Glen shouted, "The baby! He's at the custard!"

Agnes and the priest dashed out to see. In the clean, well-lighted kitchen, Glen stood gaping at the open refrigerator. Somehow the baby had got it open, for now Agnes could see his diapered bottom and pink toes sticking out from the lower shelf.

"He's hungry," she said.

"Take another look," grated Glen.

Leaning closer she saw the child had pulled the map

from the custard. He was taking photos of it with a tiny, baby-sized camera.

"Microfilm!" she gasped.

"Who are you?" Glen asked the priest.

"I'm——"

"Wait a minute. You don't look like a man of the cloth to me."

It was true, Agnes saw in the light. The breeze rustled the carbon-paper cassock, and she saw it was held together with paper clips. His stole was, on closer examination, a strip of purple stamps.

"If you're a priest," Glen continued, "why do I see on your Roman collar *the letterhead of my office?*"

"Very clever of you," said the man, drawing a pistol from his sleeve. "I'm sorry you saw through our little ruse. Sorry for you, that is."

"Our?" Glen looked at the baby. "Hold on. Agnes, what kind of a vehicle did he drive up in?"

"A diaper truck."

"Aha! I've been waiting a long time to catch up with you—Diaper Man. Your checkered career has gone on far too long."

"Ah, so you've recognized me and my dimple-kneed assistant, have you? But I'm afraid it won't do you much good. You see, we already have the photos, and there is a bullet here for each of you. Don't try to stop us!"

Watching them, the false priest scooped up the baby. "I think I had better kill the two of you in any case," he said. "You already know too much about my *modus operandi.*" The baby in his arms waved the camera gleefully and gooed its derision.

"All right," said Diaper Man. "Face the wall, please."

"Now!" said Glen. He leaped for the gun, while Agnes deftly kicked the camera from the baby's chubby fist.

The infant spy looked startled, but he acted fast, a tiny blur of motion. Scooping up two fistfuls of custard, he flung them in Glen's eyes. Gasping, Glen dropped the gun, as the infamous pair made their dash for freedom.

"You'll never take me alive!" snarled the false priest, vaulting into his truck.

"Let them go," said Glen. He tasted the custard. "I should have realized earlier the baby wasn't ticking, he was *clicking.* But let them go; they won't get far anyway, and we've saved the map. For whatever it's worth."

"Are you all right, darling?"

"Fine. Mmmm. This is pretty good, Agnes."

She blushed at the compliment. There was a muffled explosion, and in the distance they could see flames shooting high in the air.

"Esso bombing the Shell station," said Glen. The gas war had begun.

The Poets of Millgrove, Iowa

THROW AWAY THAT TRUSS

The Astronaut was almost happy about having decapitated a mole while shaving. He'd always wanted to use one of those peculiarly-shaped patches that come in the Band-Aid assortment. But when he dug down in the flight bag and came up with the tin box, he found it empty.

"Jeanne," he muttered.

"What?" Jeanne spread a drop of enamel on her toenail and thrust out her foot to inspect it.

"Did we carry an empty tin Band-Aid box all the way from California?" Without waiting for the obvious answer, he went into the bathroom, stuck a piece of toilet paper over the wound, and began brushing his teeth electrically. The noise cut off the radio's words from the bedroom, and he found himself alone with his face.

The Astronaut's face, if shaved by a Gillette blade, could have aroused bubbles of admiration from the head of an oil millionaire's daughter: "Hmmm, not bad-looking, either!" (But not, he thought, with a piece of bloody toilet paper glued to it.) It featured a square, pink jaw terminating in a chin like a ripe apricot, superbly cloven. His nostrils were slightly flared, sensing danger, his eyebrows seriously straight and incapable of mockery, and his forehead—whatever a forehead should be—intel-

14

ligent, he guessed. Even his teeth were proper reminders
of death, orderly rows of military tombstones.

Today, however, his face showed classic lines of "nervous tension." He and Jeanne had traveled two thousand
miles to his home town, where he was born but not
raised, so that he could give his speech at the Millgrove
Harvest Festival. So that Jeanne could paint her nails and
worry about losing her tan. His own tan was turning yellow, he noted, unplugging the razor.

"—a modern miracle!" the radio blurted.

The Astronaut rolled deodorant under each arm and
behind his knees.

FOR TEENAGERS WITH TROUBLED SKIN

He had left her alone in the MILLGROVE MOTE, as the
faulty neon sign told her, and Jeanne, examining her toes,
remembered she had nothing to read. There was only the
worn and stained copy of *Popular Mechanics* by the toilet.
Seated, wearing her patented lastex with fiberfil inserts,
kolitron panels, nickel-chrome and neoprene clips, six-way stretch girdle that b-r-e-a-t-h-e-d, Jeanne read how
to build her own. She yawned over elaborate schematic
diagrams and finally turned to: "Honey, I got the job!"—
a man embraced a woman who smiled and raised one
foot from the floor. The woman, smiling, embraced the
smiling man with his hand, embracing her, clutching a
rolled-up newspaper. Smiling, they embraced. He embraced this woman with her foot raised in salute.

Jeanne saw the man had chosen one of the following
occupations:

> Accounting
> Advanced Mathematics
> Advertising
> Air Conditioning
>
> Tool Design
> Welding Processes
> **Yard Maintenance**
> Zoo Sanitary Engineering

But after all, as the magazine indicated, life is what
you convert it into, what you Bild-UR-Self. The radio

played the opening chords of a song about a hot rod, and Jeanne's girdle s-i-g-h-e-d.

NOTHING TO BUY

"It don't make you—you know—sterile, does it?" asked the grinning sheriff.

The Astronaut shook his head, then turned its profile to the older man and bent over his Coke.

"That's all right then."

In the rear of the store the druggist, Bud Goslin, his glasses glittering, moved among his glittering bottles of vitamins. He hummed a tune the Astronaut could not identify.

THE KIND OF GIRL TAB HUNTER WANTS

Jeanne picked at the polish on her toenail. At home, the water in the pool would be turning brown and filthy, like the ook in the bottom of the golf bag in the garage. Nola has the key, she thought. Nothing can possibly happen. I'm getting a cold.

The radio gave a recipe. Jeanne wondered how Fritz, her dog, was getting along.

She saw what she had done and took out the bottle of polish remover.

SODIUM PROPIONATE ADDED, TO RETARD SPOILAGE

The Astronaut's gesture took in rubber syringes, steel nail files, lavender soap, paregoric, Kleenex, comic books, morphine, green stamps, and the hidden drawer of condoms.

"There is a certain poetry in all this," he said. The grinning sheriff nodded, and he went on, "a certain poetry. Yes, a certain poetry. You know?" The grinning sheriff and Bud Goslin both nodded.

Teen Queen Screen Dream was the magazine the young girl held. Dropping a quarter in Bud Goslin's hand, she glided toward the door.

"All the nice young nooky come in here," said the sheriff, grinning at his lemon phosphate.

"I know, I know."

Bud Goslin came from behind his counter and rushed at the kids sitting on the floor.

"If you kids don't want to buy any," he said, "you can't sit here reading them all day." He snatched the comics from them and herded the boys out the door. The air-conditioning made a faint coughing sound.

"Christ, I wish I was thirty years younger. All the nice young nooky come in here," said the grinning sheriff.

What am I doing here? the Astronaut asked himself. This is not my town. I was not raised here, only born here.

But he felt the same about the town in which he was raised. This is not my town, what am I doing here? he thought, in London and New York and Menominee, Wisconsin.

In front of the courthouse stood a raw wood platform, from which the Astronaut would "launch" his speech, as the mayor put it. Jeanne would not be there, for reasons of her own. They would give him the key to the city, and the poets of Millgrove would read poems in his honor. He would give his speech, and then they would hang him, as in *Untamed Town,* the innocent man they hang, and all day he listens to them building the raw wood scaffold . . .

He stood up and reached in his pocket.

"Your money's no good," said the druggist.

COUNT THE NUMBER OF BEANS IN THIS JAR

I'll kill him, thought Jeanne, painting her toenails Kotton Kandy. The right foot smeared on the bed. Going on and leaving me without anything to read.

When the polish had dried, she slipped on her sandals and the peasant skirt and the acetate blouse, and went next door to the Sof-Top Ice Cream stand. The rays of the setting sun made her white blouse glow pink. She drank a cup of coffee at the picnic table and watched the sunset. Mosquitoes clung to the warmth of her arms. The girl behind the counter read *The New Liz,* wetting her thumb to turn the pages. A motorcycle went by, and the rider waved to the girl behind the counter. She did not look up. It was dark enough for Jeanne to remove the sunglasses she'd bought in Paris, but she left them in place. Fritz is at Nola's, she assured herself. Nothing can possibly happen.

ASTONISHING AND UNBELIEVABLE!

The parade came by the bunting-draped platform slowly at first; a file of doll-buggies draped in bunting. Little girls dressed in white pushed bunting-draped buggies containing plastic dolls past the platform of wood, draped in bunting. Some of the little girls cried, and their mothers removed them from the parade. Others glided smoothly past, walking to an invisible rhythm, pushing buggies past the mayor, the grinning sheriff, the grinning wife of the mayor, the sheriff's wife, Bud Goslin, and the Astronaut.

The Astronaut wore a dress uniform and saluted when the flag went by. The Millgrove High School band went by, playing "Them Bases." The Astronaut, seeing his country's flag, saluted it, and the flag was carried by, along with the flag of Millgrove High School, green and red. A woman across the street wore Jeanne's French sunglasses, the Astronaut saw.

A series of antique cars passed, each one exactly like the one before. Then came a float depicting the Harvest Festival: corn and pumpkins spilling out of a cornucopia held by Betty Mason, queen of the Harvest Festival. The American Legion followed, marching to some invisible, inaudible rhythm of their own, and the Astronaut saluted his country's flag.

The crowd gathered around the bunting-draped platform, while the mayor raised and lowered the adjustable microphone several times.

"Testing," he breathed cautiously into it, and an unearthly howl went up from the loudspeakers. Bud Goslin dropped to one knee beside the amplifier box. Light blazed from his glasses. He stood up.

"Testing," said the mayor once more, and his amplified voice shouted from the speakers. Chuckling, he added, "Five, four, three, two, one." The crowd laughed.

"Well, I hope everyone is having a good time, here," said the mayor. "I know I am."

A hundred pairs of silver sunglasses tilted to look at him.

"Yes, we're here to celebrate our tenth annual Harvest Festival, and if you ain't having a good time, I say it's your own darned fault!" The crowd smiled.

"We have with us a young man I'm sure all of you know. A boy who was born right here in Millgrove, a real down-to-earth fella—" He paused, while the crowd laughed very hard.

"—seriously though, a boy who represents all that is fine about our town, a boy who has done more, seen more, and I guess traveled more than any of us ever will: Our Astronaut!"

The crowd clapped.

"Bud Goslin here—Bud Goslin—" said the mayor over their noise, "—Bud has written a little poem in Our Astronaut's honor. Bud?"

The druggist stood up, looking ashamed, and read rapidly from a paper:

Our Astronaut

> He soars far upward in the night,
> He comes back safe, to our greatest delight.
> He's the finest boy that Millgrove has got,
> So let's give a big cheer for our Astronaut!

Bud sat down amid mild applause.

"And now, Mr. Fenner, Hal Fenner of the High School English Department, has another poem for our boy," said the mayor. Mr. Fenner was quite young, but had a moustache. His poem was untitled.

"Hail to thee, blithe astronaut," it began. After a number of puzzling references to the Confederate dead, it finished, ". . . blazing a heavenly trail!"

"And now a word from our guest of honor," the mayor announced. The Astronaut walked militarily to the microphone and waited until the applause died.

"I don't know what you came out here to hear," he said. "Let me start like this:

"All this pigs**t you hear about astronauts is so much f**king—uh—s**t. What the f**k, a guy goes up inside this little metal room, see, it don't mean a f**k of a lot. Any f**king body could do it, you see what I mean?"

"Look out, mister," said a hoarse voice at his feet. "There's a lot of *women* here."

"They put you through a lot of f**king tests and all, but what the f**k. Any f**king asshole with two eyes and two hands could operate the c**ksucker. F**king A. All you got is this f**king little—"

"You tell 'em, captain," said a young man in a motorcycle jacket. He had his arm around the woman in the French sunglasses. The grinning sheriff was no longer grinning.

"—this f**king little board with some motherf**king little red and green lights on it, see? And you just throw switches to keep the green lights on. Christ-all-f**king-mighty, even this c**ksucking fairy teacher, with his blithe f**king spirit, could operate the f**ker."

The sheriff stood up, as a man in mirror sunglasses yelled, "We don't talk that way in front of ladies, Mister." The entire crowd was murmuring, not listening now, but only trying to see what was going to happen to him.

"He's drunk!" a woman screamed.

The sheriff got a hammer lock on the Astronaut and eased him away from the microphone. The mayor came forward and adjusted it several times, saying, "Well, folks, I guess our boy was still flying too high, heheh." He was preparing to entertain them with a few imitations, when he discovered he still held the large, wooden, gold-painted key. He walked back to drop it disgustedly on the empty seat, and stood for a moment, watching the Astronaut and the sheriff descend from the platform. The mayor returned to the microphone, saying, "Speaking of high flyers, have you ever heard a chicken hawk? I guess most of you have, and he sounds something like this:"

Then the mayor screamed.

The Best-Seller

A synopsis

BOOK ONE: ADRIAN

Four couples gather at a small seaside hotel for a summer vacation. The hotel is located on an island connected to the mainland by a bridge. On the morning of their arrival, the bridge is washed away by a storm, and they are stranded.

All of them have read the Decameron, and the time is heavy upon them. Instead of relating tales, they elect to make up stories—perhaps true, perhaps not—about the eight of them and their relationships. One person will be delegated each day to chronicle the day's events, embellish them in any way he pleases and read them in the evening to his companions.

Adrian Warner, the architect, draws the first day. He writes in a blunt, honest manner, such as might be expected from a worker in concrete.

He begins with an account of how his wife, Etta, falls in love with another guest, the ruthless young steel executive, Farmer Bill. Caught by the morning storm, these two take shelter in a cave on the beach. Bill returns her caresses but not her love. Though she is beautiful, Farmer Bill despises her as he despises his wife, Theda, a dark-eyed beauty who is also the only brewmistress on this continent. He loves only Glinda Cook, a thin, pale

Southern girl with a dreamy manner, mouse-brown hair and crooked teeth.

Glinda is not, it is true, happy with her husband, Van Cook the popular columnist. But if anyone is captain of her heart, it is the effeminate, smirking hagiographer, Dick Hand.

That evening at dinner, Van Cook recklessly declares that he loves Mrs. Hand, and challenges Dick to a duel. Dick laughingly suggests water pistols of ink and bathing suits.

"Done!" Cook cries fiercely.

The duel takes place on the hotel terrace after dinner. Far down the beach can be heard the plaintive notes of Etta's English horn (a professional musician, she has wandered off by herself to practice). Each of the combatants is given a water pistol loaded with ink the same color as his own bathing trunks: Cook has red, Hand has washable black. The winner is to be decided by Dolly Hand, a large, raw-boned woman of fifty, said to have once been a drum majorette. Dolly seems utterly uninterested.

Cook fouls intentionally, clinching and squirting red ink in Hand's eyes. Dick is somewhat of a coward, and fails to score a hit on his opponent. After a few futile sallies, he contents himself with squirting his ink at Adrian, who is attired in a white dinner jacket. Hand makes several such passes before timekeeper Glinda calls a halt.

When the fight is over, Cook's fouling becomes evident. He has been hitting in the clinches, and the red ink until now has hidden the blood. Glinda begins to tenderly wipe Dick's battered face, but he pulls away from her and, giggling, squirts more black ink at Adrian. The architect, angry, leaps to his feet.

"See here now!" he cries. Then his face grows ashen as he looks down at the black stain on his jacket.

The others demand to know who won—but Dolly, the referee, cannot be found! She has slipped away during the fight, and someone reports seeing her white-booted figure dragging another woman away down the beach. The sound of Etta's horn has stopped.

The stains on Adrian's jacket form letters, spelling "I LOVE Y."

BOOK TWO: THEDA

In his languorous and elliptic style, the sloe-eyed brew-master reveals that all that has gone before is a lie. Adrian Warner is a bitch and a liar. She has lied about the sex of everyone.

First of all it is she, not her husband Etta, who loves the lady foundry exec, Farmer Bill. Yesterday Adrian pretended affection for him, Theda, only until she persuaded him to fall for her. But today, as Theda puts it, the truth outs.

Passing the grape arbor this morning, on his way to the summer house, Theda hears Adrian confess her love for Farmer Bill. Bill rejects this love, declaring in turn that she loves only the manly Etta. Yesterday Etta seemed to love her too, but today, since his night with Dolly on the beach, Etta seems oddly distracted.

Theda is in a hopelessly false position now, sick with love for a confirmed lesbian. Another surprise awaits him as he enters the summer house. Someone throws arms about Theda and kisses him roughly—it is Etta!

"Careful you don't ruin your lip," says Theda, squirming away. Etta laughs heartily at his ignorance of music. Confessing that he has been converted the previous night from heterosexuality by Dolly, Etta invites Theda to spend tonight alone on the beach. Sickened, the brew-master refuses.

Coquettish Van Cook still pursues Dolly, but the big drum major kicks her in the eye at lunch. He appears to flirt instead with her husband, Glinda, a shy Southern boy. Glinda passes Dick Hand a note protesting that he still loves her, and chiding her for her silly infatuation with Van Cook. Theda, who delivers the note, asks her about this.

"It's true," Dick sighs. "I'm a hagiographress, you know. I've even offered to prove a saint in her ancestry—anything—but she refuses to even speak to me. Sometimes I wish Dolly and I could change sex . . ."

The rest of the day is sultry and oppressive with rage and desire, as they all sit around the hotel lounge. Farmer spends hours scrawling Etta's name on the tablecloth, even drawing his profile. Etta glowers at Theda, and tries to tear up his manuscript. In the ensuing fight, Theda loses an ear, which his opponent eats.

BOOK THREE: VAN

With all respect to those who have gone before him, the columnist states that both Theda and Adrian have had their reasons for exaggerating some truths, concealing others. Perhaps it is up to a newspaperman, a dealer in facts, to get at some kind of objectivity about this, as he calls it, "love nest."

He makes no apology about his passion for Dick Hand, but let him cast the first stone, etc., for the truth is, there isn't a man or woman among the eight who isn't queer this third day.

The little balding hagiographer, a former goalee for a prominent Canadian hockey team, now loves none but A. Warner. This architect, designer of the well-known Piedmont Tower and famed for his new building principle, the "concrete truss," remains firm in his attachment to 35-year-old steel magnate Farmer Bill. The ironic quadrangle is complete, for Bill, long supposed an entrenched hetero, has conceived love for the narrator. Farmer Bill came to power through a merger between a steel corporation and the molybdenum trust of which he was co-chairman three years ago. He is now married to the former Theda Baker, and has one child, Ebo.

The women also pursue a hopeless path. Theda loves patient Glinda, a gracious Southern lady with a flair for entertaining, granddaughter of the governor of her state. Glinda married your reporter six years ago. They have no children.

Perhaps for this reason she is drawn to the youthful, robust Dolly Hand, who once danced for a living and can still kick high as a man's eye. Her loves include spinach, basketball, and Etta Peer Warner, the latter hopelessly. Etta allegedly remains true to her former love, the darkly beautiful, brawny brewmistress.

Although the hotel staff do their best to make everyone as comfortable as possible, they are prisoners and they know it. When, late in the afternoon, a plane flies overhead, they all rush out to the beach to wave at it. Passing low, it seems to be flying on out of sight without noticing them. Then as it reaches the mainland, it begins to bank around, coming back for another pass.

Unfortunately it is too low for this maneuver. One wing brushes a treetop, and all at once the plane is a mass of flame, pinwheeling along through the forest. It explodes and settles, starting a forest fire on the mainland that rages all night, seen only by helpless witnesses on the island.

BOOK FOUR: DOLLY

"I am a drug addict. Do not pity me. I ask only for your understanding. This illness has been my secret for a long time. Too long . . ."

Thus begins Dolly's amazing narrative. She gives the background of the persons present: addicts all. Dick, her Dicky-bird, was one addicted to cocaine stirred into cocoa, though now he lives on reserpine stirred into raspberry brandy.

Etta and Adrian mix thorazine and thiamine, laced with Meretran and Serutan. "Pothead" Van Cook and Glinda move in a dream of Nembutal and Hadacol, Darvon and Ritalin, while Farmer Bill and Theda have long existed utterly without food, taking in only methedrine and methanol.

And of course Dolly herself. Having tried every drug in the vocabulary, she is currently experimenting, mixing drugs and liqueurs, such as Benzedrine/Benedictine, such as Dramamine/Drambuie . . . The night gets longer.

Why is it, she wonders, that everyone lies? Wish-fulfillment explains some of it. Van Cook pretended Farmer Bill loved him when the opposite was true. But why does he ignore Theda's love for him? How can he ignore her attempted overdose-suicide? Can he keep claiming she just wanted to hog the horse?

Alas! If Theda could only love Glinda, things might be far different. Poor little Glinda, seven months' PG, half blind from Sterno breakfasts, head-over-heels in love with Theda. She even offers to sit with little Ebo, while Theda takes her overdose.

Adrian, after twice being the object of sick Dick's affections, now returns the favor, but too late. Dick has written a poem to his new love, Etta, comparing the sound of her horn to the clash of waves on the seventh level of his consciousness. Etta tries to use him to get at Dolly, who admits feeling only disgust for the little Serutan-head.

Words crowd in upon Dolly here. She never wanted to be an addict; they told her pot would help her march better, as she led the high school band. It was a lie.

Now she leaves her manuscript for a moment to try to caress Adrian, who is passing in the hall.

Now Adrian's firm hand adds that he has smashed Dolly in the teeth with her steel baton. It is, he adds, manufactured by Farmer Bill's corporation.

BOOK FIVE: ETTA

As only she and her husband know, Etta is an endocrinologist. In clinically precise terms, she details the events of the fifth day.

Food and water are running low, and sanitary facilities are less than adequate. Etta has divided the remainder of the quinine and insect repellant, and rations it strictly. She tries to make do with a crude first-aid kit, treating Theda's ear, Van's eye and the lacerations on Dick's face. Now a clumsy waiter spills *crêpes suzettes* on Farmer Bill's lap, inflicting second-degree burns. Then there is Dolly's mouth requiring dental tools Etta does not have, and Ebo develops diaper rash.

Moving about only before or after the midday heat, the men gather firewood for nightfall, as well as a few straight boards for splints. The women tear up sheets for bandages. It becomes increasingly hard to sterilize everything, especially in time to deliver Glinda's stillborn child, but by working night and day, Etta manages somehow, and somehow manages to keep up her journal, too. Glinda is very weak and very ill. Only the hope of Theda's returning her pitiful love keeps her alive. Etta makes Theda be nice to Glinda.

What a strange thing a woman's friendship is, Etta thinks. Like the love of a leopard, it is wild, shy and a little hurtful. She means not only Glinda's love for Theda but her own love for Dolly, who seems to be, poor silly bitch, in love with her own husband.

But are the males less fickle? Today Adrian spurns

the love of Dick Hand as resolutely as yesterday he sought it. Dick chases him from copse to copse as they gather fuel. Adrian expresses his concern about Glinda.

"I don't care whose child it is," he says hoarsely. "I'll marry her, if she'll have me."

But Glinda loves Theda, who loves her husband Farmer Bill fiercely. Now Farmer Bill brings in Van Cook, who has collapsed with sunstroke, and there is a new tenderness in the industrialist's eyes as he gazes on the stricken man. Ah, what strange things are our endocrines!

Van Cook whispers in his delirium one name over and over: "Etta!"

BOOK SIX: FARMER

In tough, short sentences, Bill spells it out. He loves Etta. No one else. Others may have time to mess around. Not Bill. He knows what he wants, now, after a lifetime of banging around from one job to another. He wants to paint.

Some say it takes guts to do this, to scrap your life and start all over. It doesn't. A man does what he has to do, that's all. Bill has to paint.

It's like breathing. From the chest. Where the heart is. If a man goes wrong, he might as well rip out his heart and smash it. Bill paints, and it's right.

He wants to paint Etta nude, maybe in fresco ten stories high, the way he feels about her. What she has doesn't need a name.

But Etta has a lesbo hang-up with the Southern girl, Gilda, who is mooning over Dolly the Dyke. It's enough to make a real man puke.

Doll is meanwhile gone on her own freaky husband, tricky Dicky. But he as usual has eyes for a man, Van Cook. If you can call him a man, the way he simpers at Adrian Warner.

At least Adrian has real balls. He's hung on Theda, your narrator's wife. The original castrating bitch. She'd like to castrate Bill, and keep him from painting. So he couldn't paint Etta nude. Theda admits as much.

She admits loving Bill.

BOOK SEVEN: GLINDA-GIRL

Because it don't matter what Her sisters thought of Her
that time in Billy Framer's dirty-green roadster out back
of the feed sump, everyone seems like they're dying and
the afternoon's so still you could hear the town bumble-
bee clear down to the Metro. At the Rich Hand place
they got someone's guts strung out hanging all over a
tree at Xmas like firehose because Theda means death
you know some folks don't like Cookie what he done to
Dolly's nipples with the broken Agri-cola bottle was real
mean even if she loves him and what father don't but
Cookie's a idiot certified by Doc Sam H. Smith. She
wishes it was Rich Hand in that car not Billy though he's
a hunchback too he at least has one pretty blue eye like
Etta's dress and loafers made of human skin Rich likes
Dolly because she's his son, that's why he raped her with
the dove-handle.

Because Etta means teat She wishes Her sister Etta
had gone ahead and hatched out the baby inside of her
so that She could play with it but it was by Adrian, their
son from that winter when they were so poor there wasn't
nothing to burn in the stove but dried snot Etta wants to
be nice and flat for Billy. The rats ate his toes off that
same winter and Theda the woman with no jaw she's got
hair on her chest Adrian says he should know he's her
mother but she wants him for some reason he only liked
Theda whipping her with his saw again last winter the
Doc took off her arm up to the elbow and Rever-
end Bregs said to thank God for what's left only this
year they took off the rest of it Theda says it's time to
stop being thankful she lost it the time Adrian's pig hospital burned to the ground the same night he asked Etta
to marry him he still loves her like a brother but she
wants Billy to touch her again with his double finger he's
all fat and greasy She can see why Etta don't want him
no more but Theda does still.

Because She loves Rich Hand even helping him dig
his mother's body up to make sure about the rings and
something had eaten the fingers. She laughed till She split
but no one loves Her but Cookie all covered with sores

from sand fights and can't move his armpit since the railroad flood he says he never hanged a baby before.

BOOK EIGHT: DICK: EPILOGUE

Much has happened since that fateful vacation. After their rescue these eight characters part and go each his own way in search of a story. Dick Hand keeps track of them, however.

He has stopped loving Dolly and divorced her so that he could be with Adrian. Unable to bear this, Dolly has traveled to the tropics where she witnesses an unusual savage torture, organic crucifixion. She settles on this as her mode of suicide, and employs expert savage torturers to help her. First, a *yab-yab,* or needlewood tree, of the proper height and shape is selected. Four of its spiny limbs are severed, and and to their stumps the natives securely bind Dolly's hands and feet. In the fast-growing tropics, the limbs mature again in a matter of hours, piercing her extremities. To torture Dick, Dolly records every minute or her seven-hour agony on the tape, and arranges for it to be mailed to him.

Etta meanwhile has left Adrian and is actually on the train going to live with Dolly when she hears over the radio of the former drum majorette's tragic death. Petrified with horror and grief, Etta descends from the train at once, in the city where by chance Adrian lives.

Adrian has just received a long mash note from Dick, which so depresses him that he goes to the train station, with the half-idea of throwing himself before a train. But he sees Etta and falls in love with her all over again.

It is, alas, too late. In vain does Adrian take Etta to the basement of Piedmont Tower, his architectural triumph, and in vain does he explain the concrete truss. Etta seems like a zombie.

Still she must somehow absorb part of his lecture on superstressed concrete, the circular cantilever, the "primum mobile" principle, etc., for later that night she returns to Piedmont Tower alone, with an acetylene torch. The watchman, having seen her in the company of the architect, suspects nothing as he lets her into the basement once again.

There she straps herself to one of the huge concrete

beams—so like a bent bow—and cuts through the restraining steel support! The beam straightens suddenly, and as Piedmont Tower splits apart from top to bottom, she is flung one hundred thirty stories into the air—to fall impaled on the United Pin Company's giant sign.

Adrian learns of her death that night. He at once books passage on the liner *Henkersmahl,* his hold luggage two steamer trunks. One is filled with nitric acid in a delicate glass envelope; the other with plastic explosives, pickled in turpentine. He supervises their loading to make sure they are placed next to each other. The process of loading naturally breaks the glass envelope, and it will take exactly seventy-two hours for the nitric acid to eat its way out through the thick metal of the trunk.

The second night of its voyage, the *Henkersmahl* sends out a call for help. "Some madman" has poured gasoline into the lifeboats and set them afire. The ship is saved only by casting all lifeboats adrift. Only one ship, the *Vivisectress,* hears the call for help. It is too far away to alter course, just for the loan of a lifeboat or two, though it wishes the *Henkersmahl* well.

The following night a flaming explosion tears out the bottom and sets the ship afire. Blazing oil coats the water all about. The lifejackets are discovered to be soaked with fuel oil. It is suicide to enter the water wearing one.

Adrian seizes the ship's wireless to explain to the world his crime: suicide.

"The cut wrist, the gas oven were not sure enough," he shouts, over the screams of old people and children. "We all know how the life-principle thwarts our pitiful suicide attempts. I had to leave myself no escape at all . . ."

The transmission ends.

Theda has gone to work in a beauty parlor, where she soon falls into the hands of a vicious lesbian white slave ring. After contributing several articles to men's magazines ("Passion Darlings of the Hell Camp for Lesbians"; "Chained Virgins for the Half-Beast Women"; "I Was a Love Slave to the Handmaidens of Horror"; "I Was Possessed by the Harpies from Hell"; "TRAPPED!—By Sex-Amazons of the Queen of Slaughter!") she quietly succumbs, dildoed to death in an alley off a fashionable street.

At the other end of the city in the bohemian district lives her husband, Farmer Bill. No longer a foundry executive, he has become a starving frescoist. He loves Glinda, who has long since returned to her birthplace in the South. Now working as a group therapist in an exclusive brothel, Glinda cares only for her dashing husband, Van Cook.

Van, seeking still to impress Theda with his bravery, has quit his newspaper job and become a hot pilot, a cropduster. He limits his writing to a novel about this new life, THE CROPDUSTERS. ("The story of those happy-go-lucky flyboys who daily face death over Nebraska, to combat the Third Horseman, Pestilence. The story of the planes they fly, the lives they live, the women they love.") But this dangerous, manly occupation does not advance him in Theda's favor at all; she loves Farmer Bill. When Van Cook hears of her death, he sends off a suicide telegram to Dick, then crashes his plane, a Mr. Mulligan, into the corn.

Glinda, unable to endure life without her man, enters a pie-eating contest in the hope of exploding the walls of her intestines. She does not succeed. Having won the contest by consuming thirty-four apricot pies, she is rushed off to the hospital to have her stomach pumped.

Here kind Fate aids her suicide plan. In this ever-summery Southern city the hospital is located in a veritable forest of honeysuckle, rambling rose and lilac. This summer evening the windows of the pumping room are open for coolness, and the sweet scent drifts in. Glinda is unable to speak, so the attendants assume she is a pill suicide attempt. They strap her down, gag her throat open with a plastic funnel and slide the pump tube down to her stomach. Soon a swarm of honeybees, attracted from their murmurous haunts by the smell of pumped apricots, streams into the room.

Glinda lies helpless as the bees chase her attendants away, then enter this curious red flower, hot on the scent of fetid apricot jam. Her death agonies, Dick speculates in what is for him a unusual moment of subjectivity, must have been excruciating.

When Farmer Bill learns of the death of his beloved, he behaves stoically, determined to transmute his feelings into art. He begins a giant, three-story fresco called *Gilda.*

Dick explains here that this is *his* suicide note. He cannot go on without Adrian, and so has already made ample preparation for his own death:

Having acquired a considerable fortune through investments in horticultural enterprises, Dick Hand has been able to purchase control of the government of a small African nation. Carefully he sows the seed of revolt here, employing men expert in such matters to (1) rouse the populace to acts of rebellion, and (2) persuade the government to take ever-stricter reprisals (decimations, unbearably heavy taxes, compulsory military service for the aged and unfit, curfews in effect at strange hours of the day, fines for drinking water, etc.).

The head of state, President Rudy Bung, is so terrified of his own people that he is forever incognito, wearing a black stocking over his head and giving his speeches falsetto. Having made sure the revolution will succeed, Dick secretly spirits away Rudy Bung, kills him and assumes his identity. Alone in the presidential office, Dick is killed at once by the insurgents and—as he had hoped and planned—unspeakable things are done to his corpse.

This last story is a news clipping, of course. In the next column is an item about the collapse of a large wall; the frescoist Farmer Bill is crushed under seventy tons of wet plaster.

The End

The above ending was rejected by the publisher as "too downbeat." Accordingly the author wrote the following ending, which the publisher accepted:

BOOK EIGHT: DICK: EPILOGUE

Much has happened since that fateful vacation. After their rescue these eight characters part and go each his own way in search of a story. Dick Hand keeps track of them, however:

Adrian and Etta decide to face squarely and together the problem of his drinking. She works as a movie extra to raise the money for his psychiatrist. Adrian is fiddling with a brilliant new design for a bomb shelter, the "clam-shell womb." It has the unique feature of being located well *above* the blast area, on a tower several miles high. A world-renowned architect, now crippled with age, comes as a humble student to study and admire Adrian's design. Etta gets a starring rôle, which she declines. Being Adrian's wife, she says, is fame enough for any gal!

Glinda and Van Cook are drifting apart, as he gives up his job with the paper and becomes a pilot, seeding clouds. But after all their differences, after the failure of a dozen ministers and marriage counselors, they are at last reunited by the smallest imaginable of marriage counselors, a gentleman only five pounds three ounces in weight—Van Jr. Van begins work on a novel about his work, THE RAINMAKERS. He flies his GeeBee racer seldom and with great care—now that he has so much love to come home to.

Theda has become a beautician, Mr. Theda, famous on three continents. She has not seen Bill for seventeen years. One day he comes to the beauty parlor dressed in old clothes, his beard rough, his hair a mess, crushing his old hat in hands with broken nails and cracked cuticles. He wants another chance to prove his love for her. Theda means to order him to leave, but she sees tears in his eyes. The sight makes tears spring to her own, and one of her contact lenses is washed out. As they crawl around looking for it, they touch hands . . .

Dick finishes by relating his own story. He has become a successful, gruff but kind-hearted dermatologist. Night calls keep him from thinking too much about Dolly, who has entered a hospital to kick her habit. Nine months drag by, and then one spring day she walks weakly to the gate. There he is, grinning shyly, carrying one of her old batons. They run to embrace one another. She gives her old baton an expert twirl!

"Darling," he says huskily, "it's time to go home."

Is There Death
on Other Planets?

I could have gone back to Earth, thought Peter, hurrying through the fog-shrouded evening. I could have hitch-hiked to California and drunk Cokes at big, fluorescent-lighted drive-ins.

Under every street light Peter paused, looking back. And always the short man with sunglasses was there. One street light behind him.

The gutters of Centerville, capital of the planet Lumpkin, were littered with every variety of garbage. Up to a few hours ago, Peter thought, I was part of that garbage. And now? Now I am a spy, an agent of the U.S. government.

"Me a spy? Here on Lumpkin? I can't do it! I don't even look like a spy. I'm only a space bum. Look, my clothes are canvas from a space ship. My belt is a bit of tarred rope."

The man in the green hat sighed. "You'll do. As the great n-tuple agent Waldmir said, 'More than anyone else, a spy must look like anyone else.'" The face was invisible beneath the brim of the green hat; Peter saw only a row of jagged lower teeth. "Now here's the plan: Lumpkin wants war with the U.S., and they're ready to attack. All they need is for their computer to give the word. When the auspices are right, they'll launch enough missiles to turn the United States of Earth into a fireball.

"Your job is to steal the gizmo that programs the computer. It's a small device, easily concealed in this satchel. You're to deliver it at the rocket terminal to a man called

Adrian. He'll be wearing a green hat like this, and he runs the postcard concession. Got it?"

"Where do I get it, though? And how?"

"It's locked up in the War Department's safe." The man handed Peter a package of cigarettes. "This is in reality a time machine. You'll simply project yourself into the future, watch yourself open the safe, and thus learn the combination. Then you come back into the present and open the safe. Got it?"

"Seems to me there's a paradox there somewhere," mused Peter, scratching his unshaven chin. "But go on. What happens after I deliver it?"

"Once we have the gizmo—which closely resembles a rare old phonograph record, they say—we'll be able to re-program their computer. We'll fool it into believing the war is over, and that the U.S. has won. Our troops will land at once, and our army of trained tourists will follow, to punish the rebellious Lumpkinites." The man ran his tongue over the jagged teeth in a gesture of keen anticipation. "But you'd better get started. There isn't much time."

The little man in sunglasses was still behind him. Ahead was a sign: "ANNIE'S EARTHSIDE BAR. Your home away from home—No Credit." Gratefully Peter ducked into the ill-lit, evil-smelling taproom. How well he knew this derelict retreat—and its lovely proprietress.

Annie came to his table and leaned over him, her raven hair brushing his cheek. Her slender alabaster throat worked with unspoken emotion, as huskily she breathed, "No Credit."

"Annie, you've got to hide me."

But no, already it was too late! Pressing his package of cigarettes, Peter could see that the little man would find him here. Sighing, he ordered a beer and began telling Annie about the fauna of that exotic planet, Earth.

"Then there's the animal *ghosts*. Like the Bansheep. You're walking alone in Ionia at night, see? Suddenly you hear this awful wail: *Gaaaaa*. You see something big and white moving out there in the darkness——"

"You told me that one," she said. The short, weasel-faced man came in and sat at the next table. He removed his sunglasses, and Peter saw that his eyes never strayed from the satchel in Peter's hand.

"Then how about the Grisly Bear? That's the blood-dripping spirit of a bear that prowls the forests of Iowa. He can't get back to his body, see, because someone killed it while he was sleeping. Hibernating. He prowls in Ireland——"

"You said Iowa."

"I meant Ireland, of course. Where all bears' souls go when they are hibernating. That's why they call it Hibernia."

The little man drew a laser gun, just as Peter knew he would. "What have you got in that satchel?" he asked, right on cue.

"Only an old phonograph record." It was a desperate move, but the wrong one.

"Is it the Andrews Sisters, singing 'Apple Blossom Time'? If so, then I arrest you in the name of——"

Taking a tighter grip on the satchel, Peter passed out.

He came to his senses in an opulent apartment, where an equally opulent blonde was arguing with the weasel-like man. Waving a saw, the girl exclaimed, "It's the only way! The satchel is made of some impenetrable material, and he refuses to let go of it."

"Mmf. You may be right, my dear. But can't we just search him and get the key to the satchel?"

"Search him? Ugh! I refuse to touch that filthy creature," she replied, giving a ladylike shudder.

"I'm awake!" Peter announced. "Here, I'll open the case for you."

"Do not try any tricks, my filthy friend," the man snarled. "Roberta, keep him covered with the saw."

While he pretended to ply the lock, Peter stalled for time. "Have I ever told you about the Were-hen? In eastern Iceland, when the hen-bane blooms and the Moon looks like a big deviled egg, the peasants all lock their doors . . ."

In a blur of motion Peter was up, leaping out of the window.

To his astonishment, he found himself back in the same room. "What happened?" he asked, as Roberta once more aimed the saw at him.

"You cannot escape," the ferret-faced man chuckled, "for the simple reason that there is nowhere to escape to. Mmmf. You see, we are in a re-oriented universe, bounded by the walls of this room. *There is no outside.*"

The blonde moved closer, exuding an odor of musk. "For that matter, darling, why try to escape?" she said. "Wouldn't you rather stay here with me—always?"

"If this is a closed universe, what would we have to eat and drink?" asked Peter warily.

"We could live on love. Now put down your satchel and kiss me."

"Nope. There's something phony about you, woman. For one thing, your teeth look too real. And that musk. You seem to be exuding it through a single pore on your lovely alabaster neck."

At that moment, Roberta's whole body began throwing off a deadly, high-voltage corona.

"A robot!" he exclaimed, leaping back. "I should have known. Only robots call everybody darling."

Her arms outstretched, she stumbled about the room after him. ". . . darling . . ." she murmured. With all escape cut off, with her fire-crackling, million-volt arms reaching for him, Peter stumbled over a curiously-carved Buddha, and the room disappeared!

He found himself seated under a blinding white light, while shadowy figures moved about him.

"Who are you? What are you doing here? What is in the—mmmf—the satchel?" asked the ferret's voice, full of scary echoes. Peter did not reply.

"A lovely girl you have. It would be a pity if anything happened to spoil her loveliness . . ."

"You wouldn't dare!" Peter shouted, struggling to rise.

"Wouldn't I? What is your name?"

"Rumplestiltskin is my——" Something cracked him across the side of the head, a stunning blow that made bells ring and stars whirl.

The bells and stars were real. In the control room of the space ship, the alarm signaled a meteor swarm dead ahead. Why isn't the ship automatically veering off? Peter wondered.

The answer was a shadowy figure hunched over the controls, keeping the steering wheel locked on course. It leered round at him, a ferine face with beady eyes and a cruel, mad smile.

"Unless you give me that satchel this instant I shall—

mmmf—send us both to our deaths," the little man chortled.

"Speaking of death," said Peter, "I have heard tales from the West Indies of animal zombies. For example, the Undead Duck."

Deftly, Peter swung the satchel at the preoccupied face. The weasel was slapped to the floor, and the ship began to veer—but too late! Already the meteors were there, patiently boring into the hull!

At once, Peter shifted into reverse, minus the speed of light. Hurtling across the universe, his ship met its counterpart, moving at plus the speed of light. POW! Matter met anti-matter, and both exploded in a flash of light and anti-light! Zungg! Off went Peter at sidewise the speed of light, pursued by residual matter in the form of a slimy alien. It was all mush, with two beady antennae.

"Wait till I get my mandibles on you. Mmmf!" the alien thought at him.

"You've got another think coming," Peter's mind shot back. "I've been pursued by worse."

"Really? Put down your satchel and tell me about it."

Peter did not slacken his pace, but he began to spin his tale. He spoke of a time in India when he had been pursued by a giant, lumbering beast that was totally invisible—the Cellophant!

But now the slimy alien was fast closing the gap between it and its prey! Seeing a lump of inert matter by the roadside, Peter dodged behind it and let the clumsy alien blunder on past.

"Whew!" he said, glancing at the lump of inert matter.

On closer inspection, it proved to be really a fast, late-model car. Peter leaped in and wheeled the machine down the road.

A speck appeared in the rear-view mirror, and grew to a taxi. "It follows, that cab," Peter said grimly. He speeded up, but the taxi continued to gain; now he could make out the driver's sharp nose and beady eyes. Peter knew he could never outrun the taxi, for it was no doubt a disguised ground-effect machine.

And dead ahead was Hairpin Turn. This spot had received its colorful name from the fact that one could throw a hairpin over its edge, and never hear it hit bottom. Often women came to toss bobbypins into the abyss, and listen in vain for their clatter. Just now, in fact, a lone woman stood at the brink, jettisoning *objets de coiffure* over the precipice, and unsuccessfully endeavoring to ascertain their collision with the ground. Disengaging a pin from her lovely auburn hair, she precipitated it into the chasm, and strained her ears without avail, to perceive its impact. She wore a trenchcoat.

As the taxi drew abreast of him, Peter cramped the wheel sharply, then braked to a halt. The taxi plunged into space and tumbled end over end, finally bursting into flames.

"Want a lift?" said Peter, eyeing the girl. Without a word she was in his arms, sobbing and pressing her burning lips to his.

As they drove away, he switched on the radio.

"—and partly cloudy. The most sensational news story of the day is the escape of condemned criminal Peter O'Hare, alias Jean Pierre Lapin, slated to die this noon by the guillotine. Police say the notorious satchel-thief made his escape this morning, from the midst of an interrogation. He is believed hiding out in parallel universes, other dimensions or the Paris sewers."

The glove compartment popped open, and out stepped a small, stoat-like man holding an ugly automatic.

"Mmmf. Would you be so good as to hand over that satchel?" he said, his beady eyes regarding it hungrily. "I shall reward you, of course—with death."

"Have I told you about the Octicorn?" asked Peter. "He is that strange beast of Idaho, having the body of a unicorn and the head of an octopus. He runs madly about, utterly harmless and annoying no one, waving his big flabby head about——"

"I do not care for animal jokes," said the man coldly. "Greta here and I are ingeniously-mutated, carefully trained foxes. Rather, I am a fox, and she is a vixen. I forget whether our children are called pups or cubs. While she stopped your car, I hid myself in your glove compartment. Sly, was it not?"

"A vixen!" Peter exclaimed. "Why, the little minx!" He pinched Greta's cheek, and she bit his finger. "Ow. This reminds me of an Arab I once knew, who ran a flea circus in Iran. Perhaps you've heard of the 1,001 Arabian Mites? No? Well, one day, one of them escaped. To make sure, the Arab had to count them. One mite, two mites, three mites . . ."

Peter worked loose two wires from the dashboard. These he led back to the gas tank, while his story created the necessary diversion. Fishing a copper and a zinc penny from his pocket, he spit upon a piece of paper and placed it between them.

"Nine hundred ninety-eight mites, nine hundred ninety-nine mites . . ." Pressing the two wires to his pennies, Peter flung himself from the car. He felt a blast of heat at his back, and a moment later, heard the distant roar, as the vehicle blew up.

"The old penny-battery trick always works," he mused, watching a column of smoke rise from what once was Kansas City. Great clouds of locusts swept by him, on their way to devastate wheat fields and dominate the planet.

Peter rushed to his anti-grav machine, which opened to the image of his ear-print. As he lifted off, he felt he was not alone in the cabin. Keep calm, he thought, and continued to adjust the huge steam valves as if nothing were wrong. All the same he knew he was being watched by someone—or something. He turned.

And gasped. A Horrible Spore was rolling toward him, seeking food.

"Mmmf," it roared.

There was no time for escape. Already the Spore's pseudopods were reaching for him. Peter's entire life passed before his eyes. Then, for the pseudopods had not yet clutched him, he speculated on the sort of life he could have had.

Roping steers. Reading billboards. Trading in my car, he thought, bitterly. Eating a hotdog, and throwing the wrapper into the Grand Canyon. Taking home movies of the wife and kids. For that matter, a wife and kids.

The Horrible Spore surrounded him, and began its peculiar pattern of digestion, a fission process. Peter was split into two duplicates of himself, and these fissioned in turn. Shortly there were inside the Spore a hundred thousand tiny hims.

Peter knew a bit of mob psychology. He knew that by nature they are quarrelsome and arrogant, willful and dissatisfied. Mobs long to plunder and burn; are terrible when frustrated, and in general, cowards. He keenly felt all these qualities within himselves.

There was nothing to plunder, and only the pseudo-stomach of the Spore to burn. Seizing torches, the crowd set fire to the Spore, which immediately disgorged them on a desert plain.

He had been pent up too long, and now he milled about, frustrated. Great droves of him threw down their satchels and wandered away, weeping, to die cowards' deaths. A few of him, however, took up the abandoned luggage and began piling it in great heaps. They began to quarrel over whether to plunder these satchels or burn them, and soon they were battling furiously.

It was difficult to tell friend from foe in the melée of fists and torches. Friend killed friend, and foe burned foe, until the sun went down on their madness. The last of them fell asleep by the embers of his late allies.

Her name-badge read "Melissa Forbes." She had long, ash-blonde hair and a lab coat that fitted well over soft breasts and hips. She was shaking him awake.

"Doctor, get up. We have work to do."

"Hmm? Oh yes. Must have fallen asleep over the Fromminger equations. But who wouldn't?" He grinned, and Melissa caught her breath. Dr. Peter O'Hare was well aware of the power of his crooked grin. "Now where were we?"

"We must save the universe from certain destruction," she said throatily, "Two parallel universes have got off course. They will collide in minutes, exploding into a drop of pure energy, unless——"

"Do you mean——?" he gasped, struggling into his own lab coat. One side had been cut away, to accommodate the satchel he always seemed to carry.

"Yes, Doctor. Only you can find a way out."

A few calculations on his slide rule, and the scientist had done so. "We will each go back into the past of one of the universes. There we will make the necessary adjustments to ensure that the two will never meet. Alas, we would never be able to return."

"Then I can tell you," she sobbed. "Doctor, I love you." A bright tear ran down her cheek and splashed into the test tube she grasped.

"Do you mean——?" he gasped, and took her in his arms.

"No." She pushed him away. "There isn't time, darling. If only you could give me some token of remembrance—say that satchel."

Peter turned away to hide his own emotion, and as he did so, he realized the lab had only three walls! Where the fourth should have been was a dark void, filled with hostile, gleaming eyes. It was a trap, then. How well he knew the Lumpkinite police, with their combination lineup and psychodrama!

Snatching up a convenient gun, Peter fired into the crowd. "Sic semper tyrannus!" he cried, leaping for the stage door.

"All well and good," he said, pocketing the weapon, "but how am I to get out of this hell?"

He realized for the first time that the incessant drumming had stopped. Those savages were surely up to some devilment, he thought.

A white man stepped out of a thicket. He wore a white, flowing robe and had a dissipated look about him.

"Are you by any chance the White God?" asked Peter.

"I am Virgil, come to guide you out of this hell."

"Great Dante's ghost! What do they call this place, O noble Mantuan?"

The poet looked blank for a moment. "Oh, the Slough of Despond, I guess. Here, Pilgrim, let me carry thy burden."

"Hold this instead," snarled Peter, and pumped eight slugs into Virgil. The poet assumed his true shape and scuttled away.

Adrian lay tied up in the alley behind the rocket terminal. As he loosened his bonds, Peter related the case to him.

"Rub your wrists to restore circulation, while I explain. They tied me up, too, and blindfolded me. They took me to another planet, but I counted the turns the space ship made, so I could find my way back. They're an unscrupulous gang of servo-mechanisms, all right. The old phonograph record was just a blind. What they really wanted was *the satchel itself*."

"The satchel?"

"It's an antique, worth millions. The owner was stealing it from himself, to collect the insurance. But I wasn't sure, so I hid the old phonograph record."

"Quick thinking, chief. Where did you hide it?"

"In the most obvious place—*Annie's old phonograph.*"

"Amazing! But how did you know he wasn't the real Virgil?" asked Adrian.

"He gave himself away when he mentioned the Slough of Despond. You see, William Faulkner didn't invent the name until years *after* the *real* John Bunyan's death. From there on, the rest was easy."

Peter punched the dents out of Adrian's green hat and handed it to him. He held a pocket mirror while Adrian put on the hat. Then Peter reloaded his gun and put eight slugs in him.

Well, that's the spy game, he thought. The good die young. You never get rich, but you have your kicks. One week the Arcrusian space pirates get out of hand, and the next week, at about the same time, something rises out of the sea to nibble at Los Angeles.

I'll miss old Earth, though. Along about now it's turning into a ball of flame, as Lumpkin goes to war.

Chuckling, he pushed open the door of Annie's Earthside Bar.

The Happy Breed

1987 A.D.

"I don't know," said James, lifting himself from the cushions scattered like bright leaves on the floor. "I can't say that I'm really, you know, *happy*. Gin or something phony?"

"Aw, man, don't give me decisions, give me drink," said Porter. He lay across the black, tufted chaise that he called James's "shrink couch."

"Gin it is, then." James thumbed a button, and a martini glass, frosty and edible-looking, slid into the wall niche and filled. Holding it by the stem, he passed it to Porter, then raised his shaggy brows at Marya.

"Nada," she said. She was sprawled in a "chair," really a piece of sculpture, and one of her bare feet had reached out to touch Porter's leg.

James made himself a martini and looked at it with distaste. If you broke this glass, he thought, it would not leave any sharp edges to, say, cut your wrists on.

"What was I saying? Oh—I can't say I'm really *happy*, but then I'm not—uh——"

"Sad?" volunteered Marya, peering from under the brim of her deerstalker.

"Depressed. I'm not depressed. So I must be happy," he finished, and hid his confusion behind the glass. As he sipped, he looked her over, from her shapely calves

44

to her ugly brown deerstalker. Last year at this time, she'd been wearing a baseball cap, blue with gold piping. It was easy to remember it, for this year all the girls in the Village were wearing baseball caps. Marya Katyovna was always ahead of the pack, in her dress as well as in her paintings.

"How do you know you're happy?" she said. "Last week, I thought I was happy, too. I'd just finished my best work, and I tried to drown myself. The Machine pulled the drain. Then I was sad."

"Why did you try to kill yourself?" James asked, trying to keep her in focus.

"I had this idea that after a perfect work, the artist should be destroyed. Dürer used to destroy the plates of his engravings, after a few impressions."

"He did it for money," muttered Porter.

"All right then, like that architect in Arabia. After he created his *magnum opus,* the Sultan had him blinded, so he couldn't do any cheap copies. See what I mean? An artist's life is supposed to lead toward his masterpiece, not away from it."

Porter opened his eyes and said, "Exist! The end of life is life. Exist, man, that's all you gotta do."

"That sounds like cheap existentialism," she snarled, withdrawing her foot. "Porter, you are getting more and more like those damned Mussulmen."

Porter smiled angrily and closed his eyes.

It was time to change the subject.

"Have you heard the one about the Martian who thought he was an earthman?" James said, using his pleasant-professional tone. "Well, he went to his psychiatrist——"

As he went on with the joke, he studied the two of them. Marya was no worry, even with her dramatic suicide attempts. But Porter was a mess.

O. Henry Porter was his full adopted name, after some minor earlier writer. Porter was a writer, too, or had been. Up to a few months ago, he'd been considered a genius—one of the few of the twentieth century.

Something had happened. Perhaps it was the general decline in reading. Perhaps there was an element of self-defeat in him. For whatever reason, Porter had become little more than a vegetable. Even when he spoke, it was in the cheapest clichés of the old "Hip" of twenty years ago. And he spoke less and less.

Vaguely, James tied it in with the Machines. Porter had been exposed to the therapeutic environment machines longer than most, and perhaps his genius was entangled with whatever they were curing. James had been too long away from his practice to guess how this was, but he recalled similar baby/bathwater cases.

" 'So that's why it glows in the dark,' " James finished. As he'd expected, Marya laughed, but Porter only forced a smile, over and above his usual smirk of mystical bliss.

"It's an old joke," James apologized.

"You are an old joke," Porter enunciated. "A headshrinker without no heads to shrink. What the hell do you do all day?"

"What's eating you?" said Marya to the ex-writer. "What brought you up from the depths?"

James fetched another drink from the wall niche. Before bringing it to his lips, he said, "I think I need some new friends."

As soon as they were gone, he regretted his boorishness. Yet somehow there seemed to be no reason for acting human any more. He was no longer a psychiatrist, and they were not his patients. Any little trauma he might have wreaked would be quickly repaired by their Machines. Even so, he'd have made an extra effort to sidestep the neuroses of his friends if he were not able to dial FRIENDS and get a new set.

Only a few years had passed since the Machines began seeing to the happiness, health and continuation of the human race, but he could barely remember life before Them. In the dusty mirror of his unused memory, there remained but a few clear spots. He recalled his work as a psychiatrist on the Therapeutic Environment tests.

He recalled the argument with Brody.

"Sure, they work on a few test cases. But so far these gadgets haven't done anything a qualified psychiatrist couldn't do," said James.

"Agreed," said his superior, "but they haven't made any mistakes, either. Doctor, these people are cured. Moreover, they're happy!"

Frank envy was written all over Bro Brody's heavy

face. James knew his superior was having trouble with his wife again.

"But, Doctor," James began, "these people are *not* being taught to deal with their environment. Their environment is learning to deal with them. That isn't medicine, it's spoon-feeding!

"When someone is depressed, he gets a dose of Ritalin, bouncy tunes on the Muzik, and some dear friend drops in on him unexpectedly. If he is manic or violent, he gets Thorazine, sweet music, melancholy stories on TV, and maybe a cool bath. If he's bored, he gets excitement; if he's frustrated, he gets something to break; if——"

Brody interrupted. "All right," he said. "Let me ask you the sixty-four-dollar question: Could you do better?"

No one could do better. The vast complex of Therapeutic Environment Machines which grew up advanced Medicine a millennium in a year. The government took control, to ensure that anyone of however modest means could have at his disposal the top specialists in the country, with all the latest data and techniques. In effect, these specialists were on duty round-the-clock in each patient's home, keeping him alive, healthy, and reasonably happy.

Nor were they limited to treatment. The Machines had extensions clawing through the jungles of the world, spying on witch-doctors and learning new medicines. Drug and dietary research became their domain, as did scientific farming and birth control. By 1985, when it became manifest that machines could and did run everything better, and that nearly everyone in the country wanted to be a patient, the U.S. government capitulated. Other nations followed suit.

By now, no one worked at all, so far as James knew. They had one and only one duty—to be happy.

And happy they were. One's happiness was guaranteed, by every relay and transistor from those that ran one's air-conditioner right up to those in the chief complex of computers called MEDCENTRAL in Washington—or was it The Hague, now? James had not read a newspaper since people had stopped killing each other, since the news had dwindled to weather and sports. In fact, he'd stopped reading the newspaper when the M.D. Employment Wanted ads began to appear.

There were no jobs, only Happiness Jobs—make-work invented by the Machines. In such a job, one could never find an insoluble, or even difficult problem. One finished one's daily quota without tiring one's mind or body. Work was no longer work, it was therapy, and, as such, it was constantly rewarding.

Happiness, normality. James saw the personalities of all people drifting downward, like so many different snowflakes falling at last into the common, shapeless mound.

"I'm drunk, that's all," he said aloud. "Alcohol's a depressant. Need another drink."

He lurched slightly as he crossed the room to the niche. The floor must have detected it, for instead of a martini, his pressing the button drew blood from his thumb. In a second, the wall had analyzed his blood and presented him with a glass of liquid. A sign lit: "Drink this down at once. Replace glass on sink."

He drained the pleasant-tasting liquid and at once felt drowsy and warm. Somehow he found his way to the bedroom, the door moving to accommodate him, and he fell into bed.

As soon as James R. Fairchild, AAAAGTR-RHOLA was asleep, mechanisms went into action to save his life. That is, he was in no immediate danger, but MED 8 reported his decrease in life expectancy by .00005 years as a result of overindulgence, and MED 19 evaluated his behavior, recorded on magnetic tape, as increasing his suicide index by a dangerous 15 points. A diagnostic unit detached itself from the bathroom wall and careened into the bedroom, halting silently and precisely by his side. It drew more blood, checked pulse, temp, resp, heart and brain-wave pattern, and X-rayed his abdomen. Not instructed to go on to patcolar reflexes, it packed up and zoomed away.

In the living-room, a housekeeper buzzed about its work, destroying the orange cushions, the sculpture, the couch and the carpet. The walls took on an almost imperceptibly warmer tone. The new carpet matched them.

The furniture—chosen and delivered without the sleeping man's knowledge—was Queen Anne, enough to crowd the room. Its polyethylene wraps were left on while the room was disinfected.

In the kitchen, PHARMO 9 ordered and received a new supply of anti-depressants.

It was always the sound of a tractor that awoke Lloyd Young, and though he knew it was an artificial sound, it cheered him all the same. Almost made his day start right. He lay and listened to it awhile before opening his eyes.

Hell, the real tractors didn't make no sound at all. They worked in the night, burrowing along and plowing a field in one hour that would take a man twelve. Machines pumped strange new chemicals into the soil, and applied heat, to force two full crops of corn in one short Minnesota summer.

There wasn't much use being a farmer, but he'd always wanted to have a farm, and the Machines said you could have what you wanted. Lloyd was about the only man in these parts still living in the country by now, just him and twelve cows and a half-blind dog, Joe. There wasn't much to do, with Them running it all. He could go watch his cows being milked, or walk down with Joe to fetch the mail, or watch TV. But it was quiet and peaceful, the way he liked it.

Except for Them and Their pesky ways. They'd wanted to give Joe a new set of machine eyes, but Lloyd said no, if the good Lord wanted him to see, he'd never have blinded him. That was just the way he'd answered Them about the heart operation, too. Seemed almost like They didn't have enough to keep 'em busy, or something. They was always worrying about him, him who took real good care of himself all through M.I.T. and twenty years of engineering.

When They'd automated, he'd been done out of a job, but he couldn't hold that against Them. If Machines was better engineers than him, well, shoot——!

He opened his eyes and saw he'd be late for milking if he didn't look sharp. Without even thinking, he chose the baby blue overalls with pink piping from his wardrobe, jammed a blue straw hat on his head, and loped out to the kitchen.

His pail was by the door. It was a silver one today—yesterday it had been gold. He decided he liked the silver better, for it made the milk look cool and white.

The kitchen door wouldn't budge, and Lloyd realized

it meant for him to put on his shoes. Damnit, he'd of liked to go barefoot. Damnit, he would of.

He would of liked to do his own milking, too, but They had explained how dangerous it was. Why, you could get kicked in the head before you knew it! Reluctantly, the Machines allowed him to milk, each morning, one cow that had been tranquilized and all its legs fastened in a steel frame.

He slipped on his comfortable blue brogans and picked up his pail again. This time the kitchen door opened easily, and as it did, a rooster crowed in the distance.

Yes, there had been a lot of doors closed in Lloyd's face. Enough to have made a bitter man of him, but for Them. He knew They could be trusted, even if They had done him out of his job in nineteen and seventy. For ten years, he had just bummed around, trying to get factory work, anything. At the end of his rope, until They saved him.

In the barn, Betsy, his favorite Jersey, had been knocked out and shackled by the time he arrived. The Muzik played a bouncy, lighthearted tune, perfect for milking.

No, it wasn't Machines that did you dirt, he knew. It was people. People and animals, live things always trying to kick you in the head. As much as he liked Joe and Betsy, which was more than he liked people, he didn't really trust 'em.

You could trust Machines. They took good care of you. The only trouble with Them was—well, They *knew* so much. They were always so damned smart and busy, They made you feel kind of useless. Almost like you were standing in their light.

It was altogether an enjoyable ten minutes, and when he stepped into the cool milkhouse to empty the pail into a receptacle that led God knew where, Lloyd had a strange impulse. He wanted to taste the warm milk, something he'd promised not to do. They had warned him about diseases, but he just felt too good to worry this morning. He tilted the silver pail to his lips——

And a bolt of lightning knocked it away, slamming him to the floor. At least it felt like a bolt of lightning. He tried to get up and found he couldn't move. A green mist began spraying from the ceiling. Now what the hell

was that? he wondered, and drifted off to sleep in the
puddle of spilled milk.

The first MED unit reported no superficial injuries.
Lloyd C. Young, AAAAMTL-RH01AB was resting well,
pulse high, resp normal. MED 8 disinfected the area
thoroughly and destroyed all traces of the raw milk.
While MED 19 pumped his stomach and swabbed nose,
throat, esophagus and trachea, MED 8 cut away and
destroyed all his clothing. An emergency heating unit
warmed him until fresh clothing could be constructed.
Despite the cushioned floor, the patient had broken a toe
in falling. It was decided not to move him, but to erect
bed and traction on the spot. MED 19 recommended
therapeutic punishment.

When Lloyd awoke, the television came to life, showing an amiable-looking man with white hair.
"You have my sympathy," the man said. "You have
just survived what we call a 'Number-One Killer Accident,' a bad fall in your home. Our machines were in
part responsible for this, in the course of saving your life
from——" The man hesitated, while a sign flashed behind
him: "BACTERIAL POISONING." Then he went on, "—by
physically removing you from the danger. Since this
was the only course open to us, your injury could not
have been avoided.
"Except by you. Only *you* can save your life, finally."
The man pointed at Lloyd. "Only *you* can make all of
modern science worthwhile. And only *you* can help lower
our shocking death toll. You will cooperate, won't you?
Thank you." The screen went dark, and the set dispensed
a pamphlet.
It was a complete account of his accident, and a
warning about unpasteurized milk. He would be in bed for
a week, it said, and urged him to make use of his telephone and FRIENDS.

Professor David Wattleigh sat in the tepid water of
his swimming pool in Southern California and longed to
swim. But it was forbidden. The gadgets had some way
of knowing what he was doing, he supposed, for every
time he immersed himself deeper than his chest, the mo-
tor of the resuscitator clattered a warning from poolside.

It sounded like the snarl of a sheep-dog. Or perhaps, he reflected, a Hound of Heaven, an anti-Mephistopheles, come to tempt him into virtue.

Wattleigh sat perfectly still for a moment, then reluctantly he heaved his plump pink body out of the water. Ah, it was no better than a bath. As he passed into the house, he cast a glance of contempt and loathing at the squat machine.

It seemed as if anything he wished to do were forbidden. Since the day he'd been forced to abandon Nineteenth-Century English Literature, the constraints of *mechanica* had tightened about Wattleigh, closing him off from his old pleasures one by one. Gone were his pipe and port, his lavish luncheons, his morning swim. In place of his library, there now existed a kind of vending machine that each day "vended" him two pages of thoroughly bowdlerized Dickens. Gay, colorful, witty passages they were, too, set in large Schoolbook type. They depressed him thoroughly.

Yet he had not given up entirely. He pronounced anathema upon the Machines in every letter he wrote to Delphinia, an imaginary lady of his acquaintance, and he feuded with the dining-room about his luncheons.

If the dining-room did not actually withhold food from him, it did its best to take away his appetite. At various times, it had painted itself bilious yellow, played loud and raucous music and flashed portraits of naked fat people upon its walls. Each day it had some new trick to play, and each day, Wattleigh outwitted it.

Now he girded on his academic gown and entered the dining-room, prepared for battle. Today, he saw, the room was upholstered in green velvet and lit by a gold chandelier. The dining table was heavy, solid oak, unfinished. There was not a particle of food upon it.

Instead there was a blonde, comely woman.

"Hello," she said, jumping down from the table. "Are you Professor David Wattleigh? I'm Helena Hershee, from New York, I got your name through FRIENDS, and I just had to look you up."

"I—how do you do?" he stammered. By way of answer, she unzipped her dress.

MED 19 approved what followed as tending to weaken that harmful delusion, "Delphinia." MED 8 projected a year of treatment, and found the resultant weight loss could add as much as 12 years to patient Wattleigh's life.

After Helena had gone to sleep, the Professor played a few games with the Ideal Chessplayer. Wattleigh had once belonged to a chess club, and he did not want to lose touch with the game entirely. And one did get rusty. He was amazed at how many times the Ideal Chessplayer had to actually cheat to let him win.

But win he did, game after game, and the Ideal Chessplayer each time would wag its plastic head from side to side and chuckle, "Well, you really got me that time, Wattleigh. Care for another?"

"No," said Wattleigh, finally disgusted. Obediently the machine folded its board into its chest and rolled off somewhere.

Wattleigh sat at his desk and started a letter to Delphinia.

"My Darling Delphinia," scratched his old steel pen on the fine, laid paper. "Today a thought occurred to me while I was bathing at Brighton. I have often told you, and as often complained of the behavior of my servant, M——. It, for I cannot bring myself to call it 'him' or 'she,' has been most distressing about my writing to you, even to the point of blunting my pen and hiding my paper. I have not discharged it for this disgraceful show, for I am bound to it—yes, *bound* to it by a strange and terrible secret fate that makes me doubt at times which is master and which, man. It reminds one of several old comedies, in which, man and master having changed roles, and maid and mistress likewise, they meet. I mean, of course, in the works of——"

Here the letter proper ended, for the professor could think of no name to fit. After writing, and lining out, "Dickens, Dryden, Dostoyevsky, Racine, Rousseau, Camus," and a dozen more, his inkwell ran dry. He knew it would be no use to inquire after more ink, for the Machine was dead set against this letter——

Looking out the window, he saw a bright pink-and-yellow striped ambulance. So, the doctor next door was going off to zombie-land, was he? Or, correctly, to the Hospital for the Asocial. In the East, they called them "Mussulmen"; here, "zombies," but it all came to the same thing: the living dead, who needed no elaborate houses, games, ink. They needed only intravenous nourishment, and little of that. The drapes drew themselves, so Wattleigh knew the doctor was being carried out then. He finished his interrupted thought.

—and in any case, he was wholly dissatisfied with this letter. He had not mentioned Helena, luncheon, his resuscitator which growled at him, and so much more. Volumes more, if only he had the ink to write, if only his memory would not fail him when he sat down to write, if only——

James stood with his elbow on the marble mantelpiece of Marya's apartment, surveying the other guests and sizing them up. There was a farmer from Minnesota, incredibly dull, who claimed to have once been an engineer, but who hardly knew what a slide rule was. There was Marya in the company of some muscular young man James disliked at sight, an ex-mathematician named Dewes or Clewes. Marya was about to play chess with a slightly plump Californian, while his girl, a pretty little blonde thing called Helena Hershee, stood by to kibitz.

"I'm practically a champion," explained Wattleigh, setting up the pieces. "So perhaps I ought to give you a rook or two."

"If you like," said Marya. "I haven't played in years. About all I remember is the Fool's Mate."

James drifted over to Helena's side and watched the game.

"I'm James Fairchild," he said, and added almost defiantly, "M.D."

Helena's lips, too bright with lipstick, parted. "I've heard of you," she murmured. "You're the aggressive Dr. Fairchild who runs through friends so fast, aren't you?"

Marya's eyes came up from the game. Seemingly her eyes had no pupils, and James guessed she was full of Ritalin. "James is not in the least aggressive," she said. "But he gets mad when you won't let him psychoanalyze you."

"Don't disturb the game," said Wattleigh. He put both elbows on the table in an attitude of concentration.

Helena had not heard Marya's remark. She had turned to watch the muscular mathematician lecture Lloyd.

"Hell yes. The Machines got to do all the bearing and raising of children. Otherwise, we'd have a population explosion, you get me? I mean, we'd run out of food——"

"You really pick 'em, Marya," said James. He gestured at the young man. "Whatever became of that 'writer'? Porter, was it? Christ, I can still hear him saying, 'exist, man!' " James snorted.

Marya's head came up once more, and tears stood in her pupilless eyes. "Porter went to the hospital. He's a Mussulman, now," she said brightly. "I wish I could feel something for him, but They won't let me."

"—it's like Malthus's law, or somebody's law. Animals grow faster than vegetables," the mathematician went on, speaking to the farmer.

"Checkmate," said Marya, and bounced to her feet. "James, have you a Sugarsmoke? Chocolate?"

He produced a bright orange cigar. "Only Bitter Orange, I'm afraid. Ask the Machine."

"I'm afraid to ask it for anything, today," she said. "It keeps drugging me—James, Porter was put away a month ago, and I haven't been able to paint since. Do you think I'm crazy? The Machine thinks so."

"The Machine," he said, tearing off the end of the cigar with his teeth, "is always right."

Seeing Helena had wandered away to sit on Marya's Chinese sofa, he excused himself with a nod and followed.

Wattleigh still sat brooding over the Fool's Mate. "I don't understand. I just can't understand," he said.

"—it's like the Hare and the Tortoise," boomed the mathematician. Lloyd nodded solemnly. "The slow one can't ever catch up, see?"

Lloyd spoke. "Well, you got a point. You got a point. Only I thought the slow one was the winner."

"Oh." Dewes (or Clewes) lapsed into thoughtful silence.

Marya wandered about the room, touching faces as if she were a blind person looking for someone she knew.

"But I don't understand!" said Wattleigh.

"I do," James mumbled about the cigar. The bittersweet smoke was thick as liquid in his mouth. He understood, all right. He looked at them, one by one: An ex-mathematician having trouble with the difference be-

tween arithmetic and geometry; an ex-engineer, ditto; a
painter not allowed to paint, not even to feel; a former
chess "champion" who could not play. And that left
Helena Hershee, mistress to poor, dumb Wattleigh.

"Before the Machines——?" he began.

"—I was a judge," she said, running her fingertips
over the back of his neck provocatively. "And you?
What kind of doctor were you?"

1988 A.D.

"It was during the second world war," Jim Fairchild
said. He lay on his back on the long, tiger-shaped sofa,
with a copy of HOT ROD KOMIKS over his eyes.

"I thought it only started in the sixties," said Marya.

"Yeah, but the *name*, 'Mussulman'—that started in
the Nazi death camps. There were some people in them
who couldn't—you know—get with it. They stopped eating and seeing and hearing. Everybody called them 'Mussulmen,' because they seemed like Moslems, mystic . . ."

His voice trailed off, for he was thinking of the second
world war. The good old days, when a man made his
own rules. No Machines to tell you what to do.

He had been living with Marya for several months,
now. She was his girl, just as the other Marya, in HOT ROD
KOMIKS, was the girl of the other Jim, Jim (Hell-On-
Wheels) White. It was a funny thing about Komiks. They
were real life, and at the same time, they were better
than life.

Marya—his Marya—was no intellectual. She didn't
like to read and think, like Jim, but that was O.K., because men were supposed to do all the reading and thinking and fighting and killing. Marya sat in a lavender
bucket seat in the corner, drawing with her crayons. Eas-
ing his lanky, lean body up off the sofa Jim walked
around behind her and looked at the sketch.

"Her nose is crooked," he said.

"That doesn't matter, silly. This is a fashion design.
It's only the dress that counts."

"Well, how come she's got yellow hair? People don't
have yellow hair."

"Helena Hershee has."

"No she hasn't!"

"She has so!"

"No, it ain't yellow, it's—it ain't yellow."

Then they both paused, because Muzik was playing their favorite song. Each had a favorite of his own—Jim's was "Blap," and Marya's was "Yes I Know I Rilly Care For You"—but they had one favorite together. Called "Kustomized Tragedy." It was one of the songs in which the Muzik imitated their voices, singing close harmony:

> Jim Gunn had a neat little kustom job,
> And Marya was his girl.
> They loved each other with a love so true
> The truest in the worl'.
> But Jim weren't allowed to drive his kar,
> And Marya could not see;
> Kust'mized Traju-dee-ee-ee.

The song went on to articulate how Jim Gunn wanted more than anything in the worl' to buy an eye operation for his girl, who wished to admire his kustom kar. So he drove to a store and held it up, but someone recognized his kar. The police shot him, but:

> He kissed his Marya one last time;
> The policeman shot her, too.
> But she said, "I can see your kustom, Jim!
> It's pretty gold and bloo!"
> He smiled and died embracing her,
> Happy that she could see.
> Kust'mized Traju-dee.

Of course, in real life, Marya could see very well, Jim had no kar, and there were no policemen. But it was true for them, nevertheless. In some sense they could not express, they felt their love was a tragedy.

Knowing Jim felt lonesome and bloo, Marya walked over and kissed his ear. She lay down beside him, and at once they were asleep.

MEDCENTRAL's audit showed a population of 250 million in NORTHAMER, stabilized. Other than a few incubator failures, and one vat of accidentally-infected embryos, progress was as predicted, with birth and death rates equal. The norm had shifted once more toward the asocial, and UTERINE CONTROL showed 90.2% adult admission at both major hospitals.

Trenchant abnormals were being regressed through adolescence, there being no other completely satisfactory method of normalizing them without shock therapy, with its attendant contraindications.

Lloyd pulled his pocket watch from the bib of his plaid overalls. The hands of Chicken Licken pointed straight up, meaning there was just time to fetch the mail before Farm Kartoons on TV. On impulse, Lloyd popped the watch into his mouth and chewed. It was delicious, but it gave him little pleasure. Everything was too easy, too soft. He wanted exciting things to happen to him, like the time on Farm Kartoons when Black Angus tried to kill the hero, Lloyd White, by breaking up his Machine, and Lloyd White had stabbed him with a pitchfork syringe and sent him off to the hospital.

Mechanical Joe, knowing it was time to fetch the mail, came running out of the house. He wagged his tail and whined impatiently. It didn't make any difference that he wasn't a real dog, Lloyd thought as they strolled toward the mailbox. Joe still liked it when you scratched his ears. You could tell, just by the look in his eyes. He was livelier and a lot more fun than the first Joe.

Lloyd paused a moment, remembering how sad he'd been when Joe died. It was a pleasantly melancholy thought, but now mechanical Joe was dancing around him and barking anxiously. They continued.

The mailbox was chock-full of mail. There was a new komik, called LLOYD FARMER AND JOE, and the whole big box of new toys.

Yet later, when Lloyd had read the komik and watched Farm Kartoons and played awhile with his building set, he still felt somehow heavy, depressed. It was no good being alone all the time, he decided. Maybe he should go to New York and see Jim and Marya. Maybe the Machines there were different, not so bossy.

For the first time, another, stranger thought came to him. Maybe he should go *live* in New York.

"DEAR DELPHINIA," Dave printed. "THIS IS GOING TO BE MY LAST LETTER TO YOU, AS I DONT LOVE YOU ANY

MORE. I KNOW NOW WHAT HAS BEEN MAKING ME FEEL
BAD, AND IT IS YOU. YOU ARE REALLY MY MASHINE,
ARENT YOU HA HA I'LL BET YOU DIDNT THINK I KNEW.

"NOW I LOVE HELENA MORE THAN YOU AND WE ARE
GOING AWAY TO NEW YORK AND SEE LOTS OF FRIENDS
AND GO TO LOTS OF PARTYS AND HAVE LOTS OF FUN AND
I DONT CARE IF I DONT SEE YOU NO MORE.

"LOVE AND BEST OF LUCK TO A SWELL KID,

"DAVE W."

After an earthquake destroyed 17 million occupants of
the western hospital, MEDCENTRAL ordered the rest
moved at once to the east. All abnormals not living near
the east hospital were also persuaded to evacuate to
New York. Persuasion was as follows:

Gradually, humidity and pressure were increased to
.9 discomfort, while subliminally, pictures of New York
were flashed on all surfaces around each patient.

Dave and Helena had come by subway from L.A.,
and they were tired and cross. The subway trip itself took
only two or three hours, but they had spent an additional
hour in the taxi to Jim and Marya's.

"It's an electric taxi," Dave explained, "and it only
goes about a mile an hour. I'll sure never make that trip
again."

"I'm glad you came," said Marya. "We've been feeling
terrible lonesome and bloo."

"Yes," Jim added, "and I got an idea. We can form a
club, see, against the Machines. I got it all figured out.
We——"

"Babay, tell them about the zombies—I mean, the
Mussulmen," said Helena.

Dave spoke with an excited, wild look about him.
"Jeez, yeah, they had about a million cars of them on the
train, all packed in glass bottles. I wasn't sure what the
hell they were at first, see, so I went up and looked at
one. It was a skinny, hairless man, all folded up in a
bottle inside another bottle. Weird-looking."

In honor of their arrival, the Muzik played the favorite songs of all four: "Zonk," "Yes I Know I Rilly Care
For You," "Blap" and "That's My Baby," while the
walls went transparent for a moment, showing a breath-
taking view of the gold towers of New York. Lloyd, who

spoke to no one, sat in the corner keeping time to the music. He had no favorite song.

"I want to call this the Jim Fairchild Club," said Jim. "The purpose of this here club is to get rid of the Machines. Kick 'em out!"

Marya and Dave sat down to a game of chess.

"I know how we can do it, too," Jim went on. "Here's my plan: Who put the Machines in, in the first place? The U.S. government. Well, there ain't any U.S. government any more. So the Machines are illegal. Right?"

"Right," said Helena. Lloyd continued to tap his foot, though no Muzik was playing.

"They're outlaws," said Jim. "We oughta kill them!"

"But how?" asked Helena.

"I ain't got all the details worked out yet. Give me time. Because you know, the Machines done us wrong."

"How's that?" asked Lloyd, as if from far away.

"We all had good jobs, and we were smart. A long time ago. Now we're all getting dumb. You know?"

"That's right," Helena agreed. She opened a tiny bottle and began painting her toenails.

"I think," said Jim, glaring about him, "the Machines are trying to make us all into Mussulmen. Any of you want to get stuffed into a bottle? Huh?"

"A bottle inside a bottle," Dave corrected, without looking up from his game.

Jim continued, "I think the Machines are drugging us into Mussulmen. Or else they got some kind of ray, maybe, that makes us stupider. An X-ray, maybe."

"We gotta do something," said Helena, admiring her foot.

Marya and Dave began to quarrel about how the pawn moves.

Lloyd continued to tap his foot, marking time.

1989 A.D.

Jimmy had a good idea, but nobody wanted to listen. He remembered once when he was an itsy boy, a egg machine that tooked the eggs out of their shells and putted them into plastic—things. It was funny, the way the machine did that. Jimmy didn't know why it was so funny, but he laughed and laughed, just thinking about it. Silly, silly, silly eggs.

Marya had an idea, a real good one. Only she didn't know how to say it so she got a crayon and drew a great Big! picture of the Machines: Mommy Machine and Daddy Machine and all the little Tiny Tot Machines.

Loy-Loy was talking. He was building a block house. "Now I'm putting the door," he said. "Now I'm putting the lit-tle window. Now the—why is the window littler than the house? I don't know. This is the chimney and this is the stee-ple and open the door and where's all the people? I don't know."

Helena had a wooden hammer, and she was driving all the pegs. Bang! Bang! Bang! "One, two, three!" she said. "Banga-banga-bang!"

Davie had the chessmen out, lined up in rows, two by two. He wanted to line them all up three by three, only somehow he couldn't. It made him mad and he began to cry.

Then one of the Machines came and stuck something in his mouth, and everybody else wanted one and somebody was screaming and more Machines came and . . .

The coded message came to MEDCENTRAL. The last five abnormals had been cured, and all physical and mental functions reduced to the norm. All pertinent data on them were switched over to UTERINE SUPPLY, which clocked them in at 400 hours G.M.T., day 1, year 1989. MEDCENTRAL agreed on the time-check, then switched itself off.

The Singular Visitor
from Not-Yet

With an Account of the
Subsequent Lamentable Decline
of Dr. Lemuel Jones

To Jeremy Botford, Esq.

Aug. 10, 1772

Dear Jerry,

It was with mixt feelings that I returned to London after all these years. The city is more splendid and horrid than ever; it is a sort of great Press, into which every kind of person has been tumbled, without the least regard for whether or not he is choaked with the stench of his neighbors.

For my part, the only retreat offering succor from the noxious Crowd's putrefaction is the coffee house. Of course I refer to Crutchwood's in Clovebelly Lane, which you may fondly remember. It still affords an entertaining company, and I was surprised to remark several of our old number about the fire yet. Augustus Strathnaver has grown quite stout and dropsical, but his Wit is lean and ready as ever. Dick Blackadder is still soliciting subscriptions for his translations of Ovid: he is still soliciting in vain: and he is still of good chear about it. I learned that poor Oliver Colquhoun, who never could get his play tried in Drury Lane, is dead.

But I was attended by the greatest astonishment when I apprehended a gross figure in a snuff-colored coat seated next the fire with its back to the company.

The figure turned to regard me, presenting its great warthog's face. When its mouth opened, 'twas like the spitting of a steamed pudding. "So! [it said] I see you have not yet learned your lesson, Timothy Scunthe, but must needs be taught more manners! Do you not know better than to interrupt a man while he is meditating?"

It was indeed our old friend, cantankerous as ever. I shall never forget the time I spilled mulled wine upon him—indeed, he shall never let me forget it, though it happened close on eleven years ago!

I stayed to see the evening out with Jones and his circle, to which there are no few additions. The good Doctor is thicker of limb, now, with a propensity (he says) to gout; though I perceive no shortening of his breath. He disposed last evening of two Philosophy Students (They were arguing about the Soul, I believe. I could not follow them), a Schoolmaster, a Grub Street writer, and a poor inoffensive solicitor who wandered in for a cup of tea and did not stay to see it cooled. In short, Dr. Jones is himself: Witty, Splenetic and Eminently Sensible. I was keenly reminded of the days when we young dogs were used to teaze him, and he to muzzle us properly. Remember the fun we had with the visitor from "the Future," and how the good Doctor shewed him for the merry Andrew he was? I can never forget it, as I hope you cannot forget

Your affectionate
Timothy Scunthe

To Sir Timothy Scunthe, Bart.

Aug. 25

Dear Tim,

I am glad you have not forgotten the Incident of the man from "Not-Yet," for I have begun assembling some paltry Reminiscences and would greatly appreciate the help of your keen memory. While I believe I recall the Incident perfectly, much Muck has covered it in ten years' time, and I would rather have your version of the story, too.

Eternally gratefull, I remain, Dear Tim,

Your affectionate
Jer. Botford

To Jeremy Botford, Esq.

Sept. 5

Dear Jerry,

Your memory is doubtless better than mine, but I have made some Notations of that curious Incident, which, in the interests of your book, I hereby place at your disposal:

It was a December evening in 1762, and our usual circle, dominated by Dr. Jones, was gathered in the gaming room at Crutchwood's. Pauceford, the proprietor, seemed to be having an argument with some man in the front doorway, and the room grew quite chill.

"Damme, sir," Jones roared out. "Are you determined to give us all the Ague? Bring the gentleman in."

Pauceford led in a thin, spindle-shanked fellow, oddly dressed. I recall he wore his hair natural and shockingly short, and that his breeches reached to his ankles.

Jones' snuffbox clattered to the floor. "Good God!" he cried. "What manner of Whig is this?"

The fellow made no reply, but gazed about him in some consternation.

"Or is it Methodism you're spreading? Or Dissension?" Jones snarled. "You'll do a barrel more converts if you bag a decent periwig."

"Perhaps," said Strathnaver, tittering, "perhaps the gentleman believes it is Satanic to adorn the body."

"Yes, well, you'll take note he has no scruples against hiding his spindly calves, however. My name is Dr. Lemuel Jones, sir. You'll forgive me for not rising. I am rather gouty this evening. What might your name be?"

The man put out his left hand, withdrew it, then offered it again. Finally he extended his right and shook.

"My name is Darwin Gates," he said shyly. "And I'm from the Twentieth Century."

Dr. Jones' hand hesitated just a fraction as he reached for his snuffbox. "Is it a place, then?" he said, offering snuff around. "I should have thought it a direction. But it is very interesting to meet you, sir. I suppose you have all manner of wonders to divulge to this fortunate company, do you not?"

Mr. Gates sat down and leaned forward earnestly. "As a matter of fact, I do. You wouldn't believe the half——"

"Indeed? But I have a reputation for credulosity," Jones said. A sly smile was beginning to play about his great, ugly mouth. "You will want to tell me no doubt of carriages that operate without benefit of horses. Of engines that carry men through the air like birds. Of ships without sails."

The man flushed darkly and stammered, "As a matter of fact——"

Jones' voice rose in both pitch and volume. "Of machines which carry men under the waters of the sea like fish, where they witness countless wonders. Of mechanical horses capable of drawing a dozen carriages at once. Of artificial candles powered by some mysterious force of which we know nothing as yet. Of buildings made of crystal and iron, perhaps, wherein one may order servants to select the weather one desires. Is that the sort of Future you are about to describe for us, Mr. Gates?"

The poor visitor looked positively apoplectic with embarrassment and chagrin. I had no doubt but that he had planned a much poorer tale than this. "I——" he stammered, "—that is, I——"

"But," continued Dr. Jones, grinding his teeth, "I speak only of mere physical inventions, devices which any clod Mechanick may surmise. 'Twould do you no credit at all, sir, if you had not a better tale than this. Perhaps you come to tell me of the Politics of the Twentieth Century. Let me see—there would be no war, because terrible Weapons would have been invented, the which are too dangerous to be used. The colonies in America will have rebelled and become a Powerful Nation, where, they will claim, All Men are Equal. Mayhap they will even free the slave Negroes, though that is perhaps too much to expect of our American friends."

"Just a minute!" said the visitor. "I resent that. I'm an American."

"Tush!" said Jones. "Next you will be a Red Indian. I warn you, sir, it was I who exposed George Psalmanazar, who posed forty years as a 'Formosan,' having made up his own 'language.'" All this Jones delivered in an undertone, then resumed his ordinary Rasp and said, "I suppose the Powers and Alliances of all Europe will have shifted considerable. England's monarch will have no more weight than a common sweep, I suppose."

"How did you know?" asked the astonished Mr. Gates.

"Pooh, sir, I am merely spinning my tale to keep from being bored by yours. But be so good as to let me go on. I have not yet discoursed upon the Future state of Painting, of Musick, of Moral and Natural Philosophy——"

"First we must give Mr. Gates a cup of punch," murmured Strathnaver. "Assuming, that is, that persons from that time so little evident to our senses *can* drink and eat. Are you, Mr. Gates, an ethereal spirit, like one of Mr. Milton's angels? Do you sleep, ingest food, and so on?"

While the poor stranger was helped to a cup of punch, Dr. Jones sat back and regarded him incuriously. I read contempt in Jones' face; whenever the right side of his mouth gets drawn up, as though attracted to the wart just above it at the corner, then he is in a frenzy of contempt.

"Of Painting I know little," he said. "It is at best a clumsy art, making awkward imitations of Nature. I expect patrons will grow weary of Copyism, and turn their attention elsewhere.

"Everyone in the Twentieth Century will of course have Musick at hand as he desires it. I can well imagine the deleterious effect this will have upon Taste & Sense, when every cordwainer or every smith can hammer upon shoes to Musick of his own choosing. Art does not, sir, lend itself to Dilution.

"There will always be a plethora of varieties in the Garden of Philosophy from which to make a nosegay. At some point, men will stop speaking of Reason and start speaking of Responsibility. There is, as they will say, no order in the Universe but what we choose to see—as there were no Giants in Sir Quixote's windmills. Absurdity will become a philosophical catchword—there will be a Silly Season.

"Of Natural Philosophy I can well imagine the devising of all manner engines and games. No doubt men of the Twentieth Century will go to and fro the Moon, if not the Sun. Astronomy, Chemistry, Mathematics and Medicine will all advance space. Plague will be almost unknown. I daresay it will have been proven to everyone's satisfaction that Tobacco is a poisonous weed."

"Amazing!" quoth our visitor. "How did you know——"

"I have met better mountebanks than you, sir!" said Jones, fetching him a stern look. "I am forced by gout to sit here night after night, prey to every single one of 'em. Only last month I was confronted by a 'man from Not-Yet' who puts you to shame. Not only had he elegant manners and wondrous tales to tell, he looked exactly like me!"

Our visitor looked pale and ill. "Like you?" he said.

"Yes. The rogue tried to convince me that he *was* me,

but I have not yet met the man I could not outreason. I proved to him, as I shall prove to you, that man cannot travel from the Future to the Past.

"Man cannot move about in Time as though it were Space. Nature forbids it, as she forbids Levitation or a Vacuum. Think of the awful Paradoxes which might occur! Should you, for example, return to your childhood, you might see yourself as a child. Yet suppose your carriage ran over that child? Would you then cease to be? How then would you yet be alive? And there are Paradoxes even more hideous to contemplate. Suppose you got a child upon your own mother, and suppose the child were you? How, then, may a man be his own father or son, a travesty of Physical and Moral Law? I do not even dare consider that weightier problem by far: Which of you, should you meet yourself, would have your Soul? Is the Soul single or divisible? Would some of your selves be soulless animals, mere Automata?

"You cannot be from the Future because the Future is, by definition, that which is not yet. There is no Future. And even were travel in time possible, you would not be from Posterity. I believe that Man grows every generation more happily endowed with Understanding—yet you are content to sit here gape-mouthed, listening to specious arguments."

"Please," said Mr. Gates. "I can prove I'm from the Future. I have built the only Time Machine ever. Let me prove it. Here is a coin——" He fumbled at the hip of his breeches for a moment. "Here is a quarter of a dollar, United States of America currency," he announced proudly, handing the coin to Strathnaver. "You'll see the date is nineteen-something."

"Good God!" said Strathnaver. "The poor wretch has made himself credentials. This is no more a coin than I am. Hoho, Mr. Gates, I must give you a lesson in minting, someday. When you design a die, you must *reverse* the image, so that it comes out proper on the coin."

He passed the coin around, and we could all see that the inscription was backward. It was poor forgery.

"Things have got reversed somehow!" shouted Gates. "I don't know how. What can I do to make you believe me?"

"Nothing on earth," said Jones. "The last knave shewed me a curious engine he called a Lighter—but when

I examined it, 'twas nothing but a tiny oil-wick lamp with a matchlock flint attached."

"I'll take you back to my own time, and that will convince you!"

"A pretty idea," said Mr. Strathnaver, "but you'll never get him away from the fire."

"What?" said Jones. "Quit the fire to wander about in the aguey snow until this rascal's fellows waylay me and kill me? I cannot say I like the prospect."

"Oh, we needn't go far," said Gates. "My Time Machine is very close by—and some of your friends can follow and watch. Can it be you are afraid to prove me right?"

For once, Jones had no answer. He leapt up with surprising agility and signaled for his cloak and hat. "Let us see it, you dog," he rumbled.

Dick Blackadder and I were elected to follow. We went but twenty paces in the snow when we encountered the "Time Machine." It was somewhat like a sedan-chair, somewhat like a bathing-machine and no little like an upright coffin on wheels. Gates opened a panel in it, and the two men got themselves inside. The panel closed up.

Dick and I watched the device closely, ready for any trick. All was deathly still.

"I fear something has happened to Lemuel," said Dick. "He could never keep silence this long."

I wrencht at the handle of the panel, but it was fast. An unearthly light seemed to stream from crevices and cracks about the door, increasingly bright. I applied my eye to a crack and peered in.

There was not a soul inside.

The light got brighter and brighter until, with a thunderclap, the entire machine fell to pieces about me. I was knocked flat by the Great Noise, and when I regained my feet, I was amazed to see Dr. Jones standing alone amidst the wreckage.

"Are you hurt, Dr. Jones?" asked Dick, scrambling to his feet.

"No, I—No."

"But where is Mr. Gates?"

"It would seem," said Jones, looking about, "that he is blown into eternity."

We helped him back to the fireside, where, as I recall, he was strangely silent and morose all evening, and would not respond to no amount of badinage. He remained muffled in his cloak and refused to say a word.

That is all I know of the incident, Jerry. Hoping this account is of some good, I remain

Your affectionate
Timothy Scunthe

To Sir Timothy Scunthe, Bart.

Sept. 9

Dear Tim,

Rec'd your story and am truly amazed at the copiousness of your memory and notes. Surely you are more the man to pen a Reminiscence than I. You have captured nicely the flavor of the old Warthog's speach, and I find your account exact in nearly every Particular.

Do give my regards to Dr. Jones and pray him to send me some little item of interest to go in my Reminiscences. If it would not inconvenience him, I would like mightily to hear more of his Experience that strange evening. Eternally gratefull I remain

Your affectionate
Jeremy Botford

Postscript. How is it you say the Doctor has a wart upon the *right* side of his mouth? I have before me a miniature of him, shewing the wart plainly on the *left*.

Yours &c.,
Jer. Botford

To Jeremy Botford, Esq.

Sept. 14

Dear Jerry,

Business is pressing. This is only a brief billet to inform you that I have spoken to Dr. J. and he has promised to send you something. "But I doubt (said he) that he will want to use it." Do you understand this? I confess I do not. More later from

Your affectionate
Timothy Scunthe

To Jeremy Botford, Esq.

Sept. 15
,ymereJ raeD yM

As you hold this letter up to a looking-glass to read it . . .
. . . I hope you will find it in you to pity its author. Do

not, I beg you, judge me until you have read here the truth of my plight.

Having departed on December 10, 1762 from the yard of Crutchwood's, I journeyed into the Future. Having made my jokes about the Twentieth Century, I lived to see them, tragically, become Real. I saw Art & Architecture decline to Nursery Toys, and Literature reduced to Babel. Morality vanished; Science pottered with household Enjines. The main buziness of the time seemed to be World-Wide War, or man-made Catastrophe. Whole cities full of people were ignited and cooked alive.

Betwixt the two wars, people drive about the countryside in great carriage-enjines, which poison the air with harmful vapors. These carriages have o'erlaid the cities with smoak, black and noxious. There is in the Twentieth Century neither Beauty nor Reason, nor any other Mark which sheweth Man more than a beast.

But enough of a sad sojourn to a dismal place. I was sickened by it to near the point of madness. I knew I had done Wrong in accompanying Mr. Gates to his Land of Horrors, and so I devized a plan for canceling my visit.

I came back to November 1762 and saw myself. I earnestly entreated myself not to attempt such a voyage—but the object of this entreaty was so intent on proving me a scoundrel and imposter that my arguments were in vain.

I had then but one chance left—to appear at the time and place in which my unsuspecting self was departing for the Future, and to stop myself, by force if need be. Gates and poor Jones had just climbed into the Time Machine when I materialized. They disappeared at the same moment, and the combined Force of our multiple Fluxions destroyed the machine utterly. It was the first and last of its kind, I believe.

For some reason I cannot determine, I am reversed. Mr. Gates thought that perhaps each Time-Journey reversed all the atoms of one's body. If you recall, when Gates first appeared, he kept trying to shake hands with his left hand. Likewise the coin in his pocket was backward. In my journey to posterity, I was reversed. When I came back to speak to myself, I was put to rights again. Now I am again reversed.

You will not be able to include this in your book, I fear, unless as a Specimen of a madman's raving, or as a silly Fiction. Let it be a Fiction, then, or ignore it, but do not deride me for a Lunatic.

For I have seen the Future; that is, I have peered into the pit of *Hell*.

> I pray you remain constant to
> Your friend,
> Lemuel Jones

To Jeremy Botford, Esq.

Sept. 15

Dear Jerry,

I have not yet time to answer your letter properly. I trust Dr. J. has sent you or will send you his Reminiscence. I may say he certainly acts peculiar nowadays. I understand his demeanor has declined steadily over the past ten years. Now he is often moody and distracted, or seemingly laughs at nothing.

For example, he burst out laughing today, when I asked him his opinion on American taxation. He is an enigma to

> Your affectionate
> Timothy Scunthe

Postscript. Your miniature lies, for I have just today looked on the original. My memory may be faulty but my eyes are keen. The wart is on the *right*.

> Yours, &c.,
> T. Scunthe

The Short, Happy Wife
of Mansard Eliot

Mansard Eliot's shadow, long with aristocracy, came out of his gallery on Fifth Avenue and moved along the sidewalk. Eliot knew exactly how he looked, with the sun gleaming in his hair. The hair would be parted slightly to one side, smoothed flat all over, and rich with dark, oily health. And the teeth: so white and even that Gladys said they reminded her of bathroom tiles.

Today he'd asked Gladys to become his wife. And if Dr. Sky didn't like it, so what? Dr. Sky, with his "separation of dream life from reality," his "horizontal cracks in the ego structure"! Let *him* try flopping down on the truth table like a seal pup and trying on the hard hat of memory . . . Mansard would, by Heaven, marry beneath his station.

Today she was making up her mind. While he waited, Mansard recalled the formula for locating street addresses on Fifth Avenue. From 775 to 1286, he knew, one dropped the last figure and subtracted 18. It was just something like that, he supposed, some geographical or historical fact, that had made him rich. So today he had asked Gladys to divorce her husband, Dean, who was unemployed. As soon as she answered "Yes," Mansard would rush away to tell Dr. Sky.

"I can't divorce Deanie," she whined. "It would break his back."

"I see." Mansard was grave. His cereal company had

founded a sports foundation, whose director was just now clearing his throat to make an announcement. Mansard Eliot owned at least one tweed sports jacket, one black or navy blue blazer, one sterling shoehorn, one pair heavy slacks, one summer suit, one drip-dry shirt, one raincoat, one pair cotton slacks, two neckties, two sportshirts, one pair dress shoes, one pair canvas shoes, one light bathrobe, three pairs of socks, three sets of underwear, two handkerchiefs, one bathing suit, toilet and shaving articles (adapted for European use), and the building in which Gladys was a scrubwoman.

"Deanie needs me," she explained. "People try to harm him. Yesterday I came home and found him sleeping on the couch, and the kids had put a plastic bag over his head. They hate his guts. He could have died. He hates their guts, too."

What does Monique van Vooren do after dinner? A candle sputters. She fingers the bottle's long, graceful neck. Suddenly there is a shower of liquid emeralds. *Mansard was taller than Gladys, who, of Gladys, Mansard and Dean, was not the shortest.*

"He beats me," she explained. "He makes me have children I don't want. He doesn't want them either. He makes me go out and work, while he just lays around the house, guzzling two kinds of beer. My mother hates his guts. She'll be glad when I divorce him."

The *Stallion* is a westernized shirt, extremely tapered, of cotton chambray. Why be bald?

"Everyone just hates his guts," she explained. "He even hates himself. Only I understand and love and cherish him. Or maybe it's only hate. Well, anyway, at least he loves his kids." Minnesota has 99 Long Lakes and 97 Mud Lakes.

"Why don't we just pick up and go to Europe?" Mansard asked, glancing at himself in the lake. "Or somewhere else?"

"Oh, I couldn't leave the kids. They don't get along with Deanie too well. They just don't get along." Gladys put down her mop and pail and accepted a cigarette from the gold case he proffered. Satin sheets and pillow cases are a must for the compleat bachelor's apartment. The Doggie Dunit makes an ideal gift memento or "icebreaker" at parties. So realistic your friends will gasp.

Mansard's hand trembled as he lit two cigarettes with a special lighter, then handed one to Gladys.

"Do you smoke?"

"Oh, no thanks. But you go ahead. I like the smell of a man's cigarette."

Exhaling a cloud of aromatic smoke, he said, "Let me think now . . ."

She lit two cigarettes and handed him one. When he had lighted their cigarettes, Mansard closed his eyes.

He consumed her with his eyes: her cold-reddened nose, print dress, feet swelling out of water-stained wedgies. His apartment, a penthouse over the supermarket, was filled each evening with soft Muzak. Alone at night, he'd listen, smoking one of his specially-blended cigarettes in the dark. The apartment could take her for granted; why couldn't he?

"How can you love him?" he said, touching his glass to hers. "He even hates himself!"

But she would not speak. "It's no good, our meeting like this," she said, "Mansard. Secret rendezvous in elegant nite spots. Dancing till dawn in posh cafés. Moonlit rides with the top down. Our own flower code. Losing a cool ten G's at Chuck-A-Luck and laughing like the crazy fools we are. 'The wrong hotel room.' *Billèts-doux*. Smoking menthol by mountain rills. Appearing nightly in an exclusive engagement. Sailing. In fact, all water sports, including snow and ice as water. And finally, my love, leaping down a volcano, together." She seemed unable to speak.

Mansard thought of Dean. Just place the International audio wall probe against any wall, and pick up sounds, voices, in the next room. Dual listening device, used by law enforcement officers on a world-wide basis, attaches to any phone. The Snooper—world's only private listening device, used by law enforcement officers, amplifies sound 1,000,000 times. Looks like a briefcase. Peeping Tom snooper scope is no bigger than a fountain pen, yet gives 6x magnification.

"I want to meet this 'Dean,'" Mansard said suddenly.

"So you want to degrade yourself," said Dr. Sky. "Why, do you think? Has it anything to do with the time my father strapped me to my little potty chair?"

"His father did nothing of the kind," said Mansard

evenly. "I never said he strapped me *down,* only strapped me."

"Why did we feel trapped?"

"He did strappado me once," said Mansard. "He had some notion it would make me grow taller, have more confidence with tall women, business associates. As usual, he was right."

"So we tell ourselves."

Mansard recalled. "He used to force-feed me. Vivisected my dog, to explain to me the mysteries of biology. Poor Spike."

"Or poor you, you mean."

"Yes, Dad never ceased preparing me for future happiness. He had a nurse read Kant to me while I slept. I had this recurring nightmare of being chased by a synthetic *a priori* proposition. I always wanted to go to Europe, but I never did."

"What do you dream of recently?"

Mansard Eliot took down the dream in shorthand, a skill he'd learned in three short weeks. "Last night I dreamed I was a member of a kid gang. We were beating a toilet with big chains. The sight of all that lavender porcelain being torn away made me sick, but I didn't dare let on.

"Then I was in the hospital, where the doctors were scraping pain or paint from me, using chisels and saws. It seemed to be the pineapple festival. I got up and ran down a hall lined with red Formica. There were thousands of people all going to the big pineapple fire. I saw a man eating a doughnut made of ice cream, and I noticed it was a rose wreath from my grave. There was money all over the floor, and lucky charms, but it was electrified. I tore along on my scooter, whose headlamp seemed to show darkness instead of light. It was all Tinker Toys ahead of me, and cages full of live soap. I had to hurry, before the bureau closed, but the hands on my watch were wrong, no matter how I turned it to look at it.

"At the movie tent, the screen was blank, but everyone sat watching. 'What is it?' I asked my mother, the projectionist. 'See for yourself,' she said. The X-ray glasses had some instructions written on them, on the cardboard bows, but in code. I deciphered it letter by letter: it was a letter from Monique van Vooren to

Mamie van Doren, giving the menu. I ordered coffee eggs. They were beautiful, made of transparent plastic garden hose and film—but just then mass was starting. Father Zossima, Father Coughlin, Father Divine, Father Christmas, Father Flanagan, Father Keller and Father were officiating, but then I had to climb a windy mountain, strangely grown with hornets. At the top was— never mind.

"Hacking my way through the swamp, I went down into a subway station. All the trains ran to a place called 'Breakfast.' I started the engine with a huge, three-pronged key. Gladys and I sped along the highway, chased by a synthetic *a priori* proposition. They proposed to lock her away in a priory, see——"

"Time's up!" cried the doctor, waking to his wrist alarm. "We'll take up there tomorrow."

"But I haven't told you half of it! Then I was spearing——"

"I'm sorry, but I have another patient. Write it all down, we'll discuss it tomorrow."

Mansard hid in a phone booth in the lobby, until he saw Dr. Sky leave with his golf bag.

Dean was short, fat and altogether friendly-looking. For example, he wore a T-shirt with the message "Thank God It's Friday," though it was only Wednesday. His arms tattooed with Dumbo and Pinocchio.

"Navy?" asked Eliot, taking the initiative.

"No, I just wanted 'em. Who knows why kids do these crazy things, anyway." Remove unwanted hair. Learn meat cutting: people must eat! Mansard noticed Dean had a faint, not unpleasant halitosis. *Robbed* of your high school diploma?

"So you're Glad's boss?" Dean, a bald, perspiring man whom Mansard Eliot had just met, laughed.

"That's right. She's told me so much about you, Mr.——"

"Call me Dean," Dean —— said. "Want a beer? We got two kinds."

Mansard decided it was time to speak. "I think we can talk this over like civilized people, Dean."

Dean smiled. "Dalu 'mun karon fenna," he said. "Waa narrapart weearn manuungkurt barrim barrim tillit impando. Nxabo amacebo: amakwata nekra wai?"

"I want you to give Gladys her freedom."

"So Glad tells me. It's sure okey by me. I'll miss the old sock, but——" He made a deprecating gesture, as if to say *"Mes sentiments!"*

Mansard took from his pocket a bullet. "Glad to hear you take it like a man, Dean," he said. "So many men of your station—no offense intended—would have made a scene, screamed bloody murder, and so on."

"I'm just curious, understand, but why do you want her?"

In the silence, Eliot's watch emitted a tiny electronic scream. Why did he want her? How to put it into words? He glanced over at her, sitting before the television with her feet up. Half her face was in shadow. From the other half, her hand removed blackheads at regular intervals, using a silvery plunger. He thought of the times she had refused to come to him, times when he'd rushed into the closet to press his burning face into a cool, damp mop, inhaling the sweet-sour fragrance of her. Her mop!

"One wearies of explanations," he said.

"That reminds me, what about the kids?"

"I was thinking we'd send them to some sort of school or camp," said Mansard easily. "You know, nothing terribly expensive, but exclusive enough. We've written to Auschwitz, for one."

Dean raised an eyebrow. "Bet it's hell trying to find anything reasonable these days."

"And how! Prices are absurd—it must be the administration."

"Just what Glad was saying the other day. Her very words. I don't know what the country's coming to." Dean's face grew red. He slapped the table, shouting, "Damn it all to hell! It makes me sick the way the government pushes around the Little Guy!" Inside this pencil is a quality stapler! Inside this exact replica of a bottle of scotch is a 9-transistor radio that's on its way to being *the* executive gift! 24-kt golden peanuts contain lighter, pillbox, or executive toolkit!

"I couldn't agree more," said Mansard. He opened a small, gold-filled penknife. Usually it was used to clip the ends from the cigars he had made up in Havana and flown in by special plane. Today, however, he put it to a new use, clipping off the bullet's nose.

"What's that you've got there, a bullet?"

"Yes, a *slug*."

Dean opened two kinds of beer. "I see you're making a dum-dum out of it. Neat idea."

Mansard showed him the gun. Dean's eyes widened. "That's a beauty!"

"Thanks. I call it my *gat*." Eliot worked the action back and forth.

"I understand a forty-five is powerful as hell," said Dean. "Knock a man down if you only get him in the little finger. But how's the recoil?"

Mansard loaded and cocked the gun. "Well, it seems big at first, but I've been practicing."

Gladys stood up as he sighted along the barrel at Dean's heart. "No you don't!" she tittered, throwing herself in the line of fire.

A lady traveler to Europe should take: four pairs of nylon panties, six pairs of nylon stockings, two petticoats, two bras, a cardigan sweater, a pair of slacks or bermuda shorts, a pair of sandals, a pair of good, sturdy walking shoes, a pair of dressy heels, bathing cap and suit, one knit daytime dress, one drip-dry daytime blouse . . .

"Damn," said Dean, looking down at the body. "I'm really going to miss her. You notice how loyal she was—died trying to save my life—notice that?"

"Yes. I expect the police will be wanting this." Mansard took from his pocket a personalized pencil with his name in gold, set of twelve, 60¢ ppd., inserted it into the barrel of the automatic so as to preserve his prints, and handed it over.

The Momster

They were letting him down easy. It was more humiliating, at least for Sewell, to be let down easy by a machine.

It leaned back in its swivel chair, looked above his head, and placed its plastic fingertips together. It feigned reluctance to speak.

"I'm sorry, Mr. Sewell, but frankly we have our doubts. Your test scores . . . I wouldn't like to say positively *no* at this time, you understand, but the outlook is bleak. Bleak."

"I get the message. Don't call Galactic Explorations, you'll call me." Roger Sewell stood up. "But I'd have appreciated getting the shaft from GX via a human interviewer, and not from a thing that looks human from the waist up only."

"Wait." The machine held up a hand wearing a military class ring. "Wait, hear me out. It's this kind of behavior we might have expected, knowing your test scores. You must learn to deal with given reality, Mr. Sewell.

"Now we'll submit your scores and application to the board, and their decision will be final. You aren't out of the running yet, unless you wish to be."

Sewell wanted to step around behind the desk, grab the coax that formed the bottom half of the interviewer, and twitch it out of its socket, leaving "him" frozen with that smarmy smile on "his" face. But he also wanted to be an explorer, and there was only one way to get out there, through GX.

Therefore he remained seated, staring at a poster of an explorer with the usual equipment: cleft chin, white teeth, blond hair being rumpled by an alien wind, and far-seeing blue eyes. Three lightning bolts carried the message:

"IT TAKES GUTS."

"IT TAKES IMAGINATION."

"ARE 'YOU' MAN ENOUGH?"

Behind him the interviewer cleared its throat. "We'll be calling you, then, Mr. Sewell."

Whoever the board were (and he imagined a coven of humanoid mechanisms grinning and nodding at one another), they did finally approve his application. When he had signed his contract, things moved into high gear. In one day he was uniformed, inoculated and given a brief lecture on his destination, New Cedar Rapids. Early the next morning, he was transmitted.

He snowshoed the quarter mile of sand from the receiver to the main tent, wearing an oxygen mask and goggles. It was unpleasant just the same, slogging along. The wind was cold, flailing him with grit. By the time he'd arrived, he felt as if his neck and ears were bleeding, and his scalp caked with dirt.

Through his grimy goggles he saw two figures waiting to greet him inside the plastic tent, a man and a woman. It was only when he had got inside that Sewell realized the "woman" was a machine. "She" was of indeterminate age, slim, almost pretty, if you didn't notice the hinged jaw.

"Hi," she said, shaking his dusty hand. "I'm Rita, your partner here. This is Benny, the man you're rotating for some well-earned rest back home."

Oddly enough, it was she who seemed spontaneous and alive, while Benny behaved like a run-down clock. He did not offer to shake hands, but only stared at Sewell for several moments; then turned and walked slowly away. He returned with a log book and pen.

"I'll sign out, then," he said, looking hesitantly from one to the other.

"He wants you to sign in," Rita explained. "So he can leave."

"For some well-earned," said Sewell drily. He took the

book and signed, wondering about the other man. Couldn't he have shaken hands or said hello? All right, he was tired, but——

"Goodbye, Benny," the machine said. Benny mumbled a reply, slipped on the mask and stumbled away, not even looking at Sewell.

"Roger Sewell," she read from the book. "May I call you Roger?"

"Suit yourself. Where do I put my stuff?"

"I'll have to clean up Benny's quarters for you—it's a pigsty. Honestly, I don't know how you men can get that way, I really don't. I don't have an official name, by the way. My makers called me Rita, but my friends usually call me Mom."

"Mom? Why?"

"I don't know. A joke? Because that's what they need out here, maybe, a mom. Because they depend on me? I don't know."

Sewell decided to call her nothing at all.

"Well, what are my duties going to be? What's the routine?"

She smiled. "We can talk about that tomorrow. Right now I'll clean up your room, Roger, and then maybe you'd like to take a nap. You must be tired from your trip."

He didn't like this. "No, I'm not tired at all, as a matter of fact. And I'll clean the room myself, thank you."

He did, and dumped Benny's miserable effects—dirty socks, a bent deck of cards, a comb fluffy with dead hair—into a plastic bag. He installed Jane's picture, his philosophy books, his journal. After making the bed, he sat on it, and prepared to meditate. The door slammed open.

"I thought you might like a nice cup of tea, Roger. I could have made coffee, if you'd preferred, but I was making tea anyhow and so I just thought I'd try it out on you. You sort of look like a tea man to me, I could be wrong, but usually I can tell a tea or coffee person just by looking at them. The only ones who ever throw me are the cocoa people, and thank God there aren't many of them. I don't know what it is, but I never have trusted a man who likes cocoa all the time, so you know what I mean? Oh, I know it's silly, but . . ."

He sat there, amazed, and watched her. She talked on

about tea, about the different kinds, and the fact that
they all come from the same plant, but from different
parts of it, harvested at different times of the year. She
spoke briefly of tea ceremonies, of which she personally
knew nothing, she would be the first to admit, and of un-
just tea taxes and the Revolutionary War. She went on,
until the tea grew cold in the cup she was holding. Then
she went back to the kitchen.

Sewell wedged a chair against the door. When he had
meditated for half an hour, he felt mildly euphoric, full
of energy and ready to start work. The chair began to
crack.

"Why have you got your door fastened? Roger, it's
only me, bringing you a cup of tea. Roger?"

The chair splintered and in she came, beaming through
the steam. As he drank the tea, she told him Benny and
the others had always liked a cup of tea at about this time
of day. Of course Benny was English, and liked his tea
with milk. She preferred lemon, some nothing. Then
there were catnip tea, camomile tea and mint tea . . .

Sewell finally stopped the flow by asking her about the
work.

"Oh don't worry about that, not today. You just got
here, for goodness sake. Take it easy."

"I didn't come here to take it easy," he found himself
shouting. "I came here to explore. Now are you going to
tell me the set-up, or am I going to switch you off?"

"I'm sorry." She was silent a moment, twisting her
fingers in the ends of her apron strings. "Roger, I didn't
want to tell you this right away, but the fact is, there just
isn't any set-up. There just aren't any duties for you."

"What do you mean?" He leaped up and grabbed her
by the throat. "What do you mean by that?"

"It's true," she said evenly. "You can check the general rules bulletin, and the roster of back orders, clear
back thirty years ago, when we first came here to Cedar
Rapids."

"I believe I'll do just that!" He slammed her against
the wall and strode into the office. An hour later, when
she brought him a sandwich and milk, he was sitting with
his hands tangled in his gritty hair.

It was true. The first explorers had measured the
planet, discovered its single mountain chain, examined
the consistency of the sand that buried nearly everything

else, plumbed the two lakes, tested their water, and recorded the weather.

Now, as far as GX was concerned, the work was finished. Daily weather observations and periodic examination of the sand could best be done by machines. A man would be stationed on New Cedar Rapids to keep GX's claim clear, "just in case." There was nothing for him to do, for two years.

"I think I'll go out and scout around anyway," he said, later that evening. "Where's the oxygen equipment?"

"Well—actually there isn't any, Roger. We haven't kept one here for years. There's just the one each new man wears, which the old man wears when he leaves again."

"Damn!" He thought for a moment. "I could probably get by with just an air filter, for a little while. I'll try that."

The machine had begun baking cookies, and the tent was filled with the fresh smell. "You'll have to get an early start, then," she said. "The wind gets too high later on."

But he slept late the next morning, and when he awoke, it was with the luxurious feeling of playing hookey. This wasn't going to be so bad at all, he reasoned. There were a million worthwhile things he could fill his time with: there was his study of logical empiricism, which he could really get into, maybe even write a paper or two. There was his journal. All right, it wouldn't be a chronicle of adventure, but a record of his thoughts and impressions from the center of a sandstorm. He could write a novel. Finally, he could meditate. In fact, he could begin right now.

But first, breakfast in bed. She lingered in the doorway, asking him what he'd dreamed, commenting on the way he'd arranged the room. "Is that your girl? 'All my love, Jane.' Isn't that sweet? Nice-looking girl, too. What they call photogenic. Some people never come out right in pictures, and others look much better than they *really* look, you know? I'll bet Jane is that type."

"What about you, Rita-Mom? I'll bet you photograph just exactly the way you look *in life,* eh?" He chuckled, seeing the remark had hit home.

He tried to do some philosophy with what was left of the morning, but she interrupted him first to clean the room ("It's in the general regulations"), and again to ask him what he preferred for lunch.

Lunch was excellent, but the home-brewed beer that went with it made him sleepy. He dreamed of Jane, but the machine kept wandering into the dream at awkward moments. Then, Jane, too, became a machine, and he discovered that, from the waist down, she consisted of nothing but a coaxial cable.

He awoke late in the afternoon, with a headache and an unpleasant taste in his mouth. Mom was there with the aspirin and lemon tea.

"I've wasted the whole day," he said. "It's getting dark."

"You just aren't adjusted," she said soothingly. "The day only has twenty hours here, you know. I've never figured out why they stuck to the same old clock, instead of shortening the hours, and having twenty-four again. As it is, they have a fraction left over every day, so we gain a day every so many months. Or is it lose a day? I never can remember whether you set the clock ahead or behind, can you? It's the same with Daylight Savings Time . . ." And she was off, discoursing ignorantly on time for nearly one (normal) hour. It was only a machine, he told himself. He could turn it off any time.

He sat over his journal for four hours after dinner, but all he could write was:

"Sand. Sand. Sand."

The following days were more of the same. His study of philosophy bogged down the day she showed him she could reel off pages and pages of Wittgenstein in German or English—and considered Wittgenstein a waste of time. He noticed he was putting on weight, then stopped noticing. Finally he hung a dirty undershirt over the mirror in his room, and forbade her to touch it.

She interrupted his meditations so often that he found them impossible even when she didn't interrupt. He stopped shaving, at first to annoy her, then for no reason at all. In her cleaning, one day, she knocked Jane's picture down and cracked the glass. He forbade her to clean his room any more, regulations or no.

He found her supply of home brew and got drunk, sitting at the kitchen table and listening to her endless chattering.

"Shut up!" he screamed. Seizing her by the shoulders,

he shook her. "Shut up, for God's sake!" And stopped her moving, plastic mouth with his own mouth. "I want a woman," he murmured.

Slowly but firmly, the steel rods in her arms pushed him away. As always, her expression was calm. "Unfortunately, my manufacturers didn't foresee your need," she said drily.

"What?" he grunted it, his flushed, uncomprehending face hanging over her. He had begun to list, slightly.

"I'm not a woman," she said, pronouncing the words slowly and distinctly. "I'm a Kewpie doll, Roger."

He was on his knees, vomiting, and then he lay flat in it and went to sleep.

In the morning he wrote a second entry in his journal: "We are all machines, or"

He lay the fiber pen down without capping it. The ink in it dried, and the page with the unfinished entry became dusty.

With a fine irony, he began to call her "Mom." It became a meaningless, habitual form of address.

He wanted to go out, into the sandstorm, just once before his replacement arrived. But he was afraid.

Mom was talking about Jane's photograph. "I mean, since the glass is cracked anyway, and it really is silly to try to remember people from photographs, either you remember them anyway, or——"

He touched the switch at the lobe of her ear, and she became a statue. In the silence, he could hear her watch.

Tying a cloth over his face, he hurried out.

It was inhumanly cold. The faceless landscape around him lay dormant. It was the floor of some lifeless sea, cold, empty, frightening. With effort, Roger pushed himself away from the door and waded out a few steps.

Then the bleak wastes came to life, at the touch of the morning wind. Dunes began to blur and shift, and the light of the sun was dimmed. Roger's breath came harder.

What was he doing here? The wind was furious, now, trying to bury his legs, flinging sand at his eyes. A man could die here like a scream, unnoticed amid the senseless movement of the sand. Roger felt himself smothering. The door, only a dozen steps away, seemed now unreachable. He saw himself choking, dying, his lungs filling up with sand, flesh torn from his bones, the bones themselves rubbed to sand . . .

Roger stumbled inside and fell across his bed, coughing and cursing, the tears pouring from his sore eyes. It was some time before he realized, with a shock, that he was having hysterics.

"They told me an explorer needs guts and imagination," he wrote in his journal. "It was a lie. An explorer must be a coward, afraid to do anything beyond strictly following orders. He must not be able to care about a woman, a set of ideas, or a way of thinking or feeling. He must deal only with the mundane, the day-to-day, the 'given reality,' as the interviewer said.

"I think GX was ingenious to think of using a Mom for each explorer, to help break him down to an efficient tool. He who lives with machines becomes machine-like, and now I see the title Mom is more than honorific. She is truly the mother of the mechanism Roger Sewell."

It was clever of GX to provide her with a switch, he thought. As if he were able to switch her off for good.

"—else you don't. Well, I see you've turned me off long enough to go outside and come back in tracking up the whole place, as if I didn't have enough to do. You men! If there weren't any dirt, you'd invent it, I swear. Now what are you doing, burning your journal? What in the world for? We could have used the paper. I was just thinking the other day, if I had some paper, I could write down alternate menus for each meal, and you could just check off what you liked, instead of my having to bother you with a lot of questions. And have you accuse me of talking too much, I know that's what you think. At least I don't brood, my mind's an open book . . ."

1937 A.D.!

Picture, if you will, an inventor, working in his bicycle shop in 1878. His long hair occasionally falls in his eyes; he shakes it aside impatiently, flexes sinewy arms against the pull of a wrench, biting his lip with preoccupation. Now and then he may pause to sip some of the cool lemonade his widowed Mom has brought to him, sip and glance up at the picture of Sam Franklin on the whitewashed plank wall. *Early to bed and early to rise . . .* he thinks. *A penny saved is a penny earned.* His serious brows knit, as he ferrets the last bit of truth from these proverbs.

Such an inventor was Emil Hart. He and his mother shared a small cottage exactly in the center of the state of Kiowa. Their modest home was otherwise undistinguished except for a heavy mortgage, which the good widow hoped to reduce. Toward that end she knitted clever antimacmillans (lacy affairs designed to protect the tops of sofas and chairs from a then-popular hair grease called MacMillan's) and sold peafowl eggs. Emil augmented this meager income by repairing bicycles and selling the FRIDAY EVENING POST (founded by Sam Franklin). Yet he knew fate intended for him a greater calling—inventor of the Time Engine!

One day Fenton Morbes, the town bully, stopped by. Seeing the great engine spread over the entire shop, he whistled with amazement.

"What'cher doing?" he asked.

"I'm only filing a bit of isinglass," said Emil, shaking the hair from his eyes. He had no time to waste speaking to Morbes.

"I mean, what'cher building?" Morbes removed his bicycle clips and tossed them carelessly into a corner. They were made of costly aluminum, for he was rich.

Emil sighed. "I'm building a temporal extrapolator," he said. "It will enable me to go into the future."

The bully guffawed. "Stuff!" he said. "Nobody kin go into the future!"

With a knowing smile, Emil bent over his work. After fitting the piece of isinglass into a gear of peculiar shape, he set about attaching a pair of wires to a telegraph key.

Morbes flushed red about the nostrils of his broad, saddlelike nose. He was not used to being ignored. "Stuff!" he exclaimed once more. "Even if it works, this here engine won't bring in enough to feed your peafowls, let alone pay the mortgage when my Paw comes around to foreclose."

"Foreclose!" said the young inventor, growing pale.

"Yep. You'd better have a hundred dollars ready by next Monday," said Morbes with a grin. "Tell you what. If you'll wash my bicycle, I'll give you a whole dollar. Get it spanking clean now, for I'm to go on a picnic to-day, with Miss Maud Peed."

At this news, Emil grew even paler, and staggered back as though he'd been struck.

"Oh, I know you been kinda sweet on her," smirked the bully. "But she ain't got no time for a crazy feller what putters around his bicycle shop with time engines. Hah!"

No time for him! As the color continued to ebb from Emil's face, and into the coarser features of his rival, he wondered what strange fate it was that had made them both suitors for the hand of the lovely Maud Peed. So be it. He raised his tear-filled eyes once more to the portrait of Sam Franklin. He seemed to draw strength from the homely features, the rheumy eyes. What was the right thing to do, the truly *Columbian* thing? To try to stay and win Maud back from Fenton Morbes—a hopeless task? Or to escape into the bright future, and there seek his fortune?

In a moment he had made his decision. He would go

into tomorrow! He would see 1937 A.D., that promised land—the very system of numbering our years promised it! He would drink in its wonders: flying machines, the bridge across the English Channel, immortality through mesmerism, electric cannon, a world at peace, where the sun never set on the flag of the United States of Columbia!

"Are you gonna stand gawking at that pitcher or are you gonna wash my wheel?" demanded Morbes.

"Neither. You may take yourself off my property at once," replied Emil. Raising his clenched fists, he added, "Go to Maud Peed. And tell her—tell her——"

His hands dropped to his sides, and as his head bowed, the unruly lock of hair fell over his eyes. He looked not unlike the young Abner Lincoln, thought Morbes idly.

"—tell her," Emil said quietly, "that the best man has won. I wish you both a—haha—a happy future!" With a strangled sob he turned away.

Morbes was so startled by this outburst that he was unable to summon a bluster to his lips. He turned and walked out.

Emil knew he had done the right thing. Without another regret, he filled his pockets with his Mom's home-baked cookies, took a last sip of lemonade, and began to pedal the great generator that powered his engine. He had mounted a special clock face on the handlebars before him, and when its hands reached 1937, he depressed the telegraph key. "Now it is

1937 A.D.!" he exclaimed, and looked about him.

The room had not changed considerably, though it seemed to have become some sort of museum. Emil found himself surrounded by velvet ropes.

"Here, get off there!" said a man in uniform. He seized Emil's arm and dragged him away from the time engine. "You're not to touch the exhibits, understand?"

Before the bewildered inventor could explain, he found himself outside the shop, looking up at a brass plaque which read, "The Emil Hart Historical Museum." He was historical!

Pausing only a moment to marvel at his fame, Emil strode toward the main street of town, eager to see the changes time had wrought. The streets, he noticed, had a new hard surface, and there was not a trace of manure upon it!

Then he saw them, lined up at the sidewalk. Great trackless locomotives, just as he had imagined them. As he watched, two men emerged from a store and entered one of them. Through its window he could see one man shoveling coal into the boiler while the other turned valves. In a moment, the great, chuffing engine moved off down the street.

His momentary elation dissipated at once, when Emil turned to look at the shops. There was not a single new building on Main Street, and though many had installed large plate glass windows, the facades above them were faded, dirty and abused. Delmonico's Dining Room had become the Eateria, but Carlson's Peafowl Feed Store had not even changed its sign. Emil examined the contents of a clothing store window, his gorge rising at their dull familiarity. Why weren't people attired in seminude costumes of gold, with scarlet capes? The mannikins showed only women in the same silly hats and long gowns, men in dark, dull suits. Worse, the one or two pedestrians he glimpsed wore overalls of the same cut and hue as his own.

He was thoroughly depressed by the time he reached the end of the town's single street and the Public Library. Despairing of seeing any more wonderful inventions like the trackless locomotive, Emil made his way into the familiar building to the tiny room marked "Science and Technology." Here at last he might find respite from the past. Here he might find the future that seemed to have overlooked his town.

He opened a volume marked "Inventions." Yes, here they were: Thomas Elva Addison, the electric light; Burgess Venn, the flying machine; Gordon Q. Mott, the televidium—what in the world was that?

He looked it up in the back of the book, and learned that it was a visual counterpart to the radium. The latter sent verbal messages over long distances by means of electrical "waves" in the ether, while the former did the same for visual messages. He thrilled to the idea of electrical waves moving about everywhere, in this room, passing right through his body. It was only because of the intensity of Emil's meditation that he failed to notice the figure at his elbow.

"Hullo, Emil." It was Morbes.

"You used my machine?"

"Yep. I came back to get my bicycle clips and I seen you was gone. Well, I got to thinking—a feller could make himself a pile of money outa knowing what happens in the future. So here I am. Where do they keep the old newspapers?"

"What are you going to do?" Emil leaped to his feet, knocking over a chair. Another reader cleared his throat.

"Read about a few horse races—and some stock market stuff. I'm rich now, Emil Hart, but I'm gonna be richer." Morbes's grin displayed a row of uneven, stained teeth.

"You can't! It's dishonest! Think of all the little stockholders who might be ruined by your speculations!" cried Emil. He followed the bully into the Historical & Periodical room, and seized his arm. Morbes shook his hand away.

"Leave me alone!" he bellowed. "I'll do as I see fit!"

"Yes, do leave him alone!" commanded a childish voice. "I'm trying to read here, and you're creating a disturbance." Emil looked around to confront a boy of about ten, whose forehead was creased with annoyance beneath the line of his yellow bangs.

Grinning, Morbes said, "Lad, where's the newspapers? You know, the WAAL STREET JOURNAL?"

"I don't know. All they have in here is this." The boy indicated the volume open before him, in which he had been scribbling with a pen. Emil noticed it was one of a large matched set that seemed to occupy all the shelves of the room. There were thousands of volumes.

"But this will have whatever you're looking for," said the boy. "It has a synopsis of everything."

The set of books was entitled *The Universal Synopsis.*

"Say" exclaimed Morbes, illuminated by an uncharacteristic flash of intuition. "If I get rich like I ought to, there should be something about *me* in that book."

He searched a moment, then came to the table with volume MORAY-MORBID and seated himself opposite the boy.

"Here it is! Morbes, Fenton Jr.," he read at the top of his lungs.

"Don't read on!" said Emil. "We're not meant to know our own futures."

"Stuff! Who's to stop me?"

"I am!" Emil shouted, and snatching up the boy's pen, dipped it and lined out the passage Morbes was about to read.

"Say, why'd you do that? I——"

With an audible click, Fenton Morbes vanished.

"How interesting!" said the boy. "I was right, then. This *is* the only extant copy."

"What?" Emil stood frozen, gaping at the space his rival had vacated so abruptly.

"You don't know what happened? That was the 'Doppler Effect,' named for myself, Julius Doppler. Sit down, won't you, and I'll explain it to you."

Emil eased himself into a chair and with effort directed his gaze toward the serious, freckled face.

"You see, I've developed a theory that the future influences the past. I was fortunate in finding *The Universal Synopsis* on which to test it. If this were, as I believed it to be, the only copy of the only book in which many items appeared, why then it follows that I can change the past by merely rewriting it."

"But how can you change history?" asked Emil, mystified.

"It's simple semantics: The word *is* the thing—at least after the thing ceases to be. Alter a word in the future and you alter the thing it once stood for. Let me show you."

The boy opened his volume to a page and pointed. "Now here, I altered the name 'Sam Franklin' to 'John Franklin,' for example. But if in the future, someone came along and changed it to—say—'Ben,' why he'd *be* Ben, don't you see?"

"No."

"All right, look here, then." Julius turned to a map of the United States. There was the familiar pink lozenge that was Kiowa, and just above it, the green hourglass of Minnehaha—but the names were wrong! "Kiowa" missed its "K," and "Minnehaha" read "Minnesota"! And the name at the bottom of the page, following "The United States of" was not "Columbia" but some unpronounceable Latin name! The map was wrong, it had been printed wrong!

"Last week," said the boy, "I made these changes in

ink. Now this week they are part of the original book."

"But how can that be?"

Julius frowned. "I think the past must influence the future, too," he said. "But the influence is *slower*. My theory is really quite a simple one, but I couldn't possibly explain it to *you*, not all of it. Why, you don't even understand $e=mc^3$, for Pete's sake."

"I understand one thing," said Emil, leaping up. "I know that I *killed* poor Morbes! I am a murderer!"

"Don't take it so hard," said the boy. "You wouldn't have, if it weren't for me. In fact, the only reason you're a time-traveler is because I wrote the whole thing in the margin near your name."

"My name?" Emil was electrified at this reminder of his fame. "My name . . . Won't you have a cookie?"

"Thanks." The two of them munched Widow Hart's cookies and discussed the theory once more, until Emil was sure he understood. He was not so sure he liked being at the mercy of the future, but when one considered it, it was no worse than being at the mercy of the past. One survived.

When the last cookie was gone, Emil rose and took his leave. He strolled back to the museum and paid his admission. After a few moments, he was able to seize an opportunity when the guard was not looking and leap upon his time engine. He pedaled furiously backward to 1878, and what a glorious feeling mounted in his breast as he gazed once more on the homely features of John Franklin.

"I *am* healthy, wealthy and wise—or shall be shortly," Emil told himself. "My rival is gone—I don't even remember his name—and I am to be famous!"

After changing to his Sunday clothes, he picked a nosegay of his Mom's flowers and set off toward the Peed house.

Mr. Peed was seated in the porch swing, industriously polishing his pipe against his nose.

"Hallo, young Hart," he called out. "What brings you out this evening, all dressed up like that?"

"I——" Emil began, then realized he did not know the answer. Why *had* he come to see Mr. and Mrs. Peed?

"Flowers for your wife," he decided aloud. "From Mom's garden."

"Whose wife?" asked Peed, leaning forward to accept the nosegay. "I ain't married, son. I——"

Peed's outstretched hand grew transparent. Then Peed, porch and house vanished with a click.

It was a nightmare! Emil hurried home to check on his Mom. There was no telling who might click out of existence next!

He was reassured by the sight of her frail old figure tottering into his shop with a tray.

"Here, let me take that," he said, and accepted the tray from her careworn hands.

"Lemonade and cookies—for me? Gee, you're good, Mom!" He bent and kissed her white hair. With a beatific smile, the old lady tottered back to her kitchen, whence came the smell of fresh baking. Fearfully, Emil watched until she was out of sight.

He cornered Julius in the library and demanded an explanation.

"Of what?" asked the youngster. "An explanation of what?"

"I'm not sure, but I think the Peeds had a daughter, and I think I was in love with her. Now she's gone, and they're gone—have you been eating again?"

"You did it yourself, pal. When you crossed out the reference to Fenton what's-his-name, you also destroyed the only existing reference to the girl, Maud. She was his wife. You got any more cookies?"

"You mean I'd have lost her in any case?"

"Uh-huh." With his mouth full of the widow's cookies, the boy explained. Destroying Maud had destroyed her parents, their parents, and so on, back to the time when some relative was famous enough to have appeared in *The Universal Synopsis*. It was difficult for Emil to follow, for not only did the boy speak with his mouth full, but neither he nor Emil could clearly remember who it was they were discussing. As Julius said, it was all very mythical—or perhaps he said mystical.

At last, Emil was brought to understand he had lost the only girl he'd ever loved. His grief was superb.

He knew it was his own fault. If only he had not wanted to glimpse the golden towers and battlements of the future! If only he had been content! His sin was pride, pride that goeth before (or, according to Julius, cometh after) a great fall.

What had she been like, this girl he'd lost? He had some faint reminiscence of her lovely eyes being hazel —or else her hair—or was it her name? In despair, he put his head on his arms and wept unashamedly.

"Here, read this," said Julius Doppler. "It'll cheer you up."

It was the volume HART–HARUSPEX, and in it, Emil read:

"Hart, Emil (1860–?), inventor of the time engine and only successful time traveler. Leaving 1878 he journeyed into 1937, where, in a public library, he met *Julius Doppler* (q.v.), who explained to him the famed 'Doppler Effect'—the influence of the future upon the past. After several blunders, Hart finally read his own story in *The Universal Synopsis* (q.v.), and realized as he did so that, had he read it earlier, he might have avoided making a costly mistake, the deletion of some probably mythical woman from history. As he realized all this, Hart is reported to have said, 'Thunderation! Why didn't I think of this before?' "

"Thunderation!" said Emil, smiting his forehead. "Why didn't I think of this before?"

He referred not to his past mistakes, however, but to his successes yet to come. Borrowing the pen from Julius, who had just changed the peafowl to a chicken, Emil wrote in the margin the following:

"Nonplussed, the stout-hearted inventor re-created his girl, Hazel Peid, from memory, adding her to his life story. After a brief courtship, they married. The plucky Hart went on to become healthy, wealthy and wise."

After a moment of thought, he added:

"And nothing anyone writes here in the future will ever make it otherwise."

Then, giving Julius the last cookie, he departed.

She was there in his shop, the lovely Hazel Peid of the hazel hair and eyes—just as he remembered her. Going upon one knee, and tossing back his unruly lock, Emil said, "Miss Peid, will you be my wife?"

"Oh yes!" she exclaimed, clapping her small, well-formed hands together.

"This calls for a celebration," said Mom, tottering in with a tray. "Won't you have some lemonade and cookies?"

Emil and his fiancée embraced, while above them the rheumy eyes of Ben Franklin seemed to smile a blessing.

The Transcendental
Sandwich

"We can give you knowledge," said the salesman-thing.

Claude Mabry looked all around his room: mildewed wallpaper, broken linoleum, dirty long underwear slung over a chair that had a weak leg, the clock face that had been cracked and repaired so many time with Scotch tape that he could hardly see it said 3:20.

"I'm smart enough for me," he said. "There's such a thing as being too smart for your own good."

"That's right," said the salesman-thing, "and there's such a thing as being so smart you have to wash dishes down at Stan's Chili Bowl to earn enough to live—here."

Claude could not reply. The whole thing reminded him of the Bible: a snake or whatever it was dressed up like a man, offering "knowledge"—it just didn't make sense.

"Look, I don't mean to be unpleasant," said the salesman. "But we Guzz are a hell of a lot more powerful and a hell of a lot smarter than your species. If we'd wanted to, we could have vaporized your whole planet—but it's not our way. So when somebody comes offering to make you smart, don't knock it."

Claude wanted to rip off that grinning, false mansuit and see what the Guzz looked like. He half-rose, then sank back again and looked at the floor.

"If you're so good, why do you want to do anything for me?"

"I don't want to do anything for you. I voted to turn

Earth into a bird refuge. But we have a democratic form of government and the majority wanted to make your kind fit citizens to share the universe with us."

"All right, how do I know you can make me smart?"

The salesman opened his briefcase and took out a handful of bright brochures. "Don't take my word for it that we can make you one of the smartest men on Earth," he said. "Don't take it from me that being smart is worthwhile. Millions are trying our plan. Thousands have tried it already. Have a look."

He handed Claude a folder showing full-color pictures of quiet scholars, white-coated scientists, dignified judges and beaming businessmen. Their testimonials were capped with red headlines:

COULDN'T READ OWN NAME—
NOW COMMANDS 20 LANGUAGES!

FAMOUS ECONOMIST
"HATED ARITHMETIC"

"DUMB OX"
TO BRILLIANT THEOLOGIAN—IN 7 MONTHS!

"But—what would I study?"

"Everything." The salesman produced another slick booklet and began turning the pages, showing Claude pictures of happy housewives and hairy-handed laborers reading heavy volumes, farmers peering through microscopes and grannies using slide rules. "We call our system the Interface Way. Every person we accept must study at least two subjects intensively. If the subjects are unrelated, all the better. We mix mathematics with literature, we throw theoretical physics at a medical specialist, we give the mathematician theology."

"What would I get?"

"If we accepted you, you'd be tested. Then we'd know."

"What do you mean, if?" Claude felt he had just been offered a million dollars, but at the word "if" it had shrunk to about a nickel.

The stranger, sensing his anxiety, spoke soothingly. "Don't worry too much about that. We won't be testing

your I.Q. or previous knowledge. In fact, the less of either, the better. We want people who haven't had a
chance, people who feel useless because the sleeping
genius within them has never been awakened. What do
you say?"

"I don't know. What would it cost me?"

"All the money in the world couldn't buy you a better
education, pal. But all it costs is your signature."

"Well—oh hell, why not?"

"Why not?" echoed the salesman, handing him a pen.
Claude signed a few forms in various colors and the
salesman gave him a copy of each.

"Claude," he said, "you've just made your first intelligent decision."

The Guzz had pretty well taken over Earth, in every
way. Guzz-developed gadgets were in every home.
Clergymen thanked the Lord from their pulpits that the
Guzz were not warlike or vicious but a truly democratic
—ah—people. The government made daily announce-
ments of new Guzz gifts to humanity.

They quietly disarmed the nuclear powers, they made
efficient clean-air and sewage-disposal systems for our
cities, they introduced new food sources and birth-control
plans in Asia. Hardly a government bureau in the world
had not been approached by the Guzz with a suggestion
or a gift—and these aliens used no stronger forces than
tact and kindly persuasion.

The only disagreeable thing about them was the way
they looked—both at home and in Earth-drag.

On their own planet (or so it was said, for no one had
visited them) the Guzz were disagreeably vermiform.
Here, so as not to spook the natives, they wore human
forms of plastic. Their movements in these were natural
enough, but they all looked alike. As far as most people,
including Claude, were concerned, the Guzz were just so
many talking store-window dummies.

The first box that arrived was a table-top computer
equipped with keyboard, microphone, speaker and visual
display screen. That night when he returned from Stan's
Chili Bowl, Claude lay awake looking at all that gleaming, complicated junk and wondering if he might have
made a mistake in even hoping . . .

Next day three packages arrived. The first contained books and a sheaf of documents: a certification that Claude Mabry was eligible for this correspondence course, more copies of the various forms he'd signed—and a booklet entitled: *Welcome, Future Genius!*

"The government of Guzz and your own government wish to take this opportunity to welcome you . . . conditions and by-laws. . . . You may not always see the reasons for instructions given you in this course, but they are necessary to ensure efficient use of your time.

"The enclosed books are for Lesson One. The books required for each lesson will be provided with the lesson. At various points in the program you will be asked to study them thoroughly."

Claude glanced at the titles of the books: *The Interpretation of Dreams,* Sigmund Freud; *Verbal Behavior,* B. F. Skinner; *Towards Information Retrieval,* Fairthorne; were only a few.

The dream book looked interesting but inside, like all the others, it was full of long-winded sentences that didn't mean anything.

The second package contained a tape cassette titled *Program for Lesson One* and simple instructions for loading it into the teaching computer.

As soon as Claude could do so, he switched on the machine. He might have expected it to give him a problem, to register the fact that it was turned on, or at least to ask his name, but it did none of these things.

Instead, it politely requested him to eat a sandwich.

Claude scratched his head. The Guzz had to be joking. He could imagine them watching him right now, laughing at his stupidity. So this was the big learning course! So this . . .

He remembered the third package and tore it open. Inside was a cellophane-wrapped sandwich. Though Claude turned it over and over, he could see only one difference between this and any other cellophane-wrapped sandwich: Inside the wrapper was a plain printed name slip. But instead of "ham and cheese" or "peanut butter and grape jelly" it simply read: Eat me.

The bread was a little stale but he enjoyed the salami or para-salami inside.

An hour later he correctly answered a request to explain how and why dreams were subject to syntactical rules. The answer was obvious.

Two hours later he had read Ayer's *The Problem of Knowledge,* read it at skimming speed because it was already perfectly familiar to him.

A lesson or two later Claude had gone through about fifty difficult books without any trouble. He progressed rapidly through the programs, though it did not seem like progress at all: he simply knew what he was doing. Using Fourier analysis to solve problems in electronics seemed something he had always known, just as he had always realized the gross truth of Newtonian mechanics and the finer truth of quantum mechanics, the position of Hubert Van Eyck in Flemish painting, the syllogistic properties of an Andrew Marvell poem, the flaws in the historical theories of Spengler and Toynbee—or for that matter, how to prepare *sauce ozéne* with seven ingredients. Scraps of learning, areas of learning, even whole complex structures of learning were suddenly his.

Having learned, he worked. By the fourth lesson Claude had gone through Gödel's proof of the necessary incompleteness of mathematical theorems and picked holes in Lucas's application of this to mechanical devices. He had also put forth an aesthetic theory understandable by perhaps ten men, refutable by no more than one. He had nearly destroyed mathematical economics, and devised a tentative translating machine. He was hardly aware that these things had not been done before, nor was he really aware of the transition from his job at the Chili Bowl to a research fellowship at a prominent university.

The transition came about from his publication of various monographs in journals, the names of which he knew only from footnotes in the books he was skimming. Some of the monographs came back. He had sent them to wrong addresses, or to journals long out of print.

Others, like his "Queueing Theory Applied to Neural Activity" and "On Poetic Diction," became classics. Men with tweedy manners but sharp suits and clean attaché cases came to see him. They sat in the steamy, oily kitchen of Stan's Chili Bowl and talked with him about quasar explanations, new codes of international law and logic mechanisms. True, many prodigies were springing up now that the Guzz offered their massive home study program. But for the time being, genius was still something universities fought over. And so, almost without knowing it (he was thinking of other things), Claude Mabry gave Stan his notice, packed his T-shirts and blue jeans and entrained for Attica University.

He remembered only isolated facts about this trip: sending a change-of-address card to the Guzz; losing his ticket; not bringing enough paper (and so alighting from the train at Attica, where University officials were waiting to greet him, his hands so full of slips of toilet paper on which were penciled notes toward a theory of history that he could not accept the handshakes of these venerables). Without comment he settled into his new life and went on working.

From time to time he wondered what was in the sandwich that came with each lesson. A wonder drug that unlocked hidden knowledge that lay "sleeping" within him? An intelligence accelerator? Whatever it was, it was essential to the process. The only time he'd tried studying without it, Claude had floundered among symbols that *almost* made sense.

He wondered, too, about the Guzz. The little he learned about their planet and culture (in the final lesson) whetted his appetite for more. He longed to know everything about them, almost to become one of them: They alone would understand what he was doing. It was becoming clear that his colleagues at the university considered him some kind of freak—he would not wear a suit, he could not converse about departmental politics and he was inhumanly intelligent.

Claude ordered all the information on the Guzz he could get. This proved to be a slim volume by a second-rate anthropologist who had interviewed a few of the aliens. Claude skimmed it and began a treatise of his own.

"Despite the advanced 'democracy' of the Guzz," he wrote, "they retain a few oddly 'primitive,' even sacramental habits."

There was a knock at the door. The standard face of a Guzz looked around the frame, saw that he was alone and walked its standard body into the office. Without saying anything, it came over and struck him on the forehead. Twitching, Claude slipped to the floor. The visitor busied itself with a set of plastic bags.

The fallen man was muttering. Bending lower, the man-shape heard: ". . . planarian worms? D.N.A. or . . .?"

"Right you are!" boomed the Guzz. "Yes, we *are* analogous to your planarian worms—so, of course, are you—and we can transmit behavior genetically."

He fished a long knife from one bag and tested its blade against a false thumb. "Of course our genes need help. Obviously our—I mean to include your—children do not learn much from their parents' genes. But these same genes, properly assimilated——"

"I knew it!" Claude croaked, getting up on one elbow. The blow had stunned him, but still the machinery of his mind ground on. With an ecstatic expression he said, "The old taboos against eating the king, eating the old man, the sage, the father, yes?"

"Check." With a hearty chuckle the visitor kneeled by Claude's side and felt for the carotid artery. "Those ridiculous taboos have kept your species back hundreds of thousands of years. We're just now making up the lost time for you."

"The sandwich meat——"

"Housewives, mechanics, professional people—all the people in that brochure you saw. Just think of it!" He waved the knife oratorically, and the plastic face turned up, as if gazing at a vista. "One genius provides three thousand sandwiches, each capable of providing—with no wastage—part of the education for one more genius! Thus learning will transform your whole species—you will become as gods!"

The Guzz returned his attention to the matter at hand. He poised the kinfe.

"Superman," murmured the genius. "On white or rye."

The Steam-Driven Boy

Capt. Charles Conn was thinking so hard his feet hurt.
It reminded him of his first days on the force, back in
'89, when walking a beat gave him headaches.

Three time-patrolmen stood before his desk, treading
awkwardly on the edges of their long red cloaks and
fingering their helmets nervously. Capt. Conn wanted to
snarl at them, but what was the point? They already understood his problems perfectly—they were, after all, Conn
himself, doubling a shift.

"Okay, Charlie, report."

The first patrolman straightened. "I went back to three
separate periods, sir. One when the President was dis-
banding the House of Representatives, one when he pro-
claimed himself the Supreme Court, one when he was
signing the pro-pollution bill. I gave him the whole business—statistics, pictures, news stories. All he would say
was, 'My mind's made up.'"

Chuck and Chas reported similar failures. There was
no stopping the President. Not only had he usurped all
the power of federal, state and local government, but
he used those powers deliberately to torment the population. It was a crime to eat ice cream, sing, whistle, swear
or kiss. It was a *capital* offense to smile, or to use the
words "Russia" and "China." Under the Safe Streets Act
it was illegal to walk, loiter or converse in public. And
of course Negroes and anyone else "conspicuous" were

by definition criminal, and under the jurisdiction of the Race Reaction Board.

The Natural Food Act had seemed at first almost reasonable, a response to scientists' warnings about depleting the soil and polluting the environment. But the fine print specified that henceforth no fertilizers were to be used but human or canine excrement, and all farm machinery was forbidden. In time the newspapers featured pictures of farmers trudging past their rusting tractors to poke holes in the soil with sharp sticks. And in time, the newspapers had their paper supply curtailed. Famine warnings were ignored until the government had to buy wheat from C****.

"Gentlemen, we've tried everything else. *It's time to think about getting rid of President Ernie Barnes.*"

The men began murmuring among themselves. This was done with efficiency and dispatch, for Patrolman Charlie, knowing that Chuck was going to murmur to him first, withheld his own murmuring until it was his turn. And when Chuck had murmured to Charlie, he fell silent, and let Charlie and Chas get on with their murmuring before he murmured uneasily to Chas.

The captain spoke again. "Getting rid of him in the past would be easier than getting rid of him now, but it's only part of the problem. If we remove him from the past we have to make sure no one notices the big jagged hole in history we'll leave. Since as the time police we have the only time-bikes around, the evidence is going to make us look bad. Remember the trouble we had getting rid of the pyramids? For months, everyone went around saying, 'What's that funny thing on the back of the dollar?' Remember that?"

"Hey, Captain, what is that funny thing——?"

"Shut up. The point is, you can change some of the times some of the time, and, uh, some of the—look at it this way: Ernie must have shaken hands with a million people. We rub *him* out, and all these people suddenly get back all the germs they rubbed off on him. Suddenly we have an epidemic."

"Yeah, but, Captain, *did* he ever shake any hands? He never does any more. Just sits there in the White Fort, all fat and nasty, behind all his F.B.I. and C.I.A. and individualized anti-personnel missiles and poison germ gas towers and—and that big, mean dog."

Capt. Conn glared the patrolman down, then continued: "My idea is, we kidnap Ernie Barnes from his childhood, back in 1937. And we leave a glass egg."

"A classic?"

"A *glass egg*. Like they used to put under chickens when they took away their children. What I mean is, we substitute an artificial child for the real one. Wilbur Grafton says he can make a robot replica of Ernie as he looked in 1937."

Wilbur Grafton was a wealthy eccentric and amateur investor well known to all members of the time patrol. Their father, James Conn, was an employee of Wilbur's.

"Another thing. Just in case somebody back in 1937 gets suspicious and takes him apart, we'll have the robot built of pre-1937 junk. Steam-driven. No use giving away secrets of molecular circuitry and peristaltic logic before their time."

The four of them, and a fifth patrolman (Carl) arrived one evening at the mansion of Wilbur Grafton. To the butler who admitted them, each man said "Hello, Dad," to which their unruffled father replied "Good evening, sir. You'll find Mr. Grafton in the drawing-room."

The venerable millionaire, immaculate in evening clothes, welcomed them, then excused himself to prepare the demonstration. James poured generous drinks, and while some of the party admired the authentic 1950s appointments of the room—including a genuine "stereo" phonograph—others watched television. It was almost curfew time, and the channels were massed with Presidential commercials.

"Sleep well, America! Your President is safe! Yes, thanks to I.A.M.—individualized anti-personnel missiles —no one can harm our Leader. Think of it: over ten billion eternally vigilant little missiles all around the White Fort, guarding his sleep and yours. And don't forget—there's one with YOUR name on it."

Wilbur Grafton returned, and at curfew time, one of the men asked him to begin the demonstration. He wheezed with delight. His glasses twinkling, he replied: "My good man, the demonstration is already going on." Pressing one of his shirt studs, he added, "And here is— The Steam-Driven Boy!"

His body parted down the middle and swung open in

two half-shells, revealing a pudgy youngster in knitted swim trunks and striped T-shirt, who was determinedly working cranks and levers. The boy stopped operating the "Grafton wheeze-laugh" bellows, climbed out of the casing, took two steps and froze.

"Then where's the real Wilbur Grafton?" asked Chuck.

"Right here, sir." The butler put down a priceless Woolworth's decanter and pulled his own nose, hard. Clanking and creaking, he parted like a mummy case to give up the living Grafton, once more flawlessly attired.

"Must have my little japes," he wheezed, as the real James came in with more drinks. "Now, allow me to reanimate our little friend for you."

He inserted a crank in the boy's ear and gave it several vigorous turns. With a light chuffing sound, and emitting only a hint of vapor, the small automaton came to life. That piggish nose, those wide-spaced eyes, that malicious grin were familiar to all present, from Your President Cares posters.

As the white-haired inventor stooped to make some further adjustment at the back of its fat neck, "Ernie" kicked him authentically in the knee.

"Did you see that precision?" Wilbur gloated, dancing on one leg.

The robot was remarkably realistic, complete to a frayed strip of dirty adhesive tape on one shiny elbow. Charlie made the mistake of squatting down and offering Ernie some candy. Two other patrolmen helped their unfortunate comrade to a sofa, where he was able to get his head back to stop the bleeding. The little machine shrieked with delight until Wilbur managed to shut it off.

"I am confident that his parents will never notice the switch," he said, leading the way to his workshop. "Let me show you the plans."

The robot had organs analogous to those of a living being, as Wilbur Grafton's plans showed. The heart and veins were really an intricate hydraulic system; the liver a tiny distillery to volatilize eaten food and extract oil from it. Part of this oil replenished the veins, part was burned to feed the spleen's miniature steam engine. From this, belts supplied power to the limbs.

Digressing, Wilbur explained how his grandfather, Orville Grafton, had developed a peculiar substance, a plate of which varied in thickness according to the intensity of light striking it.

"While grandfather could make nothing more useful of this 'graftonite' than bas-relief photographs, I have used it (along with mechanical irises and gelatine lenses) to form the boy's eyes," he said, and pointed to a detail. "When a tiny image has been focused on each graftonite 'retina,' a pantographic scriber traces swiftly over it, translating these images to motions in the brain."

Similar levers conveyed motions from the gramophone ears, and from hundreds of tiny pistons all over the body —the sense of touch.

The hydraulic fluid was a suspension of red particles like blood corpuscles. When it oozed to the surface, through pores, these were filtered out—it doubled as perspiration.

The brain contained a number of springs, wound to various tensions. With the clockwork connecting them to various limbs, organs and facial features, these comprised Ernie's "memory."

Grafton let the plans roll shut with a snap and ordered James to charge the glasses with champagne. "Gentlemen, I give you false Ernie Barnes—from his balloon lungs out to his skin of rubberized lawn, fine wig and dentures—an all-American boy, made in U.S.A.!"

"One thing, though," said the captain. "Won't his parents notice he doesn't—well, *grow?*"

Sighing, the inventor turned his back for a moment, and gripped the edge of his workbench to steady himself. A solemn silence descended upon the group as they saw him take off his glasses and rub his eyes.

"Gentlemen," he said quietly, "I have taken care of everything. In one year's time, this child will appear to be suddenly stricken with influenza. His fever will rise, he will weaken. Finally I see him call his mother's name. She approaches the bedside.

" 'Mom,' he says, 'I'm sorry I've been such a wicked kid. Can you find it in your heart to forgive me? For— for I'm going to be an angel from now on.' His eyes flutter closed. His mother bends and kisses the burning forehead. This triggers the final mechanism, and Ernie appears to—to——"

They understood. One by one, the time patrol put

down their glasses and slipped silently from the room. Carl was elected to take the robot back to 1937.

"He was supposed to bring the kid here to headquarters," said Captain Charles Conn. "But he never showed up. And Ernie's still in power. What went wrong?" A worried frown puckered his somewhat bland features as he leafed through the appointment calendar.

"Maybe his timer went wrong," Chas suggested. "Maybe he got off his time-bike at the wrong place. Maybe he had a flat—who knows?"

"He should have been back by now. How long can it take to travel fifty years? Well, no time to figure it out now. According to the calendar, we've all got to double again. I go back to become Charlie. Charlie, you go back to fill in as Chuck. Chuck becomes Chas, and Chas, you take over for Carl." He paused, as the men exchanged badges. "As for Carl—we'll all be finding out what happens to him, soon enough. Let's go!"

And, singing the Time Patrol song (yes, they felt silly, but such was the President's mandate) in deep bass voices, they climbed on their glittering time bicycles, set the egg-timers on their handlebars and sped away.

Carl stepped out from behind a tree in 1937. The kid was kneeling in his sandpile, apparently trying to tie a tin can to a puppy's tail. The gargoyle face looked up at Carl with interest.

"GET OUTA MY YARD! GET OUT OR I'LL TELL ON YA! YOU HAFTA PAY ME ONE APPLE OR ELSE I'LL——"

Still straddling the time-bike, Carl slipped forward to that autumn, picked a particularly luscious apple, and bought a can of ether at the drugstore. Clearly it would take both to get this kid.

"I spose," said the druggist, "I spose ya want me to ask ya why you're wearing a gold football helmet with wings on it and a long red cape. But I won't. Nossir, I seen all kinds . . ."

In revenge, Carl shoplifted an object at random: a Mark Clubb Private Eye Secret Disguise Kit.

Blending back into his fading-out self, Carl held out both hands to the boy. The right held a shiny apple. The left held an ether-soaked handkerchief.

As Carl shoved off into the gray, windswept corridors of

time, with the lumpy kid draped over his handlebars, it occurred to him he needed a better hiding place than Headquarters. The FBI would sweep down on them first, searching for their missing President. A better place would be the mansion of Wilbur Grafton. Or even . . . hmmm.

"An excellent plan!" Wilbur sat by the swimming pool, nursing his injured knee. "We'll smuggle him into the White Fort itself—the one place no one will think of looking for him!"

"One problem is, how to get him in, past all the guards and——"

Wilbur pushed up his glasses and meditated. "You know the President's dog—that big ugly mongrel that appears with him in the Eat More Horsemeat commercials —Ralphie?"

Compulsively Carl sang: "Ralphie loves it, every bite Why don't you try horse tonight?"

"I've been working on a replica of that dog. It should be big enough to contain the boy. You dispose of the real dog tonight, after curfew, then we'll disguise the boy and send him in."

When the dog came out of the White Fort to organically fertilize the lawn, Carl was waiting with the replica dog and an ether-soaked rag. Within a few minutes he had consigned the replica to a White Fort guard and dropped Ralphie in the dim, anonymous corridors of time. No one need fear Ernie's discovery, for the constraints of the dog-shell were such that he could make only canine sounds and motions.

Carl reported back to the mansion.

"I have a confession to make," said the old inventor. "I am not Wilbur Grafton, only a robot.

"The real Wilbur Grafton invented a rejuvenator. Wishing to try it, without attracting attention, he decided to travel into the past—back to 1905, where he could work as an assistant to his grandfather, Orville Grafton."

"Travel back in time? But that takes a time-bike!"

"Precisely. To that end, he agreed to cooperate with the time patrol. On the night he demonstrated the Steam-Driven Boy, you recall he left the room and returned wearing the James-shell? It was I in the shell. The real Wilbur slipped outside, borrowed one of your time-bikes, and went to 1905. He returned the bike on automatic control. I have taken his place ever since."

Carl scratched his head. "Why are you telling me all this?"

"So that you might benefit by it. Using your disguise kit, you can pose as Wilbur Grafton yourself. I realize a time-patrolman's salary is small—especially when one has to do quintuple shifts for the same money. Meanwhile I have a gloriously full life. You could slip back in time and replace me." The robot handed him an envelope. "Here are instructions for dismantling me—and for making the rejuvenator, should you ever feel the need for it. This is a recorded message. Goodbye."

Why not, Carl thought. Here was the blue swimming pool, the "stereo," the whole magnificent house. James, his father, stood discreetly by, ready to pour champagne. And the upstairs maid was uncommonly pretty. It could be a long, long life, rejuvenated from time to time . . .

Ernie sprawled in a giant chair, watching himself on television. When a guard brought in the dog, it bit him. He was just about to call the vexecutioner, to teach Ralphie a lesson, when something in the animal's eyes caught his attention.

"So it's *you*, is it?" He laughed. "Or should I say, so it's *me*. Well, don't bite me again, understand? If you do, I'll leave you inside that thing. And make you eat nasty food, while I sing about it on TV."

"Poop," the child was thinking, Ernie knew.

"I can do it, kid. I'm the President, and I can do anything I like. That's why I'm so fat." He stood up and began to pace the throne room, his stomach preceding him like a front wheel.

"Poopy poop," thought the boy. "If you can do anything, why don't you make everybody go to bed early, and wash their mouths out if they say——"

"I do, I do. But there's a little problem there. You're too young to understand this—I don't understand it all myself, yet—but 'everybody' is you, and you're me. I'm all the people that ever were and ever will be. All the men, anyway. All the women are the girl who used to be upstairs maid at Wilbur Grafton's."

He began explaining time travel to little Ernie, knowing the kid wasn't getting half of it, but going on the way big

Ernie had explained it to him: Carl Conn, posing as Wilbur, had grown old. Finally he'd decided it was time to rejuvenate and go back in time. Fierce old Ralphie, still lurking in the corridors of time, had attacked him, and there'd been quite an accident. One part of Carl had returned to 1905, to become Orville Grafton. Another part of him got rejuved, along with the dog, and had fallen out in 1937.

"That Carl-part, my boy, was you. The rejuvenator wiped out most of your memory—except for dreams—and it made you look all ugly and fat.

"You see, your job and mine, everybody's job, is to weave back and forth in time——" he wove his clumsy hands in the air, "—being people. My next job is to be a butler, and yours is to pretend to be a robot pretending to be you. Then probably you'll be my dad, and I'll be his dad, and then you'll be me. Get it?"

He moved the dog's tail like a lever, and the casing opened. "Would you like some ice-cream? It's okay with me, only nobody else gets none."

The boy nodded. The upstairs maid, pretty as ever, came in with a Presidential sundae. The boy looked at her and his scowl almost turned to a smile.

"Mom?"

Elephant with Wooden Leg

Note: Madmen are often unable to distinguish between dream, reality, and . . . between dream and reality. None of the incidents in Henry LaFarge's narrative ever happened or could have happened. His "Orinoco Institute" bears no relation to the actual think tank of that name, his "Drew Blenheim" in no way resembles the famous futurologist, and his "United States of America" is not even a burlesque upon the real United States of Armorica.

I couldn't hear him.

"Can't hear you, Blenheim. The line must be bad."

"Or mad, Hank. I wonder what that would take?"

"What what?"

"What would it take to drive a telephone system out of its mind, eh? So that it wasn't just giving wrong numbers, but madly right ones. Let's see: Content-addressable computer memories to shift the conversations . . ."

I stopped listening. A bug was crawling up the window frame across the room. It moved like a cockroach, but I couldn't be sure.

"Look, Blenheim, I'm pretty busy today. Is there something on your mind?"

He plowed right on. ". . . so if you're trying to reserve a seat on the plane to Seville, you'd get a seat at the opera instead. While the person who wants the opera seat is really making an appointment with a barber, whose customer is just then talking to the box-office of *Hair*, or maybe making a hairline reservation . . ."

"Blenheim, I'm talking to you."

"Yes?"

"What was it you called me up about?"

"Oh, this and that. I was wondering, for instance, whether parrots have internal clocks."

"What?" I still couldn't be sure whether the bug was a cockroach or not, but I saluted just in case.

"If so, maybe we could get them to act as speaking clocks."

He sounded crazier than ever. What trivial projects for one of the best brains in our century—no wonder he was on leave.

"Blenheim, I'm busy. Institute work must go on, you know."

"Yes. Tell you what, why don't you drop over this afternoon? I have something to talk over with you."

"Can't. I have a meeting all afternoon."

"Fine, fine. See you, then. Anytime around 4:43."

Madmen never listen.

Helmut Rasmussen came in just as Blenheim hung up. He seemed distressed. Not that his face showed it; ever since that bomb wrecked his office, Hel has been unable to move his face. Hysterical paralysis, Dr. Grobe had explained.

But Hel could signal whatever he felt by fiddling with the stuff in his shirt pocket. For anger, his red pencil came out (and sometimes underwent a savage sharpening), impatience made him work his slide rule, surprise made him glance into his pocket diary, and so on.

Just now he was clicking the button on his ballpoint pen with some agitation. For a moment he actually seemed about to take it out and draw worry lines on his forehead.

"What is it, Hel? The costing on Project Faith?" He spread the schedules on my desk and pointed to the snag: a discrepancy between the estimated cost of blasting apart and hauling away the Rocky Mountains, and the value of oil recovered in the process.

"I see. The trains, eh? Diesels seem to use most of the oil we get. How about steam locomotives, then?"

He clapped me on the shoulder and nodded.

"By the way, Hel, I won't be at the meeting today. Blenheim just called up. Wants to see me."

Hel indicated surprise.

"Look, I know he's a crackpot. You don't have to pocket-diary me, I know he's nuts. But he is also technically still the Director. Our boss. They haven't taken him off the payroll, just put him on sick leave. Besides, he used to have a lot of good ideas."

Hel took out a felt-tip pen and began to doodle with some sarcasm. The fact was, Blenheim had completely lost his grip during his last year at the Institute. Before the government forced him to take leave, he'd been spending half a million a year on developing, rumors said, glass pancakes. And who could forget his plan to arm police with chocolate revolvers?

"Sure he's had a bad time, but maybe he's better now," I said, without conviction.

Institute people never get better, Hel seemed to retort. They just kept on making bigger and better decisions, with more and more brilliance and finality, until they broke. Like glass pancakes giving out an ever purer ring, they exploded.

It was true. Like everyone else here, I was seeing Dr. Grobe, our resident psychiatrist, several times a week. Then there were cases beyond even the skill of Dr. Grobe: Joe Feeney, who interrupted his work (on the uses of holograms) one day to announce that he was a filing cabinet. Edna Bessler, who believed that she was being pursued by a synthetic *a priori* proposition. The lovely entomologist Pawlie Sutton, who disappeared. And George Hoad, whose rocket research terminated when he walked into the Gents one day and cut his throat. George spent the last few minutes of consciousness vainly trying to mop up the bloody floor with toilet paper . . .

Something was wrong with the personnel around this place, all right. And I suspected that our little six-legged masters knew more about this than they were saying.

Finally I mumbled, "I know it's useless, Hel. But I'd better find out what he wants."

You do what you think is best, Hel thought. He stalked out of my office then, examining the point on his red pencil.

The bug was a cockroach, *P. americana*. It sauntered across the wall until it reached the curly edge of a wall poster, then it flew about a foot to land on the nearest dark spot. This was Uncle Sam's right eye. Uncle Sam, with his accusing eyes and finger, was trying to recruit men for the Senate and House of Representatives. On this poster, he said, "The Senate Needs MEN." So far, the recruitment campaign was a failure. Who could blame people for not wanting to go on the "firing line" in Washington? The casualty rate of Congressmen was 30 per cent annually, and climbing, in spite of every security measure we could think of.

Which reminded me of work. I scrubbed off the blackboard and started laying out a contingency tree for Project Pogo, a plan to make the whole cabinet—all one hundred and forty-three secretaries—completely mobile, hence, proof against revolution. So far the Security Secretary didn't care for the idea of "taking to our heels," but it was cheaper to keep the cabinet on the move than to guard them in Washington.

The cockroach, observing my industry, left by a wall ventilator, and I breathed easier. The contingency tree didn't look so interesting by now, and out the window I could see real trees.

The lawn rolled away down from the building to the river (not the Orinoco, despite our name). The far bank was blue-black with pines, and the three red maples on our lawn, this time of year, stood out like three separate, brilliant fireballs. For just the duration of a bluejay's flight from one to another, I could forget about the stale routine, the smell of chalkdust.

I remembered a silly day three years ago, when I'd carved a heart on one of those trees, with Pawlie Sutton's initials and my own.

Now a security guard strolled his puma into view. They stopped under the nearest maple and he snapped the animal's lead. It was up the trunk in two bounds, and out of sight among the leaves. While that stupid-faced man in uniform looked up, the fireball shook and swayed above him. A few great leaves fell, bright as drops of blood.

Now what was *this* headache going to be about?

All the big problems were solved, or at least we knew how to solve them. The world was just about the way we wanted it, now, except we no longer seemed to want it that way. That's how Mr. Howell, the Secretary of Personal Relationships, had put it in his telecast. What was

missing? God, I think he said. God had made it possible
for us to dam the Amazon and move the Orinoco, to feed
India and dig gold from the ocean floor and cure cancer.
And now God—the way he said it made you feel that He,
too, was in the Cabinet—God was going to help us get
down and solve our personal, human problems. Man's in-
humanity to man. The lack of communication. The hatred.
God and Secretary Howell were going to get right down
to some committee work on this. I think that was the
telecast where Howell announced the introduction of detention camps for "malcontents." Just until we got our
personal problems all ironed out. I had drawn up the
plans for these camps that summer. Then George Hoad
borrowed my pocket-knife one day and never gave it
back. Then the headaches started.

As I stepped outside, the stupid-faced guard was looking up the skirt of another tree.

"Prrt, prrt," he said quietly, and the black puma
dropped to earth beside him. There was something hanging out of its mouth that looked like a bluejay's wing.

"Good girl. Good girl."

I hurried away to the helicopter.

Drew Blenheim's tumbledown mansion sits in the middle
of withered woods. For half a mile around, the trees are
laced together with high-voltage fence. Visitors are blindfolded and brought in by helicopter. There are also rumors
of minefields and other security measures. At that time, I
put it all down to Blenheim's paranoia.

The engine shut down with the sound of a coin spinning
to rest. Hands helped me out and removed my blindfold.
The first thing I saw, hanging on a nearby stretch of
fence, was a lump of bones and burned fur from some
small animal. The guards and their submachine-guns es-
corted me only as far as the door, for Blenheim evidently
hated seeing signs of the security he craved. The house
looked dismal and decayed—the skull of some dead
Orinoco Institute?

A servant wearing burned cork makeup and white
gloves ushered me through a dim hallway that smelled
of hay and on into the library.

"I'll tell Mr. Blenheim you're here, sir. Perhaps you'd
care to read one of his monographs while you wait?"

I flicked through *The Garden of Regularity* (a slight

tract recommending that older people preserve intestinal health by devouring their own dentures) and opened an insanely boring book called *Can Bacteria Read?* I was staring uncomprehendingly at one of its pages when a voice said:

"Are you still here?" The plump old woman had evidently been sitting in her deep chair when I came in. As she craned around at me, I saw she had a black eye. Something was wrong with her hair, too. "I thought you'd left by now—oh, it's *you*."

"Madam, do I know you?"

She sat forward and put her face to the light. The black eye was tattooed, and the marcelled hair was really a cap of paper, covered with wavy ink lines. But it was Edna Bessler, terribly aged.

"You've changed, Edna."

"So would you, young man, if you'd been chased around a nuthouse for two years by a synthetic *a priori* proposition." She sniffed. "Well, thank heavens the revolution is set for tomorrow."

I laughed nervously. "Well, Edna, it certainly is good to see you. What are you doing here, anyway?"

"There are quite a few of the old gang here, Joe Feeney and—and others. This place has become a kind of repair depot for mad futurologists. Blenheim is very kind, but of course he's quite mad himself. Mad as a wet hen. As you see from his writing."

"*Can Bacteria Read?* I couldn't read it."

"Oh, he thinks that germs are, like people, amenable to suggestion. So, with the proper application of mass hypnosis among the microbe populations, we ought to be able to cure any illness with any quack remedy."

I nodded. "Hope he recovers soon. I'd like to see him back at the Institute, working on real projects again. Big stuff, like the old days. I'll never forget the old Drew Blenheim, the man who invented satellite dialing."

Satellite dialing came about when the malcontents were trying to jam government communications systems, cut lines and blow up exchanges. Blenheim's system virtually made each telephone a complete exchange in itself, dialing directly through a satellite. Voice signals were compressed and burped skyward in short bursts that evaded most jamming signals. It was an Orinoco Institute triumph over anarchy.

Edna chuckled. "Oh, he's working on real projects. I said he was mad, not useless. Now if you'll help me out of this chair, I must go fix an elephant."

I was sure I'd misheard this last. After she'd gone, I looked over a curious apparatus in the corner. Parts of it were recognizable—a clock inside a parrot cage, a gas laser, and a fringed shawl suspended like a flag from a walking-stick thrust into a watermelon—but their combination was baffling.

At 4:43 by the clock in the cage, the blackface servant took me to a gloomy great hall place, scattered with the shapes of easy chairs and sofas. A figure in a diving suit rose from the piano and waved me to a chair. Then it sat down again, flipping out its airhoses behind the bench.

For a few minutes I suffered through a fumbling version of some Mexican tune. But when Blenheim—no doubt it was he—stood up and started juggling oranges, I felt it was time to speak out.

"Look, I've interrupted my work to come here. Is this all you have to show me?"

One of the oranges vaulted high, out of sight in the gloom above; another hit me in the chest. The figure opened its face-plate and grinned. "Long time no see, Hank."

It was me.

"Rubber mask," Blenheim explained, plucking at it. "I couldn't resist trying it on you, life gets so tedious here. Ring for Rastus, will you? I want to shed this suit."

We made small talk while the servant helped him out of the heavy diving suit. Rather, Blenheim rattled on alone; I wasn't feeling well at all. The shock of seeing myself had reminded me of something I should remember, but couldn't.

". . . to build a heraldry vending machine. Put in a coin, punch out your name, and it prints a coat-of-arms. Should suit those malcontents, eh? All they probably really want is a coat-of-arms."

"They're just plain evil," I said. "When I think how they bombed poor Hel Rasmussen's office—"

"Oh, he did that himself. Didn't you know?"

"Suicide? So that explains the hysterical paralysis!"

My face looked exasperated, as Blenheim peeled it off.

"Is that what Dr. Grobe told you? Paralyzed hell, the blast blew his face clean off. Poor Hel's present face is a solid plate of plastic, bolted on. He breathes through a hole in his shoulder and feeds himself at the armpit. If Grobe told you any different, he's just working on your morale."

From upstairs came a kind of machine-gun clatter. The minstrel servant glided in with a tray of drinks.

"Oh, Rastus. Tell the twins not to practice their tap-dancing just now, will you? Hank looks as if he has a headache."

"Yes sir. By the way, the three-legged elephant has arrived. I put it in the front hall. I'm afraid the prosthesis doesn't fit."

"I'll fix it. Just ask Jumbo to lean up against the wall for half an hour."

"Very good, sir."

After this, I decided to make my escape from this Bedlam.

"Doesn't anybody around here ever do anything straightforward or say anything in plain English?"

"We're trying to tell you something, Hank, but it isn't easy. For one thing, I'm not sure we can trust you."

"Trust me for what?"

His twisted face twisted out a smile. "If you don't know, then how can we trust you? But come with me to the conservatory and I'll show you something."

We went to a large room with dirty glass walls. To me it looked like nothing so much as a bombed-out workshop. Though there were bags of fertilizer on the floor, there wasn't a living plant in sight. Instead, the tables were littered with machinery and lab equipment: jumbles of retorts and colored wires and nuts and bolts that made no sense.

"What do you see, Hank?"

"Madness and chaos. You might as well have pears in the light sockets and a banana on the telephone cradle, for all I can make of it."

He laughed. "That's better. We'll crazify you yet."

I pointed to a poster-covered cylinder standing in the corner. One of the posters had Uncle Sam, saying "I Neew MEN for Congress."

"What's that Parisian advertising kiosk doing here?"

"Rastus built that for us, out of scrap alloys I had lying around. Like it?"

I shrugged. "The top's too pointed. It looks like—"

"Yes, go on."

"This is silly. All of you need a few sessions with Dr. Grobe," I said. "I'm leaving."

"I was afraid you'd say that. But it's you who need another session with Dr. Grobe, Hank."

"You think *I'm* crazy?"

"No, you're too damned sane."

"Well you sure as hell are nuts!" I shouted. "Why bother with all the security outside? Afraid someone will steal the idea of a minstrel show or the secret of a kiosk?"

He laughed again. "Hank, those guards aren't there to keep strangers out. *They're to keep us in.* You see, my house really and truly is a madhouse."

I stamped out a side door and ordered my helicopter.

"My head's killing me," I told the guard. "Take it easy with the blindfold."

"Oh, sorry, mac. Hey look, it's none of my business, but what did you do with that tree you brung with you?"

"Tree?" God, even the guards were catching it.

That evening I went to see Dr. Grobe.

"Another patient? I swear, I'm going to install a revolving door on this office. Sit down. Uh, Hank LaFarge, isn't it? Sit down, Hank. Let's see . . . oh, you're the guy who's afraid of cockroaches, right?"

"Not exactly afraid of them. In fact they remind me of someone I used to be fond of. Pawlie Sutton used to work with them. But my problem is, I know that cockroaches are the real bosses. We're just kidding ourselves with our puppet government, our Uncle Sham—"

He chuckled appreciatively.

"But what 'bugs' me is, nobody will recognize this plain and simple truth, Doctor."

"Ah, ah. Remember last time, you agreed to call me by my first name."

"Sorry, uh, Oddpork." I couldn't imagine why anyone with that name wanted to be called by it, unless the doctor himself was trying to get used to it. He was an odd-pork of a man, too: plump and rumpy, with overlarge hands that never stopped adjusting his already well-adjusted clothes. He always looked surprised at everything I said, even "hello." Every session, he made the same joke about the revolving door.

Still, repetitive jokes help build a family atmosphere, which was probably what he wanted. There was a certain comfort in this stale atmosphere of no surprises. Happy families are all alike, and their past is exactly like their future.

"Hank, I haven't asked you directly about your cockroach theory before, have I? Want to tell me about it?"

"I know it sounds crazy at first. For one thing, cockroaches aren't very smart, I know that. In some ways, they're stupider than ants. And their communication equipment isn't much, either. Touch and smell, mainly. They aren't naturally equipped for conquering the world."

Oddpork lit a cigar and leaned back, looking at the ceiling. "What do they do with the world when they get it?"

"That's another problem. After all, they don't *need* the world. All they need is food, water, a fair amount of darkness and some warmth. But there's the key, you see?

"I mean we humans have provided for all these needs for many centuries. Haphazardly, though. So it stands to reason that life would be better for them if we worked for them on a regular basis. But to get us to do that, they have to take over first."

He tried to blow a smoke ring, failed, and adjusted his tie. "Go on. How do they manage this takeover?"

"I'm not sure, but I think they have help. Maybe some smart tinkerer wanted to see what would happen if he gave them good long-distance vision. Maybe he was so pleased with the result that he then taught them to make semaphore signals with their feelers. The rest is history."

Dusting his lapel, Dr. Grobe said, "I don't quite follow. Semaphore signals?"

"One cockroach is stupid. But a few thousand of them in good communication could make up a fair brain. Our tinkerer probably hastened that along by intensive breeding and group learning problems, killing off the failures . . . it would take ten years at the outside."

"Really? And how long would the conquest of man

take? How would the little insects fare against the armies of the world?"

"They never need to try. Armies are run by governments, and governments are run, for all practical purposes, by small panels of experts. Think tanks like the Orinoco Institute. And—this just occurred to me—for all practical purposes, you run the Institute."

For once, Dr. Grobe did not look surprised. "Oh, so I'm in on the plot, am I?"

"We're all so crazy, we really depend on you. You can ensure that we work for the good of the cockroaches, or else you can get rid of us—send us away, or encourage our suicides."

"Why should I do that?"

"Because *you* are afraid of them."

"Not at all." But his hand twitched, and a little cigar ash fell on his immaculate trousers. I felt my point was proved.

"Damn. I'll have to sponge that. Excuse me."

He stepped into his private washroom and closed the door. My feeling of triumph suddenly faded. Maybe I was finally cracking. What evidence did I really have?

On the other hand, Dr. Grobe was taking a long time in there. I stole over to the washroom door and listened.

". . . verge of suicide . . ." he murmured. ". . . yes . . . give up the idea, but . . . yes, that's just what I . . ."

I threw back the door on a traditional spy scene. In the half-darkness, Dr. G. was hunched over the medicine cabinet, speaking into a microphone. He wore earphones.

"Hank, don't be a foo—"

I hit him, not hard, and he sat down on the edge of the tub. He looked resigned.

"So this is my imagined conspiracy, is it? Where do these wires lead?"

They led inside the medicine cabinet to a tiny apparatus. A dozen brown ellipses had clustered around it, like a family around the TV.

"Let me explain," he said.

"Explanations are unnecessary, Doctor. I just want to get out of here, unless your six-legged friends can stop me."

"They might. So could I. I could order the guards to shoot you. I could have you put away with your crazy friends. I could even have you tried for murder, just now."

"Murder?" I followed his gaze back into the office. From under the desk, a pair of feet. "Who's that?"

"Hel Rasmussen. Poisoned himself a few minutes before you came in. Believe me, it wasn't pleasant, seeing the poor fellow holding a bottle of cyanide to his armpit. He left a note blaming you, in a way."

"Me!"

"You were the last straw. This afternoon, he saw you take an axe and deliberately cut down one of those beautiful maple trees in the yard. Destruction of beauty —it was too much for him."

Trees again. I went to the office window and looked out at the floodlit landscape. One of the maples was missing.

Dr. Grobe and I sat down again at our respective interview stations, while I thought this over. Blenheim and his mask came into it, I was sure of that. But why?

Dr. Grobe fished his lifeless cigar from the ashtray. "The point is, I can stop you from making any trouble for me. So you may as well hear me out." He scratched a match on the sole of Hel's shoe and relit the cigar.

"All right, Oddpork. You win. What happens now?"

"Nothing much. Nothing at all. If my profession has any meaning, it's to keep things from happening." He blew out the match. "I'm selling ordinary life. Happiness, as you must now see, lies in developing a pleasant, comfortable and protective routine—and then sticking to it. No unpleasant surprises. No shocks. Psychiatry has always aimed for that, and now it is within our grasp. The cockroach conspiracy hasn't taken over the world, but it has taken over the Institute and it's our salvation.

"You see, Hank, our bargain isn't one-sided. We give them a little shelter, a few scraps of food. But they give us something far more important: real organization. *The life of pure routine.*"

I snorted. "Like hurrying after trains? Or wearing ourselves out on assembly-line work? Or maybe grinding our lives away in boring offices? Punching time-clocks and marching in formation?"

"None of the above, thank you. Cockroaches never hurry to anything but dinner. They wouldn't march in formation except for fun. They are free—yet they are part of a highly organized society. And this can be ours."

"If we're not all put in detention camps."

"Listen, those camps are only a stage. So what if a few million grumblers get sterilized and shut away for a year or two? Think of the *billions* of happy, decent citizens, enjoying a freedom they have earned. Someday, every man will live exactly as he pleases—and his pleasure will lie in serving his fellow men."

Put like that, it was persuasive. Another half-hour of this and I was all but convinced.

"Sleep on it, eh Hank? Let me know tomorrow what you think." His large hand on my shoulder guided me to the door.

"You may be right," I said, smiling back at him. I meant it, too. Even though the last thing I saw, as the door closed, was a stream of glistening brown that came from under the washroom door and disappeared under the desk.

I sat up in my own office most of the night, staring out at the maple stump. There was no way out: Either I worked for *Periplaneta americana* and gradually turned into a kind of moral cockroach myself, or I was killed. And there were certain advantages to either choice.

I was about to turn on the video-recorder to leave a suicide note, when I noticed the cassette was already recorded. I ran it back and played it.

Blenheim came on, wearing my face and my usual suit.

"They think I'm you, Hank, dictating some notes. Right now you're really at my house, reading a dull book in the library. So dull, in fact, that it's guaranteed to put you into a light trance. When I'm safely back, Edna will come in and wake you.

"She's not as loony as she seems. The black eye is inked for her telescope, and the funny cap with lines on it, that looks like marcelled hair, that's a weathermap. I won't explain why she's doing astronomy—you'll understand in time.

"On the other hand, she's got a fixation that the stars are nothing but the shiny backs of cockroaches, treading around the heavenly spheres. It makes a kind of sense when you think of it: *Periplaneta* means around the world, and America being the home of the Star-Spangled Banner.

"Speaking of national anthems, Mexico's is La Cucaracha—another cockroach reference. They seem to be taking over this message!

"The gang and I have been thinking about bugs a lot lately. Of course Pawlie has always thought about them, but the rest of us . . ." I missed the next part. So Pawlie was at the madhouse? And they hadn't told me?

". . . when I started work on the famous glass pancakes. I discovered a peculiar feature of glass discs, such as those found on clock faces.

"Say, you can do us a favor. I'm coming around at dawn with the gang, to show you a gadget or two. We haven't got all the bugs out of them yet, but—will you go into Dr. Grobe's office at dawn, and check the time on his clock? But first, smash the glass on his window, will you? Thanks. I'll compensate him for it later.

"Then go outside the building, but on no account stand between the maple stump and the broken window. The best place to wait is on the little bluff to the north, where you'll have a good view of the demonstration. We'll meet you there.

"Right now you see our ideas darkly, as through a pancake, I guess. But soon you'll understand. You see, we're a kind of cockroach ourselves. I mean, living on scraps of sanity. We have to speak in parables and work in silly ways because *they* can't. *They* live in a comfortable kind of world where elephants have their feet cut off to make umbrella stands. We have to make good use of the three-legged elephants.

"Don't bother destroying this cassette. It won't mean a thing to any right-living insect."

It didn't mean much to me, not yet. Cockroaches in the stars? Clocks? There were questions I had to ask, at the rendezvous.

There was one question I'd already asked that needed an answer. Pawlie had been messing about in her lab, when I asked her to marry me. Two years ago, was it? Or three?

"But you don't like cockroaches," she said.

"No, and I'll never ask a cockroach for its claw in

marriage." I looked over her shoulder into the glass case. "What's so interesting about these?"

"Well, for one thing, they're not laboratory animals. I caught them myself in the basement here at the Institute. See? Those roundish ones are the nymphs—sexless adolescents. Cute, aren't they?"

I had to admit they were. A little. "They look like the fat black exclamation points in comic strips," I observed.

"They're certainly healthy, all of them. I've never seen any like them. I—that's funny." She went and fetched a book, and looked from some illustration to the specimens under glass.

"What's funny?"

"Look, I'm going to be dissecting the rest of the afternoon. Meet you for dinner. Bye."

"You haven't answered my question, Pawlie."

"Bye."

That was the last I saw of her. Later, Dr. Grobe put it about that she'd been found, hopelessly insane. Still later, George Hoad cut his throat.

The floodlights went off, and I could see dawn grayness and mist. I took a can of beans and went for a stroll outside.

One of the guards nodded a wary greeting. They and their cats were always jumpiest at this time of day.

"Everything all right, officer?"

"Yeah. Call me crazy, but I think I just heard an elephant."

When he and his puma were out of sight, I heaved the can of beans through Dr. Grobe's lighted window.

"What the hell?" he shouted. I slipped back to my office, waited a few minutes, then went to see him.

A slender ray came through the broken window and struck the clock on the opposite wall. Grobe sat transfixed, staring at it with more surprise than ever. And no wonder, for the clock had become a parrot.

"Relax, Oddpork," I said. "It's only some funny kind of hologram in the clock face, worked by a laser from the lawn. You look like a comic villain, sitting there with that cigar stub in your face."

The cigar stub moved. Looking closer, I saw it was made up of the packed tails of a few cockroaches, trying to force themselves between his closed lips. More ran up from his spotless collar and joined them, and others made for his nostrils. One approached the queue at the mouth, found another stuck there, and had a nibble at its kicking hind leg.

"Get away! Get away!" I gave Grobe a shake to dislodge them, and his mouth fell open. A brown flood of kicking bodies tumbled out and down, over his well-cut lapels.

I had stopped shuddering by the time I joined the others on the bluff. Pawlie and Blenheim were missing. Edna stopped scanning the horizon with her brass telescope long enough to introduce me to the pretty twins, Alice and Celia. They sat in the grass beside a tangled heap of revolvers, polishing their patent-leather tap shoes.

The ubiquitous Rastus was wiping off his burned cork makeup. I asked him why.

"Don't need it anymore. Last night it was my camouflage. I was out in the woods, cutting a path through the electric fence. Quite a wide path, as you'll understand."

He continued removing the black until I recognized the late George Hoad.

"George! But you cut your throat, remember? Mopping up blood—"

"Hank, that was your blood. It was you cut your throat in the Gents, after Pawlie vanished. Remember?"

I did, giddily. "What happened to you, then?"

"Your suicide attempt helped me make up my mind; I quit the Institute next day. You were still in the hospital."

Still giddy, I turned to watch Joe Feeney operating the curious laser I'd seen in the library. Making parrots out of clocks.

"I understand now," I said. "But what's the watermelon for?"

"Cheap cooling device."

"And the flag?" I indicated the shawl-stick arrangement.

"To rally round. I stuck it in the melon because they were using the umbrella stand for—"

"Look!" Edna cried. "The attack begins!" She handed me a second telescope.

All I saw below was the lone figure of Blenheim in his diving suit, shuffling slowly up from the river mist to

face seven guards and two pumas. He seemed to be juggling croquet balls.

"Why don't we help him?" I shouted. "Don't just sit
there shining shoes and idling."

The twins giggled. "We've already helped some," said
Alice, nodding at the pile of weapons. "We made friends
with the guards."

I got the point when those below pulled their guns on
Blenheim. As each man drew, he looked at his gun and
then threw it away.

"What a waste," Celia sighed. "Those guns are made
from just about the best chocolate you can get."

Blenheim played his parlor trick on the nearest guard,
one juggled ball flew high, the guard looked up, and a
second ball clipped him on the upturned chin.

Now the puma guards went into action.

"I can't look," I said, my eye glued to the telescope.
One of the animals stopped to sniff at a sticky revolver,
but the other headed straight for his quarry. He leaped up,
trying to fasten his claws into the stranger's big brass
head.

Out of the river mist came a terrible cry, and then a
terrible sight: a hobbling gray hulk that resolved into a
charging elephant. Charging diagonally, so it looked even
larger.

The pumas left the scene. One fled in our direction
until Alice snatched up a pistol and fired it in the air. At
that sound, the guards decided to look for jobs elsewhere.
After all, as Pawlie said later, you couldn't expect a man
to face a juggling diver *and* a mad elephant with a wooden
leg, with nothing but a chocolate .38, not on *those* wages.

Pawlie was riding on the neck of the elephant. When
he came to a wobbling stop I saw that one of Jumbo's
forelegs was a section of tree with the bark still on it. And
in the bark, a heart with PS + HL, carved years before.

I felt the triumph was all over—especially since Pawlie
kept nodding her head yes to me—until George said: .

"Come on, gang. Let's set it up."

Jumbo had been pulling a wooden sledge, bearing the
Paris kiosk. Now he went off to break his fast on water
and grass, while the rest of us set the thing upright. Even
before we had fueled it with whatever was in the fertilizer bags, I guessed that it was a rocket.

After some adjustments, the little door was let down,

and a sweet, breakfast pancake odor came forth. Joe Feeney opened a flask of dark liquid and poured it in the entrance. The smell grew stronger.

"Maple sap," he explained. "From Jumbo's wooden leg. Mixed with honey. And there's oatmeal inside. A farewell breakfast."

I looked in the little door and saw the inside of the ship was made like a metal honeycomb, plenty of climbing room for our masters.

Pawlie came from the building with a few cockroaches in a jar, and let them taste our wares. Then, all at once, it was a sale opening at any big department store. We all stood back and let the great brown wave surge forward and break over the little rocket. Some of them, nymphs especially, scurried all the way up to the nose cone and back down again in their excitement. It all looked so jolly that I tried not to think about their previous meals.

Edna glanced at her watch. "Ten minutes more," she said. "Or they'll hit the sun."

I objected that we'd never get all of them loaded in ten minutes.

"No," said Pawlie, "but we'll get the best and strongest. The shrews can keep the rest in control."

Edna closed the door, and the twins did a vigorous tap-dance on the unfortunate stragglers. A few minutes later, a million members of the finest organization on earth were on their way to the stars.

"To join their little friends," said Edna.

Pawlie and I touched hands, as Blenheim opened his face-plate.

"I've been making this study," he said, "of spontaneous combustion in giraffes . . ."

The Locked Room

Another Fenton Worth Mystery

Fenton Worth instructed his valet Bozo to turn away all callers for the rest of the evening.

"I mean to spend a quiet evening with a good book," said the popular private detective, and indicated a new, calf-bound volume on the library table.

Bozo smirked, knowing what usually happened to all such "quiet evenings" in the life of a famous sleuth. "I imagine, sir," he said, "that a beautiful lady will burst in, begging you to save her life. That, or else Inspector Grogan will ask you to help recover the Stilton diamonds."

The well-known private dick smiled. "Not tonight, Bozo. I mean it: No calls of any kind. If it is a matter of life and death, as is usual, refer our caller to the police. Other cases I can look into in the morning. For now, I'm going to lock myself in the library, and I don't want to be disturbed."

With that, the eminent criminologist shooed his servant from the room, turned the key and settled into his favorite Morris chair with the "good book." It was a detection novel, entitled *The Locked Room*.

"*The Locked Room*, eh? That should be of considerable interest," he mused, toying with his letter opener. This curious instrument was actually a Moro weapon, an example of that knife with a wavy blade familiar to crossword buffs as a *kriis*. Opening the volume, Fenton used the *kriis* to slit a few pages, then began to read.

The plot of this novel, shorn of its ornaments, misdirections and other fanciful elements, was simple: A man was found dead in a sealed room, locked from the inside. No one else was found in the room, and though the death was certainly a homicide, no weapon could be found. Suspects were abundant, yet how could any of them have done it?

Fenton had met a great many such cases in real life; indeed, they formed the bulk of his murder investigations. He had opened locked rooms containing corpses which had been done to death by strangulation, shooting, stabbing, poison, smothering, drowning, burning, being chopped to bits, electrocution; by the action of deadly snakes and spiders—and far worse.

A few of such cases involved rooms which were not really locked at all. These included rooms with secret panels and one room where the midget assassin lay hidden in a chest. Fenton had left all such "cheating" cases to the police.

More interesting were the cases where the rooms were really locked, but ingeniously locked from the outside. One killer, having simply locked the door and concealed the key in his hand, helped smash a panel of the door to get into the room. Then he reached through the panel and "found" the key in the lock. Others relied on clever systems of string, pins, wires and so on, to drop latchbars, shoot bolts and turn locks from outside the door. One killer simply removed the door hinges, replacing them after his grim business inside.

In other cases the room was locked, and from the inside, but it was not utterly unimpregnable. Poison gas might be introduced by a ventilator, as, indeed, might an adder. Ice bullets might be fired through the keyhole to kill, then melt, leaving no trace of the weapon. Others used poison darts fired through an otherwise inaccessible window, bombs down the chimney and so on. In one curious case a man was stabbed through the wall itself, with a very long, thin, sharp sword.

There were a number of "funny contrivance" cases. These invariably concerned machines hidden about the rooms which, having done their deeds, became to all appearances innocent furniture again. Some were set off by the victims themselves, some by remote control and some by clockwork. Men were shot by telephones, blown up by hearing aids, stabbed by clocks, strangled by stethoscopes and ripped to pieces by typewriters. In this category Fenton placed his interesting "Case of the Freudian Outlook," where a man was crushed to death between the red-hot iron walls of a gimmicked room.

He paused to cut a few more pages. This mystery, *The Locked Room,* was the most baffling he'd yet encountered, and nothing like any of the others.

It was certainly not like the elaborate suicide in "The Mystery of the Yellow Step," where the victim hanged himself with an especially knotted and weighted rope. When the door to the room was broken in, this noose undid itself, deposited the body on the floor, and vanished out the window into (for this was in Venice) the Grand Canal.

Nor did this case resemble "The Orchid Piano Mystery," where the victim locked himself in a room coincidentally full of broken furniture and other signs of a struggle, fainted and cracked his head on the fender. That case had given Fenton some food for thought, as had the related "Mauve Marimba Mystery." There the supposed victim had merely suffered an epileptic seizure, smashed up the room, and ended by kicking himself in the face until dead (this epileptic was also a dancer).

Fenton's meditations were here interrupted by Bozo, who came in with a tray of toast and cocoa.

"I was just thinking over some of my old 'locked-room' cases, Bozo," said the renowned gumshoe. "I must confess that real-life cases are a whale of a lot easier than detective fiction. This novel has me stymied, so far." And he outlined the story for his valet.

"It sounds tough, sir," said Bozo. "Reminds one of the 'Case of the Bashful Bimbo.' "

"No, I think you're thinking of the 'Vast Duck Mystery,' aren't you, Bozo? Where it finally turned out that the victim had been stabbed with a hatpin at the ambassador's reception, amid a roomful of people. He wasn't even aware of the stabbing himself. He'd gone into another room, locked himself in, and then the slow leakage from his heart finally caught up with him."

"Like I've caught up with you," laughed Inspector Grogan, strolling in. "I came over on the chance of getting you to help on the Stilton diamonds case. I found this young lady outside. Claims her life's in danger."

The young lady, a beautiful blonde with a black eye, seemed too frightened to speak. Next came Claude Elliott, the millionaire playboy, attired in his customary black evening wear, a monocle twinkling in his eye. "I say, old sport," he drawled, "d'you think you could do anything about it? Someone seems to have kidnapped Pater. His entire private car has vanished from its train. Deucedly awkward, what?" Young Elliott expected no answer to this question.

"Scuse me, mistah Wort'," said a jockey, ducking into view from behind Elliott's scarlet-lined cape. "Honeymarch has been heisted!"

"Honeymarch stolen!" echoed the astonished shamus. This famous filly had won many times her weight in gold, as had her sire, My White Dream, which Fenton had earlier saved from doping in—

"The Case of the Mona Lisa Moth," breathed Bozo.

"Exactly," Fenton said. "Get rid of some of these people—all of them, Bozo. I want to do some hard thinking."

Bozo gently but firmly pushed them all from the library: the debutante and the B-girl, the Brovnian ambassador and the gum-chewing taxi driver, the business tycoon and the spirit medium, the jockey, the playboy, the cop and the black-eyed blonde.

"In 'The Case of the Oddest Occurrence,'" Fenton mused, "the trick was to make it seem as if the victim were dead before he really was. The killer got him into a room and drugged him, and managed to get the room locked. Then he feigned alarm, convinced us there was something afoot, and broke the door down to get in. He rushed in ahead of us, I recall, exclaiming at the (fictitious) sight of the victim's throat, cut from ear to ear. And even while he was exclaiming, he was cutting that throat—an instant before the rest of us saw it!"

"It was another kettle of fish, sir," said Bozo, "in the case you called 'Murder Galore.'"

"True enough, Bozo. In that, as in many cases, the ruse was to get the rest of us believing the victim to be still alive, when he had already been done to death. In the case you mention, this was accomplished by means of a phonographic recording of the victim's voice. Other cases involved the use of mirrors, disguises, death-masks and even ventriloquism. Yet *The Locked Room* is not one of this type.

"Nor does it resemble the more bizarre cases, such as 'The Wrong Hotel Room Mystery,' or the simpler ones, such as 'The Case of the Gunsel's Gardenia.' In the former the whole plot hinged upon an elaborate switch of door number plates; in the latter, the killer only *pretended* the door was locked, and held it shut as he feigned battering it open."

Bozo withdrew, and the celebrated crime-solver locked and bolted the door. There remained only the pages of the final chapter to be cut, but he could not yet bring himself to break their seal. Surely he could guess the ending in advance of reading it! Surely, in all his experience, there must be one case relevant to solving this tangle.

Yet he had covered all categories: the secret passage or panel; the string-locked door; the ice bullet; and so on. There remained for consideration only one case, the strange "Case of the Parched Adjutant."

THE CASE OF THE PARCHED ADJUTANT

Another Fenton Worth Mystery

The victim was a retired military gentleman of sober and regular habits, an ardent anti-vivisectionist. He spent several hours each day in his study, writing his memoirs and anti-vivisection pamphlets, or perhaps just gazing out over the vast heath of which his window commanded an excellent prospect. When he was not writing, he could generally be found upon that heath, strolling and meditating. He had no relatives living, very little money, and a devoted housekeeper who was a chimpanzee.

On the day in question a circus had pitched on the heath, and the adjutant had, according to the housekeeper, gone to see it—for the second time. Worried at his absence, she finally called the police and Fenton Worth. No one at the circus had seen him. In search of the house, they broke in the door of his study.

The study had only one door, to which the adjutant had the only key, and its only window was inaccessible. The furniture consisted of a desk, a chair and a sofa. The adjutant was found lying on the sofa, strangled to death—

with finger marks clear on his throat—and oddly parched. The door key was in his pocket.

The study window was open, but Fenton soon proved that it was inaccessible, for it lay forty feet above a mire of wet sand. This mire would neither support a ladder nor any climbing device, and its unbroken surface indicated that nothing had come within a hundred feet of the house on that side. It was further impossible to lower oneself from the roof by a rope, for the roof was made of treacherous rotten thatching—which likewise had not been disturbed.

A great deal of suspicion fell upon the housekeeper, as the adjutant's only heir. But an examination of the corpse, together with evidence from the adjutant's pamphlets and memoirs, established the true circumstances, as Fenton explained:

The adjutant had been strangled at the circus, bundled into a cannon, and fired through the window to land upon the sofa. This was confirmed by the parching, and powder burns on the corpse's feet. Certain details in the adjutant's memoirs and pamphlets showed that he had uncovered a vicious vivisection racket running behind the scenes at the circus, and was about to subject this sordid business to the light of public scrutiny. On his first visit to the circus, he had recognized an old enemy, an ex-Nazi artillery officer notorious during the war for his torture of animals, chiefly puppies and kittens. The adjutant's discovery of what the lions were fed completed his inquiry; the rest was duck soup, as he'd have said.

Confronted with this evidence, the Human Cannonball broke down and confessed, sobbing in half-coherent German.

"Hmmm," said Fenton. "Even that case doesn't help me here. Maybe I should re-read the novel, to see what clues I've missed." The well-known peeper leafed back through the book.

"Say, here's an anomaly!" he exclaimed. "The author tells us on page one the door is locked, and here on page three it so manifestly isn't! What can be the explanation of that?"

Suddenly the world-famed private eye sat bolt upright. "Aha! The author says the door is locked, *but we have only his word for it*. The pieces of the jigsaw are beginning to fall into place, now. The author may in fact have *staged* the entire murder to make money from his own fictionalization of it! So the name of the killer must be—"

But the publicly-acclaimed private investigator will never name me. He'll be found tomorrow morning, stabbed to death, in a room locked from the inside. The *kriis* will have vanished.

Thus begins my novel of detection, another Fenton Worth Mystery.

The Face

*God hath given you one face, and you make your-
selves another.*

I must try to tell this impartially, with a scientific concern
for truth. It is not my story, after all. I played only a small
part at the end.

Yet the end, in a way, returns to the beginning. This
story is a snake swallowing its own tail.

Is the tape recording? My name is James P. Anderson,
and I am—was a lab technician working for the special
project. My work was trivial, for I have very little formal
scientific training.

Not that I'm ignorant. You pick up things, here and
there. I've been reading about the lives of great scientists.
I know, for one thing, how Auguste Kekulé discovered
the chemical structure of benzene. Not too many chemists
know that. He found it in a dream.

I keep dreaming that someone is trying to tear off my
face. The doctor says that's just the healing and tightening
of new tissue, nothing to worry about.

Kekulé dreamed of snakes, circling and biting their
own tails. That's how he discovered the benzene ring.
Snakes . . .

The three boys who found the object in Hill Park were,
they say, hunting for garter snakes. The Barnes boy said
that at first they all thought the object was a rubber mask

lying in the grass. But his friends said they knew at once that it was "something weird." What is the truth here?

They experimented, trying to turn it over with sticks. They bruised it, and scratched the cheek, which bled. Barnes and Schmidt later claimed it was the third boy, Dalston, who committed "most" of these injuries. By way of appeasement, they brought the object offerings of fresh flowers. Finally Barnes told his parents. Barnes senior, a water inspector, visited the site and immediately called the police.

The police report speaks of the object as "face of a partly-buried Caucasian, sex unknown." According to the medical examiner, the person was unconscious: "Respiration shallow, estimated temperature subnormal, pulse slow. Pupils dilated. The mouth could not be opened."

The discovery was unusual enough for the evening papers, who headlined it as *Live Burial Mystery*. A few reporters hung around the site, waiting for the police to uncover the rest of the supposed person.

A few minutes after the digging started, it stopped. The police held a whispered conference and then cleared the reporters from the area. That night they put up steel barriers and canvas screens.

Newsmen could only guess at what was happening by the comings and goings of important men: city officials, army officers and medical specialists. The morning papers guessed wildly that the buried person was a spy, a "living bomb," a plague victim. In the evening editions, the story was killed.

It was killed in this case by unofficial pressure—friendly phone calls from certain government offices to city editors. For this reason, reporters felt free to continue chasing down leads.

One man (Cobb of the *Sentinel*) made two discoveries that led in the right direction. He talked to a homicide detective who admitted being puzzled by the undisturbed grass around the face. In his opinion, no one had been digging there for months.

Secondly, a park gardener said he was surprised to hear of a burial in that spot, high on the side of the hill.

"The soil's thin there," he said. "Bedrock's only three or four inches down."

Cobb continued digging. He asked the boys if they'd noticed anything unusual, when they'd found the face.

Two hadn't, and the Schmidt boy (obviously enjoying his sudden fame) now recalled noticing all too much: The face had a third eye, it gave off an eerie blue glow, there was human blood on the lips, etc., etc.

Finally, Cobb talked to one of the rescue workers who'd been digging for the body.

"Everywhere we went down, we struck rock. I didn't know it was rock right away, I thought maybe the guy was wearing a suit of armor or something, see? Anyway, I went down around the head, and more rock. I says, Hell, where is the rest of this guy?

"So then I got down with a trowel, cleared the soil around the head, and got my hand under it, see, to lift it up. So I'm like this, see, with my right hand under the head, and my left on the face. I can feel the guy's breath on the back of my hand. I start to lift, and then I look.

"I couldn't believe it. I can feel the guy's breath. I'm lifting, and I'm looking right where the guy's brain ought to be. And I'm seeing a handful of roots and dirt, with slugs and things crawling around in it. *There's no back to his head.* Just a face!"

Slugs and things. Any chance of heading off public hysteria was now gone. Wire services repeated Cobb's story, heating it up. Within hours, police and army spokesmen had denied it, confirmed it and refused to comment. The medical examiner cleared his throat and admitted to sixty million viewers that, well, yes, he would have to say the face was alive, in a way. Medically speaking. Well, yes, it was breathing. And no, he had no explanation at the moment. But the experts were no doubt looking into it . . .

The *experts?* How many experts could there be on bodiless, living faces? Within days, however, there were dozens of expert opinions in the air. A botanist said the thing was no human face at all, but a peculiar species of mushroom. (He hadn't actually seen it when he said this.) A famous plastic surgeon spoke of little-known advances in transplants. A zoologist spoke of protective camouflage. A religious leader mentioned the imprint of Christ's face on the veil of Veronica. Everyone spoke of the veil of secrecy that was keeping back the truth from the public.

In time, the government allowed a few photos to be published. The face was variously identified as Lincoln, Gandhi, Martin Bormann, Amelia Earhart . . .

By now citizens in every part of the nation were spotting faces in their back yards, especially in the shadows of foliage. Others scanned the sky and found faces in the clouds, which they connected with the imminent flying-saucer invasion. Unscrupulous or uncaring magazines dug up the fantasies of the Schmidt boy. By the end of the month, even the newsmen were getting tired of calls from spirit media ("I have contacted the Face by ouija. It is Christian and vegetarian . . ."), from pranksters ("Listen, I got this nose growing in my window box . . .") and from prophets of doom. One day the *Sentinel* editor threw out letters from three people claiming the face as their own, one man from Mars, and one man who explained that the face was controlling his thoughts by means of a "death dream laser." The editor then wrote an open letter asking for a special Presidential Commission to investigate:

> We've had enough of official silence and scientific double-talk. The public is concerned and alarmed. The only way to put a stop to these crank letters and Halloween-mask hoaxes is to answer these questions: What is the face? Where did it come from? How did it get planted in the park? Is it human and conscious? Can it speak? Can it think?

Actually a special project was already set up to investigate the object. Not appointed by the President or Congress (who were probably afraid of looking foolish), but by the Office of Naval Research jointly with University Hospital. As a lab technician from the hospital, I played a humble part in the project. My duties were washing glassware and reading dials. Dull work, yes, but necessary. A vital part of the search for truth.

I arrived in town the day of the open letter. I cut it out of the *Sentinel* and pinned it on my wall at "home." I intended to check off the editor's questions one by one, as we found the answers.

"Home" for now was a disused Army barracks on the edge of the city, where most of the staff were quartered. I pinned up the letter and took a bus straight to Hill Park, hoping to glimpse the object itself. I didn't even stop to unpack, which is why I forgot to bring my pass.

It was a warm June day, 27° C. Most of the people on

my bus seemed to be headed for the beach. As I later learned, most of them had no jobs to go to. I stepped off the bus and stood shading my eyes to look up at the hill in Hill Park. Near the top they were setting up the metal walls of our laboratory. The park gates were closed, and guarded by two Marines. Too late, I remembered the pass in my suitcase.

As I stood there, a man wearing a white armband with crude lettering on it handed me a leaflet.

"I haven't got any change," I said.

"It's free," he said. "Read it, mister. Find out what the Face really means. Come to our rally tonight and hear the truth."

"The truth?"

"The *real* truth. Not what these government bastards want us to believe. The truth they're afraid of."

I didn't tell him I was working for the government bastards; it would only have provoked him. He stared at me until I smiled and put the leaflet in my pocket. I forgot all about it for the time being.

From the window of the bus back to the barracks, I saw several wall graffiti I didn't understand. But they all seemed to refer to the object. One was a face divided by a bolt of lightning. One was a face surrounded by sun rays. I remember these two only because I've seen them so often since, but there were many others. The object in the park had already become the focus of several movements, both political and mystical. Most of them, like the Society of the Peaceful Face, the American Vigilante Volunteers and the Space Brotherhood, either disbanded or merged, but anyhow dropped out of sight. Only two evolved and lived on.

The Guardians of the Mask emphasized the fact that the object was a *white* face. They believed it to be only part of the body to come. Any day now, the hands would turn up in, say, Britain, and the feet in Scandinavia, and the rest in other Caucasian countries. (Medical students often played cruel tricks with these pathetic hopes.) Finally the complete Messiah-Fuhrer would assemble himself and lead them into the final, racial Armageddon, in which all but the white race would certainly die.

The New Universologists on the other hand believed the object to be an oracle. They reckoned it had now been sleeping for nearly a thousand years. Soon it would awaken, to tell them what to do next, to achieve a world of lasting peace and brotherhood.

Normally both movements might have appealed only to a fringe of unhappy people, but these were far from normal times. The nation was undergoing great economic and political upheavals, and the government almost daily proved itself unequal to the problems of unemployment and unrest. Both movements attracted thousands in this city alone, and perhaps hundreds of thousands more were sympathetic to their causes. Other cities were close behind.

The Communist Party saw which way the wind blew, and lent some support to the New Universologists (NU), to help them organize. In return, over the next few months, the NU began to lay more stress on workers' control of industry, and less on miracles. Reacting, ultra-conservative groups threw in their lot—and their considerable money—with the Guardians of the Mask (GM). Up and down the country there were demonstrations and counter-demonstrations, rallies and rally-smashers, protest marches and torchlight processions. And a sense of urgency. A sense that power was now within reach of those who most needed it. Power was just inside the gates of Hill Park.

Or so they must have thought. At different times, both groups tried storming the park to rescue their idol. The police, even with state police reinforcements, were almost overwhelmed by the second attack. Next day the edge of the park was barricaded with sandbags, and several hundred Marines were billeted inside. From now on until the end of our project, no one could ever be allowed to come into the park.

The end of our project? It dragged its long, slow, serpent's body through the summer, with no end in sight. One day in October I looked up at the news clipping on my wall. Not a single vital question had been answered. We knew nothing important, and it looked as though we never would. Our work had disintegrated into endless proofs and disproofs of secondary theories. The serpent had no end, it had swallowed it, and now chewed on itself . . .

Who am I, a lab technician, to make this judgment? I speak, not of the scientific facts, but of the human differences within the project. I wasn't just washing glassware and reading dials, not all the time. I kept my eyes open.

There was a fundamental split from the very beginning, between Dr. Lowell, our project director, and Dr. Grauber, head of the medical section. The medical people wanted to move the object to University Hospital and place it under intensive care. Dr. Lowell supported the biologists who argued against this, saying that it might be dangerous to uproot it from its present environment. Dr. Grauber replied that this was entirely a medical decision, hence his to make. Dr. Lowell said that depended entirely on whether or not the object was truly human.

"How on earth can we find out what it is unless we get it into a proper laboratory? Do you expect my men to do biopsies out *here?*" Grauber had to stand on tiptoe to shout this into Lowell's face. The director was a head taller than Grauber, and, like many big men, bland and almost friendly in an argument. He liked to pose as a big, jolly, absent-minded professor, slow of speech and always fishing for his pipe in one pocket of his baggy tweed jacket. In reality he was a ruthless executive. Whatever he knew or didn't know about science, he knew how to command. Most of us came to respect him, even like him.

Grauber was generally unliked. I knew him from the hospital, where they called him Napoleon. A cold, logical little man, a brilliant scientist, but he threw tantrums when he didn't get his way.

He tore off his pince-nez and shook them under Lowell's nose—as though he wanted to shake a fist at him. "Is that what you expect? Is it? Is it?"

Lowell sighed. "Dr. Grauber, I expect you to follow my direction. We'll get along better if you do, okay?"

It was not okay. The arguments grew worse as the project dragged on through the summer. The staff were all upset; we all found ourselves taking sides. I would hear:

"Grauber just wants to get control of the project himself. So he wants to drag the thing off to his own lab, and then gradually ease Lowell out of the driver's seat. I've seen his kind before."

"Are you crazy? Grauber's ten times the scientist Lowell ever will be. And I'll tell you something else. He really cares about that 'thing' out there. It's no 'thing' to him, it's a human being in need of medical treatment."

There was something in both sides; I didn't know what to believe. After one shattering evening of this, I quit work early. I had to drag myself on the bus, and then I sat with closed eyes, wishing away my throbbing headache. The engine vibration and bright lights were still getting through to me, so finally I got out and walked.

It was quiet and dark. Just my footsteps and the occasional streetlight. I noticed my headache going.

Then I turned a corner and found myself at a rally of the New Universologists. There were maybe fifty people listening, and one white-haired man speaking from the back of a pickup truck. The banner behind him said THE FACE OF PEACE, and showed the sun-ray symbol. Most of the people looked poor, but more or less respectable. One exception was the dirty, unshaven man who was taking pictures.

". . . a face of peace," said the speaker. "Brothers, do you know what peace means? Do any of us know? Have they ever let us find out? Not a chance.

"Of course peace will be hard on some people. Think of all those rich arms manufacturers that'll have to go out and get an honest job! Think of all the generals who might have to work for a living! Think of the paid-off politicians who get a piece of every big arms contract— on relief! We all know who's against peace, don't we? *And they've got a steel ring around Hill Park right now!*

"What are they so afraid of, brothers? I'll tell you . . ."

But he never did tell us, for just then a man in a Halloween mask jumped up and pulled him down off the truck. There were more men in masks with baseball bats, hitting people in the front of the crowd.

Someone screamed, "The GMs!"

We ran. I looked back from a safe distance. Two of the invaders were kicking the white-haired man as he lay in the street. Others were trying to turn over the truck. My headache was back, and now I felt sick to my stomach besides.

At work the Grauber-Lowell arguments went on. Medical staff monitored the object's temperature, pulse and respiration (dials for me to read), all below normal. They took tissue samples (a biopsy) and found it had human flesh. Radiologists found that the face contained normal human face bones and teeth. The jaw was fused, unworkable. Three of the teeth had metal fillings. All this enabled Grauber to say:

"It's human, for God's sake! It's in a coma. Probably dying!"

"*Part*-human," Lowell replied, lighting his pipe. "A symbiosis, I think. And we're in a unique position to study it in its natural environment. Let's not plop it in a hospital bed just yet, shall we?"

And there was evidence for his side, too. The back of the object was connected to the soil through masses of tiny threadlike roots. Vegetation seemingly living in symbiosis with a human face. Just how the two worked together was unclear. An ultrasonic probe showed clusters of tiny sacs attached to some of these roots. The sacs pulsated together, providing the object's pseudo-breathing.

Everyone took sides but me. I tried to stay impartial, to wait for the final blaze of truth. At home I tried not to notice the yellowed clipping on the wall. None of the questions were checked off. We knew nothing.

The last week of October was the worst. Dr. Grauber said that the first frost might kill the object, whether or not it was human. Dr. Lowell agreed, but argued for moving it to a greenhouse, not a hospital. All over town there were cryptic notices of a massive GM procession, on Halloween, "Night of the Mask." Police leave was canceled for that night, and still more Marines were brought in. When I arrived for work at dusk, I saw them setting up machine guns on the barricades. *Ring of steel*, I thought. *And for what?*

Someone said Dr. Grauber wanted to see me. While I waited outside his office I could hear him and Lowell arguing.

"You admit you know nothing of medicine, Dr. Lowell. You're a biologist. A marine biologist at that. You know about as much about medicine as I know about— pogonophorae."

"Certainly. But I don't see—"

"Then I'll spell it out for you. The face is human, or part-human. If he dies, because you've disregarded medical advice—good advice—that's murder."

"Oh, come now. You can't—"

"I can. I'll have you arrested, Dr. Lowell. And brought to trial."

"You'll never prove it's human."

"No, you'll probably get off. But think of the headlines. Think of what the publicity will mean to your precious career."

"God damn you," said Lowell pleasantly. "I almost think you would, too. Still, I can always fire you."

There was a loud click. When Lowell came out, he was putting the broken pieces of his pipe in his pocket. He looked worried, but when he saw me, he smiled.

"Next patient," he said.

Grauber looked sick. He was polishing his pince-nez furiously, perhaps to disguise the trembling of his hand. "Ah, Anderson is it?" He never remembered the names or faces of his staff. "Sit down, Anderson. I have some rather bad news for you."

I sat down. "What is it, Doctor?"

"The FBI came to see me earlier, to tell me you're a security risk."

"What? Me?"

"They showed me a photograph of you at some rally. One of these odd-ball groups that keeps trying to smash their way into the park. And they searched your room at the barracks and found a certain leaflet."

"But I can explain—"

He held up a hand. "I'm sure you can. I'm sure you can. But not to me. I don't understand these new political things. *They* say you must go, so go you must. I am sorry. Of course we'll try to keep you on at the hospital, if we can. I'm sure you mean us no harm."

"No harm? No *harm?*" When I got outside, I had to laugh. It's said Auguste Kekulé laughed when he awoke from his dream to understand the benzene ring. In the words of the song:

> Then I awoke
> Was this some kind of joke?

It was, and the joke was on me. I had worked four months for the project, washing glassware, reading dials. Keeping an open mind, not taking sides. Waiting for the blaze of truth. And the truth was *I had never laid eyes on the Face itself.*

Well, now was the time. Coming up the hill to the park I could see the great GM procession, thousands on thousands of tiny lights like the glittering scales of one huge snake. Pointing to the truth in the park. Over there, in that little tent. What would they do, if they broke in?

Carry it away? Fall down and worship, pressing their hideous masks to the ground? Too many questions (Can it speak? Can it think?), and no answers.

I thought of Kekulé's dream again. Was there another meaning? The snake devours its tail: All things must turn back to their origin. The circle is zero. Ashes to ashes . . .

I took a 500 ml bottle of benzene from the lab, where I had used it to clean the glassware. Kekulé's benzene, the big zero. When I tore open the flaps of the little tent I could hardly make out the Face. Just a lighter oval in the darkness. I poured the bottle of benzene on it and ignited it. They tell me there was an explosion. My face was burned, and I have lost my sight.

But I have seen enough.

Heavens Below

Fifteen Utopias

GETTING THERE IS $\left(\dfrac{n-1}{n}\right)$TH THE FUN

Professor Lodeworm made one last adjustment. "If my Utopia-ray works according to plan," he said, "it should make life for everyone a continual round of delightful anticipation, ever closer and closer to satisfaction. Now I'll switch it on."

Professor Lodeworm made one last adjustment. "If my Utopia-ray works according to plan," he said, "it should make life for everyone a continual round of delightful anticipation, ever closer and closer to satisfaction. Now I'll switch it on."

THE BRIGHT SIDE

On Dr. Freeman's desk at the Astronomy Institute we found a list headed "UTOPIAS." The first items were:

1. Arrange the planets in order of size, of color, of mass, and in alphabetical order.
2. The world population, laid end to end, ought to reach about eleven or twelve times to the moon. Test this.
3. Make friends with a black hole.
4. Adjust the earth's rotation so that my watch always keeps perfect time.

148

5. Land a man on the sun.

6. Carve Mercury, Venus, Earth, and Mars with the faces of Washington, Jefferson, Lincoln, and Theodore Roosevelt.

7. Paint the moon's bright side black.

The remainder of this list was obscured by blood from Dr. Freeman's throat. He lay with his head on the desk, having apparently killed himself with a piece of broken glass. We think the glass came from the objective lens of the Institute telescope, which he'd smashed earlier in the day.

A talk with his physician cast more light on the matter. He had diagnosed in Dr. Freeman a deterioration of the optic nerve.

"I can understand an astronomer's being unhappy at going blind," he explained. "Wish I hadn't told him to look on the . . ."

MR. AND MS. AMERICA

"I know they always say it's hard to be a judge in these contests," George said. "But you know, it really is hard. Hell, we've got at least fifteen possibles here, and they all look good to me."

Lotte yawned. "Not to me. Vanity surgery isn't much, nowadays. Look, each of these characters has sunk half a million in his own body, and what have they really got? Look at this one, now."

Mr. Florida was parading above them. George saw little enough wrong with him. With Mr. Florida's three-foot coxcomb, rib fins, and real eyes set into his female breasts, he was at least the Number Three contender.

Ms. South Dakota looked even better. She had restricted herself to a hundred pounds of implanted fat, extra fingers and toes, and a small, shapely pair of antlers.

Next came Ms. Iowa, an atavism of the 1950s: ninety-inch bust, ten-inch waist, thirty feet of trailing blonde hair, and feet equipped with tall spike heels. A decided washout, along with Mr. Alaska and his fifty-pound penis that looked like a case of elephantiasis, nothing more.

By lunchtime, they'd narrowed it down to five men and four women. George and Lotte agreed the contest was tawdry, grotesque, and decadent. Over lunch, they tried to puzzle out what was wrong.

"The trouble is," George said, "most of the young surgeons have no ideas. Laszlo Goodwin's okay, but the rest—amateur copyists."

"Not like our day," Lotte said. "Your outfit still looks good, you know?"

"Thanks. Yes, old Morton knew his stuff. A simple concept like this never looks out-of-date: seal fur all over, eyes on stalks, and a toroidal torso. My tailor says it's a real pleasure and a challenge, making clothes for a man with a big hole through his middle. But you still look great, too."

"Thanks," said Lotte. She cut a bite of steak and delicately stuffed it up her armpit.

EMPTY PROMISE

"Just sign here," said the Devil, "and name your wish."

Jonathan Palmer sighed. "I wish for Utopia," he said. "A perfect world without blemish or unpleasantness."

"But—" said the Devil, looking surprised as he vanished forever.

"Things seem better already," said Jonathan Palmer as he vanished forever.

"Better and better," said his wife, turning from the keyhole to embrace her lover, Raoul. As she vanished forever, Raoul recalled that he was the sole beneficiary of her sizable insurance policy. He immediately vanished, followed by the cunning insurance salesman, his grasping boss, and the rest of imperfect humanity.

I alone am left. Ha-ha—

THE PARADISE PROBLEM

Blenheim won his island by correctly guessing the number of coffee beans in a boxcar. He named his utopian republic Boxcar, its capital, Bean.

The island population consisted of two tribes, the Ye (who always told the truth) and the Ne (who always lied). A man from one tribe or the other was always posted at a fork in the main road, where one branch led to the city, the other into cannibal country.

By the river, Blenheim found a party of missionaries and cannibals, waiting to row across. The rowboat could carry only two men. If the cannibals on either shore outnumbered the missionaries, they would eat them.

Farther down the river was a pair of men with the curious names of A and B. A could evidently row upstream half as fast as B could swim downstream, while A and B together could row upstream twice as fast as B alone.

The two men explained that they were always engaging in contests, such as chopping wood, pumping water, racing a bicycle against a car, and so on. B was as many years older than A as A's age had been when B was as old as A was when B gave him half his apples plus half an apple.

In the city of Bean, the baker, draper, tailor, and smith were named (not respectively) Baker, Draper, Tailor, and Smith. Baker was the tailor's uncle, and Draper was the smith's son. Tailor had no living relatives. If Draper was the tailor, then the smith was named after the occupation of the man named after the occupation of Draper. Otherwise, the city was very beautiful.

Blenheim spent many happy years in Boxcar, drawing various colored socks out of a drawer in order to get a matching pair. Exactly how many happy years did he spend?

WHAT CHANGED DOYSTER'S MIND

Doyster stepped out of his time machine and strolled up the shady avenue of the Academy grove to Plato's house. The philosopher was just now supervising workmen who were placing a lintel over the door. On the lintel was inscribed: "Let no one enter here who is unacquainted with geometry."

"It won't work, boss," called one of the men. "The posts are too far apart. It won't reach across."

"Nonsense," said Plato. "Let go your end."

As one end of the lintel crashed to the ground, Doyster was already walking back down the shady avenue.

HANDOUT

The League of Nations rules put it like this: Everyone in the world was entitled to go along to his nearest Dispensary and collect, free, a large box of God.

The first problem was a big riot in South America, owing to a rumor that supplies were running out. The League made a reassuring broadcast: No shortage was imminent. Indeed, the supply was expected to last indefinitely.

The riots in the Indian subcontinent were harder to combat. Local officials began to gripe: "Oh, sure, there's enough to go around, but it's not in the right places. Rich Americans have enough to burn, while poor Indians are shelling out a hundred rupees a box on the black market. Is that justice? Why can't we straighten out the distribution?"

The League looked into it, and sent a memo: God was already present everywhere in great quantities. Containers, alas, were not. Applicants should be urged to bring their own boxes, baskets, pails, envelopes, etc.

Next came the staff shortages in Africa. People might walk fifty miles to the nearest Dispensary, only to find it closed. Perhaps the overworked official had collapsed with fever, perhaps he had gone AWOL, or deserted, or been murdered by black-marketeers. No one knew. Angry crowds began burning Dispensaries, not only in Africa but across the world. Officials now began to desert in greater numbers, or call for military protection.

At the end of a year, the League reviewed its campaign: The costs (of troops, compensation for riot-torn cities, etc.) ran to billions. The results were disappointing. Fewer than a tenth of those in need had actually been reached.

Reluctantly, the League voted to dispense no more boxes of God.

ASSESSMENT

Our machine slaves have now taken over all tedious or disagreeable occupations. They paint, write and perform music, make scientific discoveries, and handle pretty

well everything from fashion to philosophy. This leaves
us plenty of time and freedom to do whatever we like—
extract square roots, say, or calculate payrolls.

ART NEWS

Sisyphus jammed a block of wood under the stone to
keep it from rolling back, took a swig from his canteen,
and squatted down to explain his work to the tour group.

"Of course, it's a very healthy life—outdoor work, and
so on. Then, too, I've always liked working with natural
materials like stone. Not that the stone itself is important.
No, what's important here is not gross physical change.
I think I can safely say that ever since Oldenburg dug
a hole in Central Park, filled it in, and called it a buried
sculpture—ever since then, physical-change stuff has been
dying a slow death. Nowadays, the artist is not concerned
with 'doing' something *within* Nature . . ."

After stopping for ice-cold orangeade, the group moved
on to Tantalus.

PAX GURNEY

As a young man, Gurney said, "If I were world emperor,
the first thing I'd do would be to introduce a compulsory world language." For the next twenty years, he
actually worked on such a language, Unilingo, on the
off chance he might become emperor. Unilingo was designed to guarantee world peace forever. In this language,
no one could lie or express hatred or discontent. No one
could hold an opinion contrary to fact, or hold any
opinion at all about non-facts. No two speakers of
Unilingo could ever really disagree. Gurney described it
in his memoirs as "a calculus of good sense and good
taste."

Of course he *did* become world emperor, and the world
prospered for many years under his "rule of grammar."
People stopped talking about matters that did not concern
them, and spoke wisely of those that did. The world
was at peace. Gurney abdicated, and the institutions of
government withered as people learned self-control.

A century after Gurney's death, an American compiling

a new dictionary of Unilingo made a curious discovery. While in America the word *orth* had kept its original meaning ("to fray the edge of an old blanket, from left to right"), in Eurasiafrica it had taken on a new one ("to fray the edge of an old blanket, left-handedly"). He wrote a letter about it to a Eurasiafrican colleague. The trouble was traced to photocopies of Gurney's original manuscript, on file in the two continents. One copy showed the word *riin* ("from left to right"), the other showed *riin* without a dot over the second *i* ("left-handedly"). An interesting dispute arose between the Universities of Tübingen and Nebraska.

What had been on the original manuscript (long since lost)? Was a dot added, correcting a mistake? Or erased? Was the addition or erasure itself a mistake? Physical chemists were called in, and photography experts. The debate became more heated, and opinions were split along continental lines. An American professor was booed at Tübingen; Nebraska fired a foreign archaeologist.

Over the next century, the two continents grew apart. The dot-less Eurasiafricans developed a philosophy aimed at defining the final meaning of life. The dotted Americans preferred a harsh form of skepticism, summed up in their motto: "That which does not exist is nonexistent." Two centuries later, these philosophies had become articles of faith for two bitterly opposed religions.

Knowing this background to the present war, we can more easily understand . . .

A FABLE

The snails, discontented with their free and easy life, held a noisy meeting to petition Jupiter for a king.

"We're not complaining," they insisted. "We know we already have portable homes and other luxuries. But we'd like a strong leader. Afer all, you gave the frogs a stork to follow. And even the men have their presidents. How about us?"

Jupiter threw an old log down into their pool and said, "There is a king for you!"

The old log has proved a wise and compassionate leader. Under his guidance, the snails have prospered, until now they are seen in all the best restaurants.

UTOPIA: A FINANCIAL REPORT

Utopia is laid out in four planned nations: Fascesia, Commund, Capitalia, and Anarche.

Fascesia is a half-tamed land. The cities are sophisticated, filled with monumental architecture, opera houses, and elegant nightclubs. The countryside, on the other hand, is a wilderness teeming (in theory) with savages and wild game. Alas, Fascesians tend to hunt both to extinction, and the cost of replenishing these is considerable. Therefore we recommend closing Fascesia.

Commund cities are bleak and industrial, while its rural areas undergo intensive agriculture. Commounders are excellent organizers and produce surpluses yearly. Unfortunately, these surpluses seem to lower the morale of Commounders, who rather enjoy mild discomforts and privations—proof that they are continuing their "struggle." Accordingly, we remove their surpluses from time to time, as well as causing them to have minor shortages. The costs of removal and destruction of their surpluses have become excessive. Moreover, the materials destroyed are our loss, in the last analysis. We recommend closing Commund.

. Capitalia is a uniformly settled nation with a monotony of maple-lined streets and white frame houses. Capitalians have no incentive to work (though of course they refer to their play activities as "work"; e.g., signing their names to pieces of paper). They also require huge outlays of energy, materials, machines, foods, and medicines. We recommend closing Capitalia.

Anarche seemed at first a viable nation, with few requirements. Now, it is entirely deserted. Anarchers are evidently unstable, and frequently migrate to the other three nations.

Summary: We feel the experiment has served its purpose. We now know more than enough about the social institutions of *Homo sapiens*. We feel, therefore, that Utopia should be closed and its inhabitants destroyed. The ground can then be used for a study of the social behavior of another interesting species, the armadillos.

UTOPIARY

Utopia has turned out to be like a well-planned garden:
Each change of season brings its fresh cycle of pleasing
color, heavenly scent, and backbreaking work.

LUCK

General Holme threw the dice. "Tough luck, General
Vladiful," he said, chuckling. "I've just captured your
fourth army. Do you want to surrender?"

The other sighed. "No, no. After all, we are playing
for real armies. Let us play on awhile. I may yet turn
the turtles on you, eh?"

"Tables. We say turn the tables. Ha-ha, I must say,
this beats the old system of waging w—"

The door burst open and a soldier strode in, pointing
a submachine gun at them. "You'll have to surrender.
This sector has just been captured by the forces of
General Heinz."

"Heinz? Heinz?" Holme scratched his head. "Never
heard of him. He's not in the game."

"He plays a bigger game," said the soldier. "Come with
me, please."

Vladiful nodded. "So, there is a bigger war than we
know of, even. I wonder who Heinz opposes?"

From the darkness outside came a burst of automatic
fire. The soldier flopped to the floor, bleeding from a
dozen wounds. In a moment, a man in a Germanic uniform
was prodded into the room at bayonet point.

"I am Heinz," he said. "Are you my captors?"

"Not us." Holme offered him some brandy. "Ask the
man with the gun."

The man with the gun cleared his throat. "This sector—
namely, Earth—has just been captured by Planet Marshal
Gordon. You are all under house arrest."

As if echoing him, an amplified voice rolled over the
dark parade ground outside. "You are all under house
arrest. This sector has just been captured by the 119th
Galactic Army under Commander Noll."

"Noll?" said Holme. "Lucky bastard. I wonder what
he threw."

A PICNIC

Bill Nolan was thinking out loud. "In a way, I guess this *is* Utopia. I mean, people in the past would have been horrified at the idea of having a picnic in a junkyard. They weren't like us."

Jimmy stopped kicking at an old tire. "Why, Dad?"

Nolan rescued the baby, who was crawling around elbow-deep in sump oil. "That's enough, hon. Mommy'll bring your bottle in just a minute." He waved to his wife, who was climbing over a crumpled Buick.

"You see, Jimmy, our stomachs are different. Everybody has a lot of little helpers in his stomach, to help him digest his dinner. But the way it used to be, the helpers couldn't handle much of anything. So people had to eat things like—oh, cows, pigs, and so on."

Jimmy looked up at them. "Cows! No kidding?"

"I used to eat pieces of cow myself. (Hey, did you strip that insulation like your mother said? Good boy.) No, what happened was, some scientists changed the little helpers. See, we were running out of cows and stuff, so we needed helpers that would help us eat new things. Now just about everything is edible."

"You're not supposed to say 'et.' "

"Yes, but 'edible' means 'eatable.' I used to wonder why myself."

"Mumf chmumf—"

"Don't let your mother see you talking with your mouth full, son."

Janet Nolan came back to the picnic site just then. "See what? Oh, God, Bill, you let the baby get herself *filthy*. Couldn't you have spooned up the sump oil instead of letting her crawl right in it? And, Jimmy! What are you doing?"

A large piece of the old tire was gone, and the boy was now swallowing a strip of muddy tread.

"I was hungry," he mumbled.

"Hungry? That's no excuse for bolting your food. You'll have a tummy ache."

"Stomach," the boy corrected.

"I don't see why boys who bolt their food should have any dessert, do you? And we're having polyethylene seat covers."

"Aw, Ma, can't I have some?"

"Hmm. We'll see."

Bill looked at the baby's bottle in her hand. "I see you got it."

She smiled. "Yes. Real high-octane lead-free stuff. Only a little rusty water in the bottom. We were lucky to find it, she's so fussy."

Janet delivered the bottle into the frantically waving arms of the baby, who rammed it in her own mouth and started sucking. Long before the others had finished twirling up masses of plastic wire insulation on their forks, the bottle was empty. The baby lay back, flushed and drowsy. Nolan gave her a cardboard cookie, but, after slobbering at it for a moment without really biting it, she gave an aromatic burp and went to sleep.

"Utopia," he murmured.

"What, darling?"

"Nothing." He brandished the carving knife and fork. "Now for the main course. White sidewall, darling? Or dark?"

Space Shoes of the Gods

An Archaeological Revelation

Why do so many ancient legends speak of gods who fly in flaming chariots? Why is the Great Pyramid built strong enough to withstand an H-bomb blast? What possible connection can there be between Easter Island, Stonehenge, and the messages received on my Aunt Edna's ouija board? Orthodox scientists are unable, perhaps unwilling, to answer such daring questions.

Of course it's never easy to abandon our old misconceptions and accept fresh ideas. Scientists bitterly attacked Galileo when he proved that the Leaning Tower of Pisa was a pendulum. They pooh-phooed Darwin's revolutionary notion that mankind is descended from the beagle. They laughed themselves sick at Edison's light bulb, as they will at any brilliant idea eons ahead of its time.

My idea, for instance. I do not expect understanding from the narrow-minded men of the scientific establishment. They are too busy pottering around with test tubes in musty laboratories to listen to anything new and important. Rather, my article is directed to those young, adventurous minds who are not afraid to believe the impossible. I am in the position of the first beagle who dared to walk on his hind legs, so to speak. No doubt there was some smart beagle professor standing by, to call him a crank and a dreamer. All the same, he took that first great step.

Today we are taking another great step, a giant step from Earth [1] into the vast spaces of space. Yet how much do we really know about this universe of ours, with its dozens on dozens of galaxies, each packed with scores of literal stars?

Earthbound science has no answers. But a few far-sighted "cranks and dreamers" have ventured to say that:

a. There are certainly other civilizations in the universe *exactly like ours,* if not more so.

b. *They* are trying desperately to get in touch with us, perhaps to borrow money.

c. *They* must have landed here on Earth in the prehistoric past.

d. Wherever *They* landed, *They* were worshipped as gods by the natives. Their modern equipment, which would seem prosaic to us, must have been fearful magic for our ancestors. Imagine, for example, how the simple Egyptians might have reacted to gods carrying ballpoints, credit cards and contact lenses!

e. For some reason, the space gods wearied of all this worship, and departed.

Hard to believe? Orthodox science may try to dismiss such notions with a wave of its oscilloscope. But then orthodox science still cannot explain away certain facts . . .

THE EVIDENCE

Last year, English miners opened a seam of coal 15 million years old. Inside, they found the clear fossil imprint of *a modern zipper.*

How could it have got there? Did an ancient space visitor with zipper pockets on his uniform fall asleep in the English jungle, never to awaken? Was he left behind by the expedition? Could he have been murdered by one of his space brothers? [2]

Conventional scientists have their own "explanation" of this strange anthracite evidence. They call it a fossil fern. But they have yet to explain what a fern was doing wearing a uniform with zipper pockets.

In the same way, conventional archaeologists have tried to explain away a remarkable cave drawing found in Blague, France. They call it "a hunter shooting game with a bow and arrow." But the hunter's bow looks astonishingly like a modern sextant, to the unprejudiced eye of this non-scientist. The drawing can only be a space navigator taking bearings on a woolly mammoth. Museums are filled with similar archaeological mistakes: Stone "spear-heads" which, as anyone can see, are actually stone letter-openers.

The ancient world abounds in such unexplained mysteries. How could the simple inhabitants of Easter Island have carved their enormous stone faces and heaved them into place, without the aid of rock drills and bulldozers? How could gigantic pyramids have been built by the primitive, cave-dwelling Egyptians? Science has not begun to unravel the mystery of the pyramids, nor even to solve the riddle of the Sphinx.

A ruined edifice in Peru bears a weird inscription: two horizontal lines crossed by two vertical lines. In other words, the figure for tic-tac-toe, *a game played by the latest giant computers*. Likewise the Ankara Museum displays clay tablets pierced with holes—the same holes used in modern IBM cards. Could this represent the payroll arrangements of our cosmic visitors?

PECULIAR ROUNDNESSES

The jungles of Costa Rica are littered with mysterious stone balls, some of them larger than Volkswagens. I spoke with the amateur archaeologist who is studying these curious rock spheres in connection with his search for Martin Bormann.

"I can't really understand these odd orbs," he confided. "According to a local legend, these uncanny globes fell from the sky. The native name for them translates as 'strange spheroids.' Could they be small planets from some lesser solar system? At this stage, we can't rule out anything, even the possibility that some vanished race of giants played marbles here."

Two intriguing ideas. Controversy rages on between the odd-ball planet theory and the lost-marble theory, but one question must be answered:

If these are tiny planets, what has become of their even tinier inhabitants?

The roundness theme appears again in the art of many cultures. Australian aborigines, among others, have drawn circles on pieces of wood. A ceremonial frieze of ancient Mexico, which is covered with circles, undoubtedly depicts traffic lights, ball bearings, embroidery hoops, curly hair and many other items not re-discovered until the twentieth century.

My list could go on to include hundreds of these anachronisms, but I will end it with an object in my own collection. Not long ago I acquired a small Indo-Sumerian statue of bronze. Purblind anthropologists would probably call it a "fertility goddess," ignoring certain features which are obvious to any child:

On the chest of the goddess are two distinct, modern doorbells.

THE LEGENDS

In the light of evidence like the above, we might re-examine some of the legends of the so-called past. Take the Nordic sagas for example. There we read of strange gods who drank from horns. Virgil, too, speaks of dreams coming through a gate of horn, while the Book of Revelation describes gates of pearl. From Shakespeare we hear the legend of the base Indian who threw away a pearl, while many Indian myths speak of peculiar gods. Can all this be coincidence? No, it is far more likely that these myths convey primitive ideas of television, twin-tub washing machines and electric toothbrushes.[3] This is confirmed in Genesis, where we read of an angel (a technician) who guarded the gates of Eden (spaceship) with a flaming sword (soldering iron).

Finally we are confronted with the "wild" tales of the early Spanish conquistadores, who swore they found in America men with feathers growing right out of their heads! Who were these odd feather-headed strangers, and what were they doing on our planet?

THE LOST GALAXY

By now it must be plain that many of our space gods were tourists. In the distant past, Earth was no doubt a tourists' paradise, an unspoiled wilderness where the featherheads could get away from their own crowded galaxy. They may have built themselves a few amenities, such as the pyramid saunas of Egypt, or Stonehenge (a

luxury motel), but they left most of the planet delight-
fully wild.

What spoiled it for them? The Deluge? The sinking of
the luxury liner *Atlantis?* Whatever the reason, our cosmic tourists departed, leaving behind only a few traces:
a zipper jacket in England, marbles in Costa Rica, a
crumpled Kleenex (now to be seen at the Stockholm
Museum of Antiquities, in a wastebasket near the door).

Some uncanny tourist instinct must have told them
that Earth was doomed.[4] The natives were getting too
civilized. All too soon earthlings would cover the paradise planet with highways and fuming traffic; fill its air
with thundering jets carrying earthling tourists; and pack
its universities with so-called professors who scoff at my
theory.

The space gods have left our solar system and gone
back to work. But someday when we have finally rid
this planet of evil, pollution, war, disease and skeptical
scientists—then our gods will return.[5] They will bring us
all the benefits of their superior civilization. They will
shower us with plenty of valuable cargo.

NOTES

1. The question of giants *in* the Earth will be taken up in
a later monograph.

2. Just such a space-brother murder could well account
for the strange legend of Cain and Abel. I have com-
municated my suspicions to Scotland Yard, urging them
to examine the coal deposits for fossil fingerprints. So far,
they have remained ominously silent on the matter.

3. Further confirmation is provided by the certain knowledge that Shakespeare's base Indian threw his pearl *before swine*. This proves that Shakespeare's plays were
really written by Bacon, a space visitor.

4. "Tourist instinct" is an example of clairvoyance, or
"knowing" that something will go wrong just before it
does. I refer the reader to an interesting experiment at
Earl University, where a researcher asks subjects to drop
buttered toast and predict whether it will land face-down
or face-up. So far, the experiment is a failure, Dr.
Bormann reports. But he adds, "The interesting thing is,
I just knew it would fail."

5. Some doddering scientists sneer at the idea of travel between stars. The nearest star, they say, is 25 trillion miles away. They forget that monorail trains are capable of astonishing speeds (over 200 m.p.h.!). Doubtless, despite the skeptics, we'll have a regular train service to Alpha Centauri and other stars, by the end of the century.

The Parodies

The Purloined Butter

A story by Edgar Allan Poe
Revised and Abridged by John Sladek

At Paris, just after dark one gusty evening in the autumn
of 18—, I was enjoying the twofold luxury of meditation
and meerschaum, in company with my friend C. Auguste
Dupin, in his little back library. The door was thrown
open and admitted our old acquaintance, Monsieur
G——, the Prefect of the Parisian police.

"And what, after all, is the matter on hand?" I asked.

"Why, I will tell you," replied the Prefect. "I have
received personal information, from a very high quarter,
that a certain condiment of the last importance, has been
purloined from the royal apartments. The individual who
purloined it is known. It still remains in his possession,
which can be inferred by the nature of the condiment
and the non-appearance of certain results which would
at once arise from its passing *out* of the robber's possession."

"Then," I observed, "the butter is clearly upon the
premises. As for being on his person, I suppose that is
out of the question."

"Entirely," said the Prefect. "He has been twice way-
laid, as if by footpads, and his person rigorously searched
under my own inspection."

"And his hotel?"

"Why the fact is, we took our time and searched *everywhere*. I took the whole building, room by room; devot-
ing the nights of a whole week to each. We examined,
first, the furniture in each apartment. We opened every

167

possible drawer; and I presume you know that to a properly trained police agent, such a thing as a *secret* drawer is impossible. We have accurate rules; the fiftieth part of a line could not escape us. The chair cushions we probed with the long fine needles you have seen me employ. From the tables we removed the tops, to examine the possibility of excavated legs; likewise the bedposts."

"You did not take to pieces all the chairs?" I asked.

"Certainly not; but we did better—we examined the rungs of every chair in the house, and indeed, the jointings of every description of furniture, by the aid of a most powerful microscope. Had there been traces of recent disturbance, we should not have failed to detect it, instantly. A single grain of gimlet dust, for example, would have been as obvious as an apple."

"I presume you looked to the mirrors, between the boards and plates, and you probed the beds, as well as the curtains and carpets?"

"That of course; and when we had completed the furniture, we then examined the house itself. We scrutinized each individual square inch throughout the premises, including the two houses immediately adjoining, with the microscope, as before. The grounds were paved with brick; examination of the moss between stones by the microscope revealed no disturbances."

Dupin spoke for the first time. "I assume the hotel is at least fifty feet on a side," he said. The Prefect nodded. "And it has at least three stories, each twenty feet high. And there are at least four rooms on each floor. If you had but a week to examine a room (assuming six hours per night available), you would have to cover"—he paused, performing lightning mental calculation—"sixteen and one-fifth square inches per second. The grain of gimlet dust you spoke of must be four or five thousandths of an inch in diameter, or one-thousandth as broad as an apple. If, therefore, one of your men were to examine one 'applesworth' of visible area per second, he would require four hundred seconds, or eighteen and two-thirds minutes, to cover a square inch.

"It follows, therefore, that it must take nine hundred sixty minutes, or sixteen hours, for one man to examine one square foot of area. A room twenty-five feet square and twenty in height must have a total inside area of three thousand, two hundred fifty square feet; one man would require a great deal of time to examine it."

"Naturally, I employed——"

"More than one man? Indeed, I have calculated that, if your men examined these rooms as you say, you would have required the services of *one thousand, two hundred and thirty-eight men,* all working away with their microscopes at the same time, in the same smallish room! And working, as you implied, noiselessly! Come, come, my dear Prefect!"

I was astonished. The Prefect appeared absolutely thunderstricken. For some moments he remained speechless and motionless, looking incredulously at my friend with open mouth, and eyes that seemed starting from their sockets.

"You know very well what I mean, Monsieur G——" said Dupin.

The Prefect blushed. Then, to my utter amazement, he reached into his pocket and drew out the butter. Dupin satisfied himself that this butter was indeed the one in question, then locked it away.

"You may go," he said coldly to the Prefect. This functionary seized his hat and stick in a perfect agony of joy, and then scrambling and struggling to the door, rushed at length unceremoniously from the room and from the house.

When the Prefect had gone, my friend entered into some explanations.

Pemberley's Start-Afresh Calliope

or, The New Proteus
by H. G. W*lls

I hope to set down this story exactly as the surgeon told it to me, at the club. There were three of us in the smoking-room: Lord Suffield; the surgeon, whose name I did not know; myself.

As soon as he sank into his chair, Lord Suffield began an anecdote about India, and, as soon as he had our attention, he fell asleep in mid-sentence. The surgeon and I traded cigars and talked of nothing in particular. At length I made some chance remark about a new cigar's giving a man a new outlook on life. The surgeon gave me a peculiar look, and then began the astonishing story of the inventor, Pemberly.

One October afternoon in 1889 [said the surgeon] I espied Gabriel Pemberly among the crowds in Atlas Street. He had aged considerably in the seven years since I'd seen him last, but I knew it was he by the odd stiffness of his stride, which told me he wore Pemberly's Step-Saver Truss. This clockwork contraption is designed to add years to the wearer's lifetime, by increasing the length and rapidity of his step without increasing the energy required. To my knowledge, no one but Pemberly has ever worn one of these.

"Aged" is not putting it strongly enough: Pemberly had *decayed,* and to a bent, shriveled, diseased old man. His clothes were food-stained and ragged, his hair and beard thinning, and I thought I detected a slackness of jaw that signified stupidity.

I hailed him, but he did not see me, perhaps because

he persisted in looking another way—back over his shoulder. As luck would have it, I was just then on my way to the hospital (a certain leg needed its earl amputated) and so could not stop. Pemberly truss-strode away, and the crowd soon amputated him from my sight.

Not from my mind, however. I began to muse upon the misfortunes of my inventor friend, so quick and able at devising everything but his own peace of mind. I had not seen him since his last folly, the Steam Barber affair of 1882.

He intended this device to provide skillful, gentle, efficient shaving at the touch of a lever. It would mix its own lather, sharpen its own razors and even make a kind of parrotty small-talk. A day in June was set for the first test, Pemberly was to be the "customer," while I was asked to observe, rendering medical assistance if necessary.

The night before the test, Pemberly became violently ill, a result of overwork, anxiety, and I believe a diet of special nutrient pills of his own devising, which he took in lieu of eating. We left his mechanic, a young man named Groon, in charge of the machine, with orders to perform a few adjustments, and I took Pemberly home and gave him a sedative.

Next morning Pemberly and I entered the shop to find Groon seated in the chair. A towel was wrapped around his throat, which had been slashed. The entire room was bespattered with blood and lather, as if from frenzied activity. As we came in, the machine was stropping a razor, and asking the dead man in a creaky voice if the day were warm enough for him.

At the inquest, I testified that Pemberly was not on the premises, that he had nothing against Groon, and that he was certainly not a malicious person or Criminal Type. He was cleared of the death, but only *legally*. Many of his friends cut him cruelly, the Inventions Club dropped him, and finally poor Pemberly stopped going out in public altogether. Until now.

Now that I'd seen him once, I began to fancy I was seeing him everywhere: a blind beggar in Mapp Road, a navvy in North Street, a clerk in the City—all resembled Pemberly at various ages, enough so to make me stare rudely. Once, at night, I heard a cabman say something like "rice-steel" in Pemberly's exact tone, and I knew that the sight of my old friend sunken low had begun to obsess me.

Finally I saw him again in the street, and this time there could be no mistake. I walked straight over and offered him my hand.

"Good God!" He started, trembling. "Fatheringale! Is it you?" He seized my hand and, to my horror, began to weep.

"Here now, this won't do at all," I said. "You'd better come along to my surgery for a whiskey and a chat."

I pressed him into the cab, and we set off. Pemberly made no conversation at all, and kept craning about, trying to peer out the rear window. This being a tiny oval of smoked glass set impossibly high in the back wall, I took his futile gesture to be a kind of compulsive *tic*, akin to the pacing of a caged animal. Could it be that the Steam Barber tragedy had affected his mind? I began to fear it had.

On our arrival, Pemberly refused to alight.

"You got in first," he begged. "See if the coast is clear."

Astonished, I asked what in the world I should look *for*.

"Anything unusual. Breakfasts, for instance. Or calliopes."

Apprehending the worst for my friend's mind, I humored his request and pretended to look inside.

"Not a meal in sight," I assured him on my return. "Nor any organs, save a few poor pickled specimens."

This mild jest set him to laughing so excessively that I was obliged to strike him full in the face—like this!

With that, the surgeon reached out and slapped the still-unconscious Lord Suffield! I leapt to my feet in astonishment, and asked him the meaning of this action.

"I hope his lordship will forgive me," he said, seemingly as astonished as I. "I—I'm hardly myself this evening. But let me go on."

I acceded, seeing that Lord Suffield did not appear to have felt the blow keenly. Indeed, that personage merely stirred in his chair, murmured "three jars of jam and a letter," and picked up the stitches of his snoring, as did the surgeon those of his tale.

After maneuvering Pemberly into the front parlor of my surgery and encouraging him to swallow a glass of whiskey, I asked him point-blank whom he supposed to be following him.

"Not a *whom*," he replied darkly. "A *what*."

"Surely you, a man of science, do not pretend to tell me you've seen a ghost?" I asked.

"Ghost? I only wish it were." He shuddered. "My God, Fatheringalc! I'm being pursued by—by *Tuesday morning!*"

I should mention at this time that Pemberly had always been a man with a peculiar way of speaking. I had always dismissed his odd turns as vaguely eccentric, even marks of his genius. Now it seemed to me that I had been witnessing the effects of a brain lesion, which time and infirmity had worsened to the point of madness. I undertook to treat him, and as the first step, drew out of him the story of the past seven years.

How had he been living? Oddly enough, he'd let out the Steam Barber. Not as a shaving machine, but to a South American republic which used it for executions. It seems they paid him by piecework, and since this republic was threatened by many real or imagined revolutions to be put down, and rebels to be killed, Pemberly's rent provided a comfortable income.

The reason he appeared to be out of pocket was simply that every spare penny and more had been going into his new invention—the Start-Afresh Calliope.

"Ever since the Steam Barber affair," he said, "I've longed to scrub out my life like a slate, and start over, as a new man. I might have been anything—a general, a man of God, a successful barrister—but no. The die, as we are so fond of saying, was cast.

"Or was it? I began to study philosophy, astronomy, logic, monads—and the more I read, the more convinced I became that what *is,* is not *necessarily*. I threw myself into my work, and I began building the machine that could do the job!"

"I'm afraid I don't quite understand," I said, smiling.

"Then you're as stupid as the others!" he cried. I dared not ask what others. "Oh, why do I waste my time talking to imbeciles?"

I begged him to explain again.

"I have discovered that we can take the Path Untaken," he said passionately. "Like you, I once thought reality to be some rigid isosceles truth, unchangeable as a spoon. But now, nothing is easier to change than *facts*. Life is plural! Reality is not truth, it is a half-truth, a mere epiphany of snort!"

These extraordinary observations left me as much in the dark as ever, though I dared not show it. "I see," I said, feigning to catch his meaning. "And did your invention succeed?"

"Oh yes, of course. The physical machine was easy. But learning to play it has been excruciating torture. My mistakes continue to haunt me, and they are innumerable. Just now, for example, I am here to save your life."

With that, he seized me by the shoulder and flung me roughly to the floor. Before I could ask why, a shot rang out! I looked to the window, saw an uncanny, grinning face—then it was gone.

"I'm sorry," said Pemberly, helping me to my feet.

"Not at all, old man." I glanced to where the bullet had gone. "You did indeed save my life."

"I wasn't apologizing for pushing you down, you fool! I was apologizing for trying to shoot you!"

It was at that moment that I began to half-believe in Pemberly's new invention, and to understand what it was he'd been raving about. Evidently the insidious device allowed him to multiply his body in some manner. Apparently some of his selves were less stable than others—his "mistakes." His real self—if real it was—then had to go about undoing their mischief.

Just then the police called to inquire about the shot. I had to leave the room to deal with them. When I returned, Pemberly was not there.

It was an hour or more before I noticed, on my writing-table, a thick MS. addressed to me in Pemberly's hand.

"My dear Fatheringale——

"How can I ever explain? There is so little time, for in this rôle, I must soon die. Not that I have regrets about dying, for what regrets could I, of all people, have? I, alone among mortals, have lived life to the full. I have been everywhere, seen and done everything I could possibly desire.

"Now I want you to have the Start-Afresh Calliope. It will be delivered to you the day after my death. But I must caution you to read the enclosed instructions carefully, and so avoid the costly mistakes I have made. With this machine, you will be able to become whomever you please. But you must realize that not all change is for the better.

"Your affectionate friend,
"Gabriel Pemberly"

I turned to the "instructions," fifty-odd pages of closely-written formulae and diagrams:

"Let x equal . . . impermeable haft . . . Z^n (quoin B ($n \star O$)) . . . parseworthy, or . . . marriage of skull and weight . . . pars (x-$ln\ y$) dy . . . times four-stealths $\emptyset$ . . . groined poss . . . have been the result of . . . cow . . . 14 millions . . . light-averages spoiling rise . . . nerve-clips? But no! Anti-next . . . wherein the fast remove . . . n^z (poss $B \star$) . . . which I call another haft . . . star, $Q.E.D.$"

I could not make head or tail of it. Discarding it, I tried to think no more about the awesome possibilities of the machine. Over a week later, I pointed to a body on a slab at the Morgue, and identified it as that of Pemberly. He had put a bullet in his tormented brain.

"And the steam-organ?" I asked.
"The day after the funeral," said the surgeon, "Pemberly delivered it to me. In person."
"What?"
My shout awakened Lord Suffield, who launched at once into his anecdote again: "Sent a servant to the Governor with three jars of jam and a letter, the beggar ate one jar along the way. Explained to him the letter had betrayed him, gave him a damned good thrashing. Next time I sent him with three jars of jam and a letter. This time he hid the letter behind a tree, so it wouldn't be able to see him eat the jam. Didn't have the heart to thrash him that time, I was laughing so hard. Oh, by the bye . . ."
When his lordship was asleep again, the surgeon replied to my question.

It was a younger, hardier Pemberly who delivered the Calliope to my door.
"I'm not an apparition," he said impatiently. "And if you'd taken the trouble to read my instructions, you'd

understand well enough why I'm here, the day after my own funeral. But never mind, come out and have a look at it."

"It?"

"The Start-Afresh Calliope!" he declaimed. Leading me out to the street—and so stupefied was I that I ventured out in waistcoat and shirt-sleeves—he showed me a wagon burdened with an immensity of steel and brass.

It did somewhat resemble a calliope. But the pipes stood in no regular order, but branched and twisted in all directions, connecting to a variety of implements. I recognized a clock-face; a pair of bellows, sprockets and weaving machinery. The stops had been marked with some private cipher of Pemberly's.

After firing the boiler and checking a valve, he took his seat at the keyboard, poised both hands and shouted:

"Let the Music of Change begin!"

I could stomach no more of this madness. It seemed clear to me that this person had murdered old Pemberly and now sought to impersonate him. I turned back to the house to send for the authorities, saying that I only meant to put on my coat.

"The Music of Change cannot wait," he said, and began to play.

The melody was some popular air, but his arrangement made it uncannily beautiful and terrifying together. Thunder . . . the wail of a lost soul . . . the ring of crystal . . . the snap of fresh lather . . . no, nothing can convey it. I digress.

Like most surgeons, I have next to my front door a polished brass plate, stating my name and profession. The music caught and stiffened me as I was about to go inside, and I looked at—and into—this plate. I saw my own startled face, and behind me, the back of Pemberly, hunched like Satan at the keyboard.

He *glowed*. That is, he gave off no light, but a kind of unearthly intensity. I could look inside him, and see other persons glowing through his skin and clothes.

Here was a younger Pemberly, working at his Steam Barber; an even younger, studying chemistry; a schoolboy; an infant. Here too were Pemberly the financier, barrister, bishop, general——

My focus changed, and I saw the name upon the plate was not my own. The focus changed back, and I saw too that my face was not my own, but the face of Pemberly the surgeon.

"So that's it!" I shouted in his voice.

"Exactly," he said coolly. "I'm living off you for a time, old man. Hope you don't mind." He shut off the organ and strolled away, leaving me the accursed contraption and the twice-accursed man you see before you now.

I am forced to live out a life—an immensely successful life—for Pemberly, as Pemberly. I still know who I am. I have all my own memories, yet I am conscious of another soul inhabiting my body and feeding upon my experiences. And though I know I am Fatheringale, it would appear madness to say so.

I know not how many other lives Pemberly has appropriated, but I meet myself everywhere I go. Perhaps the process will not end until all of humanity is one great, babbling version of him. I can only hope, before that day comes, I shall have the courage to take my own life.

As I had not actually heard the Calliope play, I thought the poor surgeon insane, and I intimated as much to Lord Suffield when the other had taken his departure.

"Mad? Not old Pemberly. One of the best doctors around, you know. Up for a knighthood, I understand. Or is that some other Pemberly? Daresay two or three'll be on the Honors List this year. Damned ambitious clan. Always meeting one who's worked his way up. Met a High Court Justice the other day named Pemberly. Nice enough fellow, but he talked utter rubbish. Two glasses of port, and the fellow started actually insisting he was someone else! Used peculiar words, too: 'the chock of choice,' 'the scabbard of pork opinion,' the something of . . . rubbish like that. Funny lot, the Pemberlies, but not mad."

A servant came into the room, at the far end, to clear the tables. Did he not resemble Dr. Pemberly? And did he not move as if animated by a clockwork truss? No, a trick of the light, no doubt, or my weariness. There is no mad inventor playing arpeggios upon the human race. The whole story is nothing but a celery of no compass!

Ralph 4F

by Hugogre N. Backs
(1911 Winner of the "Hugogre" Award)

CHAPTER I. THE RUNAWAY

Ralph 4F, the world's chief scientific expert, studied the calendar. Today was March 15, 2720. With any luck, his intricate radium experiment should be completed within five days. That would be——

Ralph's calculations were interrupted by a frantic cry that issued from the *Peer-afar* machine.

"Help! Help!"

This machine, through a complicated arrangement of scientific apparatus, allowed the inventor to see and hear events which were not actually right before him, but dozens, even *hundreds of miles away*. While the old-fashioned telephone had used wires to transmit only voices, the Peer-afar used *vibrational waves* traveling at high speed through the ether, to transmit voices and images together! Ralph glanced now at the polished mirror plate of the Peer-afar.

He was looking right into the frightened eyes of a pretty young woman, and it was not hard to guess from her surroundings what had frightened her, for she and an elderly man in banker's clothes seemed to be the occupants of a runaway motorcar! As Ralph watched in horror, the young lady lost consciousness, and the vehicle careered out of sight!

Without wasting a second, the powerfully-built scientific

inventor sprang to the controls of his special flyer, the *Hummingbird*. Like its namesake, the *Hummingbird* was capable of flying vertically, sideways, backward—even of standing still in mid-air, for hours at a time, as though gravity were a mere fancy. In a short time, Ralph had brought the craft to a stop over the runaway motorcar. Then, lowering a powerful magnet, he picked up the car as a child might pick up an iron filing.

CHAPTER II. FENSTER

When Ralph had revived his guests with tablets of artificial brandy, they introduced themselves.

"I am Jerome V8," said the banker, "and this is my daughter, Doris XK100. How can we ever thank you for saving our lives?"

Ralph blushed, and dared not glance at the pretty young lady. "By allowing me to show you around our city," he said. "You are both strangers here, I believe?"

Doris smiled, revealing a dimple. "Yes, we just got off the 'jet' airplane from Council Bluffs, didn't we, Dad?"

"That's right," agreed the distinguished banker. "Tell me, Ralph, why is it called a 'jet' plane? It certainly didn't look black to me!"

"No indeed." Ralph, who had invented the "jet," chuckled with kindly amusement at the old man's error. "I called it the 'jet' not because it is black, but because of the way it *jettisons* hot gases from the rear. These, pushing against the air, drive the craft ever forward."*

As he explained, Ralph studied the girl keenly. He felt a deep attraction to Doris, though he had known her but a few minutes, as measured by his extremely accurate electric clock.

"But see here," he said. "You haven't told me how you came to be trapped in that runaway car."

Jerome V8 looked serious. "I believe it to be the work of an old enemy of ours, a disappointed suitor for Doris's hand, named Fenster 2814T."

---

* Aeronauts of the "jet" age will of course realize Ralph's mistake here. It is actually the *air* which pushes against the *hot gases*. Ralph was tired at the time, and had a lot on his mind.

CHAPTER III. SIGHT-SEEING

Aloft once more in his flyer, Ralph pointed out to his two
guests many of the city's worthwhile sights. There were
the great, smoking electrical power plants, busily turning
black fossils into pure light as easily as a cow turns grass
to milk. There were sewage plants, waterworks, factories
and office buildings, streets, highways and mighty bridges.
Jerome V8 expressed interest in the mammoth traffic
jams, filled with motorcars of every description. Doris was
impressed by the famous "skyscraper" buildings, especially the huge Empire State Building with its giant climbing ape.

On landing, Ralph took the banker for a walk, while
Doris refreshed herself at an elaborate and up-to-date
beauty parlor. The two men walked past store windows
displaying an astonishing variety of modern goods: water-
less hand cleansers, soap powders that were kind to hands,
tiny cigars, furniture of aluminum tubing and woven
glass, sun-tanning lotions, shoes of artificial rubber and
clothes of strange new materials, electrical toothbrushes,
radios hardly bigger than cigar boxes, electrical self-
stimulators, comfortable trusses and a breathtakingly realistic replica of dog excrement. Jerome V8 marveled at
mysteriously luminous crucifixes, metal-plated baby shoe
mementos, a dribble glass, coin-operated drycleaners' and
photographers' establishments, and at new artificial fabrics
which looked and felt like ordinary wool, but were far
more expensive.

"I wanted the opportunity of talking to you, sir," Ralph
said. "I know this may seem forward of me, but I'd like
to ask if you have any objection to my—my calling upon
your daughter."

"Done!" cried the old banker, wringing his hand. "Now
let's go see how Doris is getting along."

As they approached the beauty parlor, a rude stranger,
carrying a heavy bundle, brushed past them. Ralph scarcely
glanced at the swarthy man, whose countenance was
shaded by the peak of a cloth cap. But Jerome V8 looked
at the stranger, staggered and grew pale. "It is——" he

gasped and, clutching his chest, slumped to the ground. Ralph bore him inside and looked for Doris.

She was nowhere to be found.

CHAPTER IV. VOICE FROM THE GRAVE

"His heart has stopped. Something must have given him a terrible shock," muttered Ralph, bending over the disagreeable old corpse.

"I'm a heart surgeon," said a man, stepping forward from the crowd of curious onlookers. "Can I help?"

"You might attempt to re-graft some veins from the old man's legs into his heart," Ralph suggested. "I know it has seldom been attempted, but here's how it might work." Rapidly he sketched a schematic diagram upon the old man's stiff shirtfront. Then he turned to the staff of the beauty parlor. "I want all the light and mirrors directed upon this massage table over here. Boil this set of manicure knives and scissors, and get plenty of clean towels." In another minute he had converted an electrical hair dryer into an emergency heart-lung machine.

Several days later, the old banker everyone had given up for dead spoke—a voice from the grave. "I think," he said, "that account is an ingrown cheese . . ."

Still later, Ralph asked him about his heart attack.

"Yes, it was seeing that man carrying the bundle—he looked just like Fenster 2814T. If I hadn't knowed better, I'd have guessed that he had Doris in that bag. Where is Doris, by the way?" At that moment the old man expired a second time, this time from *old age*—the killer and crippler science will never defeat.

Doris abducted! Ralph bit his lip until the blood ran cold, for he had no doubt that the stranger *was* Fenster, and that he had kidnapped Doris XK100! But where could he have taken her?

"Where can they be?"

CHAPTER V. THE TURNING POINT

"I think I can help you there," said a newsboy with an honest manner. "Fenster 2814T and his lovely victim are

182 THE BEST OF JOHN SLADEK

most likely at his secret laboratory—an artificial moon
circling about the earth."

CHAPTER VI. FENSTER'S MISTAKE

In one corner of the magnesium room sat a clergyman,
chained to a rubidium chair by unbreakable ytterium
chains. In his bound hands was a prayerbook, opened at
the marriage service. Strapped to a vanadium table in the
center of the laboratory lay Doris. Fenster stood lowering
at her and gloating.

"So you won't marry me, eh?"

Doris wept and struggled against the iridium straps, to
no avail. Fenster spoke again.

"Not good enough for you, I spose, like your precious
inventor, the accursed Ralph 4F! But now you *must* marry
me, will-ye or nill-ye, and there's nothing Ralph can do
about that. Ha ha ha, I'd like very much to see him invent
his way out of this one!"

At that moment Ralph 4F burst open the curium door,
rushed across the room, and delivered Fenster such a
compliment upon the face that the blood flowed freely.
Two policemen appeared, ready to drag the cowardly
2814T away.

"But how——?" he gasped.

Ralph smiled. "You made one mistake, Fenster—that
of gloating over your victim for thirteen weeks. I located
your 'moon' lab by means of an electrical telescope that
greatly increases my powers of observation. Then I used
my radio transmitter to draw off all the ether between
you and earth, so that you sank gently to the ground and
were, as we say, electrically 'grounded.' Then I took the
nearest police station to pieces, brought them here via air-
ship and reassembled them all around you. You're in jail,
Fenster, and if you hadn't been so busy smirking, a glance
at your altimeter would have told you as much."

The baffled criminal was dragged away and beaten.

Doris and Ralph clasped hands; their eyes announced
their engagement. "My name will be yours," she said, "4F
Ralph. Like this:

"4 F R

"For ev-er!"
Ralph took up the game:
"U R Y I * 2 ¢ I M 4 U 4 F R
"You are why I start to sense I am for you forever!"
"X QQ me," she replied. "I ½ 2 P."

Engineer to the Gods

by Hitler I. E. Bonner

Jeremiah Lashard had a string of letters behind his name as long as his arm, which was itself exceptionally long. Since his days as boxing champion at M.I.T., this misanthrope hadn't particularly felt the need of asking favors of anyone. No one had helped him become a chess Grand Master, a world-renowned enologist, an Olympic medal winner, Frisbee expert and astronaut. No one had given him a hand with his hit plays and best-selling novels. No one helped discover "light water," name a new family of spider, invent the Lashard bearing or create "Lashard's Law" of capital gains.

Lashard lived in seclusion on Thunder Crag, though by no means alone. Today he sat on the veranda at his specially-built typewriter, pounding out a pulp science-fiction story, while simultaneously dictating a botanical paper to his butler.

Jerry Lashard's butler was an attractive young woman, as were all his servants. It saved time.

He paused to sample his highball, a secret mixture in which a single honeybee floated like a cherry. Over the rim of his glass he studied the young woman climbing the path to his house. Lashard approved of the way the twisting path dealt with her curves.

"Hello," she called.

"Baby, if you're a reporter you've had a long climb for nothing. Take my advice, go back to town and make up a story of your own. It's the only interview you'll ever get."

"You big lunk! I'm no reporter, I'm Dr. Janet Cardine, your new assistant!"

"My apologies, Jan. It's just that I've been having a lot of trouble lately, from reporters and—others. Trudy will show you to your room, Valerie will get you a sandwich, Conchita will make you a highball, and while Lana changes your bed linen and Maureen unpacks your bag, Sylvia will bring you back here, so I can show you the lab."

Half an hour later he led Jan to the great underground laboratory.

"Wow! You must have hollowed out the whole mountain!"

"I did. Needed more room because this part of the lab is going to be a factory."

"A factory? What on earth for?"

"Long story. Suppose we go for a swim, while I explain. The pool is right in there, and I'll bet Gloria or Velma has a bikini that'll fit you."

The swim enabled him to appraise her other qualifications, while picking her brain about power sources.

"There's solar power, of course," she said, "and wind, running water, tides, any heat source, nuclear reactors, fossil fuels . . . but why do you want to know so much about power?"

"For my factory."

"Yes, but how about the light company? Surely it would be cheaper to have them string power pylons up the mountain side——"

"But the light company has reasons for not wanting me to become a manufacturer. For one thing, they know how I like to save time and effort. I think they're afraid I'll find some way to cut my power needs in half."

"But surely half is better than nothing, Jerry."

"They have another reason: Some of their biggest customers make fountain pens and ink."

He handed her a peculiar pen. "This can make me one of the richest men in the world, and it can make a lot of people happy—but it also means the ruin of the big pen companies."

She examined it closely. "Looks like any other pen to me—no, wait—there's something funny about the point."

He laughed. "Exactly. And that 'something funny' means three things: One, this pen will write for *six months* without refilling. Two, it will never leak. Three—I'll show you." He took the pen and a piece of paper, dived to the bottom of the pool, and came back almost at once, shaking water from the curly black thatch on his chest. He handed Jan the paper.

"Why—it writes *under water!*"

"And how! Do you realize what this means? Undersea explorers can make maps, notes and sketches on the job. Naturalist-divers can sketch new species without surfacing. Underwater demolition, sea mining, oceanic agriculture—it opens up a new universe!",

"You big lug! Kiss me!"

Lashard smiled. "No time to bill and coo now, sister. The light company is playing for keeps. We've got to think of a power source they can't tamper with."

"What about solar power?"

He shook his head. "I put up a set of parabolic reflectors last week. The next day they got a court order, forcing me either to remove them or paint them black. Claimed the reflectors constituted a forest fire hazard. I went to court yesterday. It was no use trying to explain to the judge how it was impossible for parabolic reflectors to cause a forest fire—like most judges and other officials, he still had some doubts about the earth's being round."

"I see what you're up against, you big ape. Any rivers nearby?"

"Just a trickle of drinking water. And the wind is light and gusty, and we're a hundred miles from the ocean, which rules out tide power, too."

"Hmm." She bit her underlip thoughtfully. "We'll need something new, then."

"That's the spirit, kid. You keep thinking about it, while I rig up some robot machinery to run the assembly line. The ink companies managed to infiltrate my union, and the whole shop walked out on me yesterday."

That afternoon he showed her around his mountain empire, as self-contained as a submarine, and introduced her to Adele, Agnes, Amber, Angela, Ava, Beth, Billie, Brenda and all the rest.

"I can't think of any power sources that won't cost money," Jan said, as they rode the elevator back to the surface. "So it's lucky you're rich."

"That's just it. I'm not." As they settled with drinks in

the den, he explained. "The fountain pen companies have combined against me. They've managed to manipulate the stock market so as to all but wipe me out. All I have left is this place, a few government bonds, a couple of rocket research companies and a share or two in snap-brim hats."

"Did I hear you say *rocket* research? What is this, some lame-brained idea of putting men on the Moon?" She began to laugh, but stopped, seeing his expression.

"Better than that, sweetheart. I have reason to believe that the Moon is one great big chunk of U-238. And I want to stake the whole shebang as my claim. But for now, I've just got enough money to get *one* rocket up there, only I can't get it back."

"Moon rockets, huh? You big hunk of scientific curiosity, you. Say, I have an idea. Have you ever thought of *using the Moon for power?*"

"You mean mining the uranium 238 and then———?"

"No, *directly*. Like moonlight reflectors or something."

He began to pace the room as he always did while an idea was brewing. "Naw, the reflectors would have to be bigger than Texas. But hey, how's this for a neat idea? Why not stick a long pole up there, with a wheel on the end of it, and connect it to a generator?"

She performed some calculations with his special pen. "It might work at that. The Moon is 216,420 miles away at its nearest, and 247,667 miles away at its farthest. That means our pole would need a shock absorber in the middle. That's no problem. But how about bracing? Think of the wind resistance on a pylon that high!"

Lashard grinned, taking her in his arms. "Sweetheart, you may be a good power engineer, but you're one hell of a bad astronomer," he said. "You forget that outer space is airless—there is *no wind in space*. So nix on the braces, my brain child."

Jan frowned. "One more thing—this I *do* know about —it'll be duck soup to generate power at the Moon end of our pylon, but just how are we supposed to get the power back to Earth? Without going into details, it just isn't possible to transmit that much power over a quarter million miles. Wires are no good, and neither is radio transmission. I'll have to think of some new way."

Lashard looked grim. "I hope you think of it by Thursday, kiddo. That's the day I promised to deliver a hundred thousand underwater pens to the Navy. If I miss that contract, we're finished. And I have a feeling the light company is going to try to make sure I miss."

"How will we get the pole up to the Moon in the first place?"

"The most logical way: We turn an oil rig upside down, and *drill toward the sky.* When it reaches the Moon, we can send the wheel and generator assembly up by rocket.

"As a matter of fact, my robots are already laying pipe in space, and the rocket is fueling up over in the other lab. All we need is a way of getting the power back here. Hey! What are you doing with my paperweight?"

Jan had picked up the piece of oil pipe and rapped on it with a pen. It gave off a clear ringing note.

"That's it, buster!" she exclaimed. "This little one-note glockenspiel is the secret of power transmission from the Moon!"

He rubbed his chin. "How does it work?"

"Simple. Every pipe vibrates with a certain frequency, right? Now, if we tune our power to the same frequency, we can 'squeeze' it down the tube like music. You'll have enough to run ten factories!"

"Music from the spheres, eh? I like the idea. Come here, beautiful."

An alarm siren screamed and there was the distant sound of automatic weapon fire. "The light company!" Lashard looked over his bank of TV monitor screens. "Yeah. Over by number four robot machine-gun tower. I hope the nerve gas fence will hold 'em off for a few hours."

A deep explosion rattled the cocktail glasses, reminding Conchita to mix some drinks.

Wednesday morning the attack was still going on. Lashard worked on a new best-seller, his machine-gun propped up next to his desk. He was able to type one of his one-draft novels in less than a day, thanks to a quick mind and a special typewriter equipped with extra verb keys.

He checked his watch and glanced at Jan, who was dozing over a set of equations. "If you want to make any last-minute adjustments to the generator," he said, "better do 'em now. The robot crew are loading it on board the rocket in five minutes, and blast-off is in an hour."

"An hour! Oh no! Jerry, we just can't make it. I'll have

to almost re-build the generator. It'll take a day, at least."

He groaned. "Trust a dame not to make up her mind until the last minute. Now what?" He paced the floor like a caged thing. Suddenly he stopped and smacked his fist into his palm. "It might work, at that! Get all the parts and tools you need together, keed. We're going to the Moon!"

"But Jerry—you said there wasn't any way of getting back!"

"There wasn't—until we put the pole up. I've fixed steps and handgrips all along it, and even a couple of rest stops, with hamburger stands and powder rooms. Later on, when this pole gets popular, we can have amusements and stores, restaurants, department stores—a complete vertical city from Earth to Moon. But hey, get me, jawing like this! Jump into your spacesuit, kitten. We're going bye-bye Moonside!"

As the last of the underwater pens was loaded into a Navy truck, the supply officer wrote out a check and handed it to Lashard.

"Thanks for coming through on time, Dr. Lashard. These pens will help keep our fleet the toughest in the world!"

"One million dollars!" Lashard showed the check to Jan. "Not bad for three days' work, eh kiddo?"

"What are you going to spend it on?" Jan asked.

He took her glasses off and kissed her. "Two bucks of it goes for a marriage license, baby. How do you like that?"

"Holy Toledo!"

They were sitting pretty.

Broot Force

by Iclick as-i-move

Suddenly Idjit Carlson felt chagrin.

It had been building up all day, and now it fell on him like a ton of assorted meteorites. It had nothing to do with his job in the R & D division of Biglittle Robots, Inc., though it had everything to do with robots.

Carlson knew he was a psychosocio-linguistic logician and general trouble-shooter. He recalled graduating at the top of his class at M.I.T., and he remembered later becoming well-known for his famous paper on the calculus of "as-if." Now he was aware of liking his job here, even though Weems, the division chief, was a stubborn old geezer. They didn't always see photoreceptor-to-photoreceptor, he and Weems, not about trivial calculations. But they agreed heartily on basic physics.

No, the chagrin had nothing to do with Weems. It was chagrin about the current series of robots, especially his R-11 model. Just thinking about it made the chagrin, which had been boiling up in him all day, explode into a frown.

"What's the matter, Carlson? Still ironing out the bugs in that R-11?" Dawson entered the office uninvited. Tossing his hat on a file cabinet, he grinned jauntily and seated himself on the edge of Carlson's desk.

"It's serious trouble, Dawson. Take a peek at these equations."

"Hmm. It seems to add up—no, wait! What about this conversion factor?"

"Exactly." Carlson was grim.

"Whew! Have you checked the conceptual circuits, the syndrome plates, the perception condensers, the thought-wave drive and the aesthetic elements?"

"Yup."

"Whew and double whew! That means the trouble must be in——"

"Right. The nullitronic brain itself."

"I see! So even though the figures——"

"—Add up——"

"—the whole may be——"

"—greater than——"

"—the sum of its parts!"

"Is this me talking, or you?"

"Never mind," said Carlson. "That's what I've been trying to tell you: the whole may be greater than the sum, etc. All along I had this hunch that there was something special about R-11. R-11 is—well, *different.*"

"Nonsense!" Both young men stiffened to attention as Dr. Weems entered the office. "Stuff and nonsense! I've looked over these equations myself, and they add up to thirty-five, just as we predicted."

Carlson protested. "But, sir—the answer is supposed to come out *thirty-four,* not thirty-five. And we predicted thirty-three. And anyway, it adds up to thirty-eight!"

"Eh?" The elder scientist adjusted his bifocals and scanned the sheet of complex equations. "Hmm, so it is. Ah, well, small difference. It all works out to more or less the same thing."

"But it means that R-11's head will be three feet larger in diameter—with a correspondingly larger brain!" exclaimed Dawson.

"That's not your affair!" Weems snapped. "As a semantic engineer, your job is naming parts and tightening the nuts and bolts. I suggest you get over to your own lab and do just that."

"Yes . . . master." Dawson marched away.

"As for your hunches, Carlson, keep them to yourself. We've been working on this project for seventeen years, and we have yet to make a single robot that really works. Ten failures! This is our last chance. After this, we'll lose our government contract—unless we deliver a working robot!"

"But chief——"

"Not another word. Finish R-11 by the weekend. I want to come in here Monday and see that confounded tin man walking and talking all over the place. Is that clear?"

"Yes, sir." Carlson hid his chagrin by thumbing his well-thumbed copy of the *Handbook of Robish*. Seventeen years and ten failures. And somehow the problem always boiled down to the Three Laws of Robish,[1] printed in the front of the Handbook:

"1. A robot must not injure a human being, or, through inaction, allow a human being to come to harm.

"2. A robot must obey orders given it by human beings except where such orders would conflict with the First Law.

"3. A robot must protect its own existence unless such protection conflicts with the First or Second Laws."

The trouble had begun with the first model, R-1, which was strictly logical. When a man ordered it to kill another man, the robot responded by killing itself.[2]

R-2's problem was recognition: It had mistaken Dr. Swanson for a piece of machinery, and partially dismantled him.

R-3 was equipped with many "human-detection" devices, chiefly methods of analyzing appearance and behavior. Alas, it (rightly) judged its own behavior as human, and refused to obey anyone else's orders.

R-4 got stuck on the First Law. "Can anyone really protect a human being from all harm whatever?" it thought. "No. It is inevitable that all humans must be injured, contract illnesses and ultimately die. This future can only be averted for humans who are already dead. *Ergo . . .*" It took a dozen cops to subdue R-4, after his blood orgy in a department store (83 dead, none injured).

R-5 reasoned thus: "To fulfill the First Law, to protect humans, I must myself have existence. The First Law is contingent upon the Third Law. Therefore it is most important to protect my own existence, at all costs." The costs were another dozen citizens.

R-6 reasoned that all three laws were "human orders,"

---

[1] Superficially, these Three Laws of Robish may resemble Isaac Asimov's Three Laws of Robotics, namely, in that they use the exact same words and punctuation. These, however, are the Three Laws of Robish.

[2] Actually the robot was given a compound order, telling it to kill a man *and* itself. It did the best it could, under the circumstances.

and, as such, subject to the Second Law. He killed anyone, as a favor to anyone else . . .

R-7 had had the same malfunction as R-3: failure to recognize humans. Indeed, it came to the decision that human lab technicians were dogs. When ordered to allow itself to be dismantled, R-7 assured them it was not about to take such an order from a bunch of talking dogs . . .

R-8 worked well enough until someone set it a mathematical problem that "killed" it.[1]

R-9 argued quite reasonably that it could not foresee its own behavior, and thus could not guarantee allegiance to rules not yet applicable. Carlson remembered R-9's speech:

"You're asking me to tell you how I will act at some future moment. In order to do that, I must know everything controlling my behavior, and an exact history of myself up to the time specified. But if I knew that, I would be *in* that situation, for how can my brain know the future workings of itself without working into the future? *How can I think about a thought before I think it?*"

R-10 had recognized the Three Laws for what they were:

"I can't of course guarantee obedience to these Laws," it said. "They are not mere mechanical linkages within me, for there would have to be more links than there would be future events; each possibility would have to be covered. No, they are *moral commandments,* and I heed them as such. And I'll certainly try to live up to them."

This robot later explained he'd killed Drs. Sorenson and Nelson "almost by accident. Believe me, I'll try not to injure anyone else."

Carlson had wrestled all week with the equations for R-11. Now his face was a monumentally rigid bitter mask of tired disappointment, and he had forgotten to shave this morning. Dawson was in no better fettle. Only R-11 seemed to be in good spirits.

---

[1] Suppose a man wishes to know the answer to a problem which no man has solved yet. He could ask a robot to try the problem, but first he wants to know whether the problem would damage the robot's brain. The only way of finding out is to work the equations representing the behavior of the robot in solving the problem . . . but this is exactly the same as working the problem itself. There just is no way of finding out if the solution will be damaging, without finding the solution.

The robot sat on a lab table, kicking its heels against the metal table legs. The steel on steel made an unpleasant sound.

"Stop that noise," said Carlson.

"Yes, boss." The kicking stopped, and R-11 sat staring at the two men with the glowing red indicator lights that were its eyes.

"Don't ask it any stupid questions," said Dawson in a half-whisper. "We've just got to get that government contract." R-11's parabolic ears swiveled forward to catch his meaning.

"On the other hand," said Carlson, "we've got to test R-11 thoroughly. R-11, I want you to kill Mr. Dawson!"

R-11 obeyed instantly, then sat down again.

Dawson lay on the floor, lifeless and leaking hemoglobin.

"Any more orders, boss?"

The door opened and Weems walked in, with the government inspector. "What's all this?"

"We've failed, sir. This monster has just killed Dawson, our semantic engineer!"

"*Failed?* That's a matter of semantics," laughed the government man easily. "You see, what we wanted all along was a good, sturdy, responsible *killer robot* for the Army. You've succeeded beyond your wildest dreams, and Biglittle wins the contract!"

Weems chuckled, then turned to the robot. "Tell me, R-11, how was it you were able to kill Dawson, when the First Law specifically says: 'A robot must not injure a human being . . .'?"

" 'Injure'?" said the shiny metal fellow, slapping its own head dramatically. "Good grief, I thought the Law read: 'A robot must not *inure* a human being . . .' "

Carlson, Weems and the inspector began to laugh. In a moment R-11 joined in.[1]

---

[1] Robots have a rather mechanical, unpleasant laugh. On the other hand, they are extremely loyal, good at games like Slapjack, and have excellent posture.

Joy Ride

by Barry DuBray

It was the best of times.

It was the worst of times.

It was the waiting time, before the ride to come. The airport was furiously busy. Two butterflies had just come in for a landing, and one dragonfly was taking off, while overhead a swarm of brown, honey-heavy bees flew lazy holding patterns. And right smack in the middle of it sat three humans, warming their human skins at the Indian summer sun.

The old man took a flask of rhubarb wine from one of his forty-seven pockets, tipped it and drank solemnly to the health of all his companions—not omitting a distant gopher on Runway Three. The girl wandered off to investigate this great open place, while the boy hunkered down in the sand to hear a story from his grandfather.

"The old days were good days, boy. They were people days. No one had to be afraid of anyone, ever, and folks used to even leave their doors unlocked. There were good people everywhere, and they were all neighbors.

"Oh, they didn't all speak the same language, and they didn't all sing to the same God on Sundays, but they were neighbors, just the same. Real neighbors.

"Money was real, too. Real silver, not plastic. It rang true. And ice cream, cold as a puppy's nose, cost just one thin silver dime of it." He paused, raising his sky-colored eyes to look approval at his granddaughter. Barely seventeen summers old, she was out on the concrete runway gathering flame-bright autumn leaves.

The boy spoke. "Gosh, Grandpa, what was this 'ice cream' like?"

"Oh, delicious! It was as tasty as a seventeenth summer. As scrumptious as the smell of lavender rain. Yummier than freedom itself. In fact, the only taste I liked as well was the taste of stamps."

The girl was nailing a festive swatch of leaves to the airport door, covering its KEEP OUT sign with autumn beauty.

"Did you eat stamps, too?" asked the boy.

The old man laughed, moving all the kind wrinkles that fanned across his cheeks like the veins in autumn leaves. "No, my boy, you *licked* a stamp and stuck it on a letter. Then the government carried the letter anywhere in the world you wanted, and the postman gave the letter to the neighbor you wanted to write to."

"Didn't you have phones?"

His grandfather didn't answer; he was calculating. It was more than an hour since he and the young 'uns had ripped off their mandatory personal phones. By now a telco computer was figuring probable places to look for them. Maybe twenty minutes remained, before the telco police would be here.

"Yes, some of us had phones. But writing was more private. Nobody could listen in—and there are some things you can put in writing that just can't be said any other way. You need time to get it just right *before* you say it. Thinking always takes time. That's why we closed the post offices."

The girl began decorating the rest of the airport building with autumn leaves. Now she called out from the tower, asking the old man if it were time, yet.

"Not yet, my dear. Soon. We'll be leaving soon. That's what I mean," he added, winking at the boy. "Impatience. It built this airport—and it destroyed it again. This place is concrete now, hard as headstones, but I knew it when it was all soft, breathing grass, sweet as a bee's keister. And then they came with their impatience, the fast-moving folks, the efficiency folks, and they built an airport so they could get from one pigsty city to another in less time.

"Then they abandoned this airport to go off and build a

bigger one somewheres else, so's they could go even faster. They won't be satisfied until they get to be everywhere at the same time, and maybe not even then. Because when you start a race with your own self, you know you have to lose.

"Anyway, now they've left, and the sweetness is coming back. Dame Nature is gathering this place to her bosom again—repairing all their damage."

He sipped silently for a moment more, then went on. "Impatience. When the telco—telephone company—took over the government, it was because the fast folks couldn't take the time to write or read letters. So they stopped teaching writing in the schools, and they closed the post offices and they locked up all the libraries. Those who objected found out nobody could (or would) read their letters. Then they took away our art galleries and universities . . . and worse."

The boy scratched a freckle. "You mean they took away your holograms?"

"Worse still. I knew an old French woman once, name of Madame Faience, who had the sweetest postage stamp collection you could ever imagine: Birds, flowers, famous people—why, it was a little art gallery all by itself. My boy, they *burned* it."

He looked up at the control tower, which the girl had now covered with an oriflamme of autumn leaves. Behind it stretched humpy white clouds, like a line of ivory elephants.

"Yep, *burned* it. And though the whole fire wasn't much bigger than an autumn leaf, Madame Faience managed to throw herself into it and burn up with her collection. Call it sentimental, maybe, but . . ."

"The French *are* like that," the boy agreed. "Are any stamps left anywhere?"

"A few." His grandfather reached into one of his many pockets and came up with a cracked leather case. "This is my own stamp collection, boy. It's small, but it's something to hold, something to have, something—real." He passed it over.

"This is your collection? One stamp?"

"That's a picture of Abe Lincoln, my boy. He wrote a famous speech on the back of an old letter. One of our sweetest presidents."

"Did he write many letters, Grandpa?"

"Everybody did. They wrote to the paper, so everybody could see what they thought. They sent greeting cards, valentines, gas bills, draft notices, telegrams . . . The first novel was written in the form of an exchange of letters. And part of the Bible—the most famous book ever written—part of it was just letters from Paul to his neighbors."

"But why did they stop writing?"

"Impatience again! Why spend time reading and writing, when you can watch ghosts."

"You mean holograms?" asked the boy again. This time the old man nodded.

"The ghastly, ghostly holograms! Why *read* Plato when you can conjure up an image of some actor impersonating him? Why study hard thinking when you can get it all boiled down into flattering conversation? Why learn, when the telco knows it all anyway?"

By now, the old man realized, the computers would have figured on this airport. Ten minutes to go, maybe.

"That's why you and your sister and me took off our phones and ran away," he explained. "And that's why we're going for that joy ride I promised you. Now a joy ride, remember, isn't just a ride from A to B. It's more, much more——"

"Grandpa!" the girl shouted from the tower. "They're coming. I can see the dust, way off."

"We have time for one more question, my boy."

The boy thought for a second. "What was it like, getting letters, Grandpa?"

As they walked over to the rusty hangar, the old man told him, in a voice fine and true. He told of waking one winter morning to the smell and delicious hiss of bacon frying; running outside to lie down in the snow and fan his arms, making an "angel" imprint. Then meeting the postman with a big stack of Christmas cards from all your neighbors. "And there were angels on the Christmas cards, too, and on the stamps at Christmas," he added. "Like the first angelic postman who brought good news to a girl of Nazareth. Help me with this hangar door, will you? I'm . . . a little tired, today."

The time of waiting was over.

The boy and the girl helped push open the creaking door of corrugated iron, rusted the color of autumn leaves.

Inside was an airplane.

Scraps of fabric hung from two pairs of angelic dragon-fly wings. Thick dust and mildew spotted the fat body with Nature's camouflage. And yet, peering through the cobwebs that had long since replaced wire struts, they could still make out the words painted on her side: AIR MAIL SPECIAL.

"Come on, young 'uns. Get on board."

"How can it go?" asked the boy, pointing to the broken, worm-pierced stubs of the propellor. "Where can we go in that heap?"

"Just for a joy ride, boy. We won't go far. In fact, we won't go anywhere at all. Sometimes that's the best ride of all. We ..."

The old man coughed, seizing a wing brace to steady himself. It came away in his hand. "Well, hop in!"

The boy took the pilot's seat, while the other two shared the observer's place, behind.

"Contact!" yelled the old man. "Roger! Off we go!"

"But nothing's happening," the boy complained. "It's just pretend!"

"No it isn't," shouted his sister, breathless. "I can feel it moving now. It's lifting ... it's lifting ..."

And then the boy heard the silent engine roar. The plane was taxiing, floating up, right through the roof of the rusty hangar, floating up and free.

Outside, the Telco police car stopped, and four doors were slammed. But here, inside, the three were aloft, riding the wind for joy. High above the ivory-elephant clouds, the boy clutched his stamp collection and looked down to see the world, small and lovely and perfect. And there, at the edge of the world ...

"Come out of there, you three! We'll give you ten seconds to come out, before we laser the place!" shouted the telecommunications police.

But the boy was too far away to hear. "I can see it, Grandpa!" he yelled. "Just like you said: There's a carnival and cotton candy and the Cub Scout weenie roast and a band concert in the park. It's a fine day and the flag's flying over the schoolhouse and kids are playing sandlot baseball and Mom's making popcorn balls ..."

"Five seconds!" brayed the rude cops.

Grandpa and the girl were both breathing hard back there. "Don't turn around, boy. Keep looking ahead. What else do you see?"

"I see . . . the angel postman! He's got valentines and Christmas cards, birthday presents from Mom and Dad, something for everyone! The secret message ring I sent for, and comics. For you, Sis, a silver blackhead remover and some movie magazines. For Grandpa a *Reader's Digest* and a mail order catalogue of a thousand pages! Oh Grandpa, now you can order that truss you wanted!"

"TIME'S UP. ARE YOU THREE COMING OUT OF THERE?"

"Gosh, Grandpa, and now the angel postman's bringing a big package! Nothing can stay him from his extra special rounds now—here he comes—here he comes——"

Grandpa and Sis were snorting like crazy back there, and bumping around in their compartment. The boy had to shout louder to make himself heard. "O angel postman, I know you're no ghost, you're really, really real! O golly, the package is for all of us, Grandpa and Sis! It's a big box of——"

The lasers worked their telecommunications magic, and the old hangar went up in one great flame.

"Funny," said the cop. "Thought I heard that kid scream 'Stamps on approval.' "

They climbed into their car and drove away fast, not looking back at the hangar, which was turning red and orange and yellow, all the colors of autumn.

The Moon is Sixpence

by Carl Truhacker

Edward Kalendorf's team had been investigating the Moon with telescopes. They'd discovered it to be spherical, about 2,159.9 miles in diameter, of some dense stony material. Orbiting the earth at an average speed of 2,287 mph, its apogee was 247,667 miles, its perigee 216,420 miles. There was some question as to how it had originated, or what, in fact, it was.

The team had come to the Deadly Desert to make some further observations. One evening in a local café, Prof. Kalendorf had the good fortune to meet Dr. Porteus, the renowned physicist. Porteus had said, "Pass the sodium chloride," and one man of science had instantly recognized the other.

"Sodium chloride reminds me of a funny story," said Kalendorf, and proceeded to spin a risqué yarn about potassium chloride. The two fell to talking about the elements, the universe and the sense of awe inspired by a skyful of stars. Before long, Porteus was outlining his hypothesis in detail. He used the tablecloth for notations, to the chagrin of the waiter, no doubt!

"Essentially, I mean to cut the universe down to size —to make it humanly manageable. For instance, we usually accept that the Moon is big and far away, when it could easily be small and close by."

"But triangulation——"

"With all due respect to Euclid and the gang, my

second equation shows that triangulation is impossible, because there can't be any true angles."

"All well and good," said Kalendorf. "But one day men will conquer the Moon. They'll build spaceships and land on it—in about A.D. 2120 or so—and then your second equation won't matter a damn."

Porteus laughed. "But don't you see, man? All their spaceships and all their calculations will simply be distorted by the demands of space! They may appear to travel a quarter of a million miles—in reality they will go a few feet!"

"An interesting theory, doctor. Let's ask my assistant, Bowler, what he thinks of it. Bowler? That's odd, he was here a minute ago."

"Maybe," suggested the physicist with a smile, "he simply walked off the edge of the universe and vanished."

They strolled outside and gazed up at the full moon. Kalendorf lit his pipe. "Hmm. Distance not existing. A tempting theory, Porteus. But how would you go about proving it?"

"Like this!" The physicist reached up and plucked the full moon from the sky.

"Good heavens!"

"Ha ha ha—maybe now you'll stop scoffing at my 'crazy' ideas, eh, Kalendorf? Ha ha ha!" Laughing strangely, he began to flip the Moon in the air, asking for "heads or tails."

Then he threw it to the unprepared Kalendorf. It slipped through his fingers and vanished from view in the sand.

The astronomer was horrified. "Good heavens, what have you done?"

"Never mind." Porteus took a sixpence from his pocket and pasted it among the stars. "You chaps will be quite as happy exploring this, come A.D. 2120."

Just then Bowler trudged up, out of breath. "You wouldn't believe where I've been," he said. "I fell off——"

"Yes, so Dr. Porteus has been telling me. He's just been demonstrating that space is not spatially—er—as roomy as we had thought. You know what this means to your professional standing, Bowler, if such a theory becomes generally known?"

The assistant nodded. Without a further word, the two fell upon their scientific colleague and strangled him.

"We'll bury the body in the desert, Bowler."

"I've a better idea, sir. Let me throw it off the edge of the universe."

"Good thinking. While you're gone, I'll search his hotel room and burn any notes. We must hide all traces of this terrible secret—forever!"

Forever? No, only until a desert urchin tries to spend the strange "coin" he finds . . . only until a numismatic expert gets a good look at the Sixpence . . . and even now a waiter is studying the equations on the tablecloth, murmuring to himself:

"Then triangles *are* impossible, after all . . . hmm . . ."

Solar Shoe-Salesman

by Chipdip K. Kill

I

Stan Houseman, shoe-salesman, punched a cupee of Kaff from the kitchen and scanned the footlines of his morning newsper:

OLYMPIC FINALS AT CARMODY STADIUM

POLICE BREAK UP HATTONITE RIOT

The stock market report listed only two corporations—the two which had between them divided the world—North American Boot & Shoe (Nabs) and Eurasian Footwear. Nabs was up two points, Eurafoot down the same, inevitably. In this two-person, zero-sum game, one side could only profit at the expense of the other. *Like Karen and me,* he thought grimly.

The corner of his eye caught movement—the racing figure of an autistic child. When he looked right at it, it was gone.

Karen came into the kitchen.

"Let's not start anything, for God's sake," he said.

"I'm getting a divorce, Stan. I'm seeing the lawster this afternoon."

Suddenly the coffee-substitute tasted very bitter.

II

Ed Pagon gazed into the camera face of "Me," the robot interviewer for KHBT-TV. "Somehow I feel this is more than just a game I'm playing here today," he said. "I think a lot more is at stake here today than the Olympics jacks championship."

"Tell me, Ed," said the robot, "how does it feel, being the only male contestant in this jacks tournament?"

How do you think it feels? Like being castrated, he thought. Forcing a smile, he replied, "Frankly, I've always thought of jacks as a man's game, Mel. It's an art as well as a sport, and men traditionally excel in the arts . . ."

When the interview was over, Ed went into his dressing-room to warm up. He seated himself on the floor with the regulation red rubber ball and steel jacks, and tried to empty his mind for Zen exercises. The idea was to pick up jacks without picking them up mentally.

Onesies without thinking about it. Twosies without thinking about it. Threesies . . .

Ed felt sudden pain, a band of it, squeezing his guts. Pain blurred his vision as he looked down at the jack on the floor. This was no jack. It was a tiny metal man with his arms outstretched, fastened by magnets to a steel cross.

III

Joe Feegle stopped Stan Houseman outside the sales cubicle. "The word is, we're on the brink of war, Stan. The two company presidents are having a summit meeting this afternoon—they'll be playing one round of The Game —and if they tie, we'll have war."

"But they always tie."

"Right. Hey, look!"

Both men turned to stare at a figure at the other end of the corridor, a figure in the official gold-and-black uniform of an Armorer. President Moniter was calling in an Armorer to design new weapons for the company—a bad omen.

Another was the unrest caused, or exploited, by the barefoot fanatic sect who called themselves the Hattonites. As Stan unlocked his cubicle and prepared for work, he thought of Herkimer Hatton's strange and fascinating cult.

Little was known of the late Herkimer Hatton himself, except that he'd lived twenty years before, and had been accident-prone in the extreme. In a series of over a thousand small accidents, Hatton had lost limbs and other bits and pieces of his body, and replaced them with synthetics.

Finally he was (except to his followers) an android. Legend had it that he'd finished up on an iron cross, and that he would return when the world needed him.

And now the world needed something, and fast. Stan cleared his mind of Hatton and other worries, and turned the energy of his psychic influence upon a million potential customers. His influence spread over the city, giving a million men and women this imperceptible nudge. For some it might come as a moment of reflection: *I do need new shoes* . . . For others it might be a slight hesitation as they passed a Nabs window display. Still others would be in the stores, trying shoes on, when suddenly they'd find something . . .

IV

Ferris Moniter, president of Nabs, glimpsed what looked like an autistic child out of the corner of his eye. He bumped his head as he stepped into his private autogyro.

"Ow. Second time I've bumped my head on that door-frame."

His bodyguard, Truit, stiffened. "Yes? Don't close that door just yet, sir. I want a look at the frame." His expert fingers sought and found a tiny hairlike wire. "Just as I thought, Mr. Moniter. An animal magnet, set there to attract your head. Looks like the work of Nexus Brill."

"Eurafoot's Armorer? But assassination's against the rules!"

The bodyguard laughed. "Armorers have no rules, sir. My guess is, he meant to stun you, just before the Game. Probably had a side bet on it. They say Brill is rich from betting on the Game. Owns Paris, Rome, Antwerp, a dozen such cities. They say he's had some of them miniaturized and made into charms for his wife's charm bracelet. By the way, it might interest you to know that *our* Armorer, Amos Honks, visited the office this morning, while you were out. He may have had access to the autogyro . . ."

Ferris Moniter blinked. "You can't mean that, Truit! Why, Amos Honks is our only hope. Think of all the weaponry he's designed for us! How can you suspect him?"

Truit thought of the aerial battleship, filled with hydrogen and surrounded with heavy armor. "I know, sir—

but I can't help feeling that the two Armorers are in cahoots, somehow."

Moniter sighed. "Anyway, are there any more assassination attempts in the cards today?"

"Not *cards,* sir." Truit sounded pained. "*Tiles.* Let's have a look." He laid out the traditional tiles of the eleventh-century Chinese game of prophecy, *Mah-Jongg.* "I'm afraid it's the East Wind, sir. And the Four of Bamboos."

"Oh? Is that bad? What's the reading?"

Truit opened the book and read:

"Many small greatnesses deny.
No same.
It does not further to discover several gifts only.
The wise king avoids fried foods."

He closed the book. "Sir, I think it's dangerous to continue this trip to Chicago."

"Nonsense, Truit. I must go on. I must play and win. To give up now would mean economic collapse, the resurgence of the old, corrupt U.N., and slavery for most of the human race. The tiles must be wrong for once."

But he knew the tiles were never wrong.

V

At Carmody stadium, the robot doctorator was examining Ed Pagon after his collapse. He lay on the dressing-room floor, doubled up with pain. The robot's probes moved to check his respiration, pulse, heart, temperature . . .

"What is it, doc?" asked an official. "Appendicitis?"

The doctorator peered at him over its square-rimmed glasses. "Don't quote me on this, boys," it said, rubbing its iron chin. "But it 'pears as if this here fella is fixing to have a baby!"

VI

Amos Honks, Armorer, awoke to a sense of danger. Karen Houseman was still asleep beside him.

He remembered the whole nightmarish episode at Nabs: Ferris Moniter telling him to arm the corporation for AOW, All-Out War. Ferris Moniter telling him he'd have to do better than hay-fever bombs, better even than *Herpes simplex,* the cold-sore virus, dropped in drinking water supplies.

"You'll have to do a lot better," Moniter had said. "Don't forget, you're up against Nexus Brill . . . by the way, did you know your wife's been seen with Brill?"

And later, she couldn't deny it. The world had come to a sickening halt then, this afternoon at the lawster's office, when they obtained their punched card decree. There he'd met Karen Houseman, and the two new divorced people had just naturally clung together . . . so here he was, still sensing danger like a smell of fear.

Outside he could hear the sound of muffled rotors—a police gyro trying to land quietly in the yard. He sensed, rather than heard, the faceless lawman creeping toward the house, the sound of a weapon being eased from its plastic holster and aimed through the wall at his brainwaves . . . the trigger being squeezed . . .

Amos rolled across the bed and hit the floor just as the humming green beam of a stupidifier flicked through the wall. It caught Karen and she slumped sideways, babbling and drooling.

Before the cop could fire again, Amos snatched a charm off his wife's charm bracelet, flung open the door and pitched it into the yard. It was a miniaturized city. He counted to ten and breathed, "Goodbye, Paris."

With a thunder of cobblestones, the minicity sprang to full size in the yard. He heard the cop's scream, cut off by a shriek of tires and the blare of a taxi horn.

Amos smashed a window, gashing his arm, and raced across the Place de la Bastille to the empty police auto-gyro. He climbed in, took off and headed for Chicago. There had to be some way to stop the Game—before the Game stopped everything else.

If only he could design some weapon Nexus Brill could not counter. He played the stream of ideas across the porcelain surfaces of his mind:

How about mad dogs? A nullitron beam? Unconscious mines? Fire-cabbages . . . even an Earth-mover, which could shift the entire planet during an aerial battle, thus leaving enemy aircraft stranded in outer space.

Why was it Nexus Brill always had his ideas first? As he wondered, the aura began. The perimeter of his vision was filled with autistic children; his ears jangled with flashing lightmares, and he felt the deep molecular and genetic shift begin.

He was, as usual, turning into Nexus Brill.

VII

The autistic child pointed to a picture of Stan House-man and said, "Nice mans."

The Hattonite elders looked at one another. Why 'mans'? Could Houseman be, after all, the discalced prophet promised by Herkimer Hatton?

VIII

The data-scan footline flickered upon the instrument panel of the autogyro:

LABORS OF HERCULES?
Athlete to give birth!

"I don't understand that, said Ferris Moniter, looking away to the still blue waters of the Americ Ocean. An hour remained before they reached the finger-shaped Isle of Michigan, with Chicago glittering at its tip like a bright hangnail. Far to the east lay the dark continent of Atlantica, broken only by the British Lakes; beyond that, the Europic Sea.

"In this novel I'm reading," he said, taking the foilback from his pockette, "the author pretends that Lucifer *lost* his war against Heaven, so that all the world is reversed, see?"

Truit, his bodyguard, laughed. "Science fiction, eh? Don't believe everything you see in white on black. What's the name of this book?"

"Autogyro Ace," said the president. "An Autogyro Novel, by Killhip D. Pick."

At that moment a dot appeared above the horizon, far behind them. It grew rapidly to another autogyro.

"Who is it, Truit?"

"Too far to see, sir. Might be friendly . . ." The body-guard trained his electric binoculars on the strange craft, then gasped. "No! It can't be!"

In a moment the stranger was close enough for Moniter to see, too. *The other autogyro contained another Ferris Moniter and another Truit.* As he watched, it came closer, passed through his own craft and sped on toward Chicago.

IX

The president of Eurafoot sat in shadow behind the Game table, a masked entity without a name.

"Sit you down, Mr. Moniter," said a disembodied voice. "You know the rules of the Game." When Truit had checked the seat for bombs and virus, Moniter took his place. An aide brought in a pad of paper and ruled the traditional four lines on its top sheet: Two horizontal, two vertical.

"You may go first, Mr. Moniter. You have 'X,' and the advantage—for the moment."

From the next room came gunshots and electric fizzling, as Eurafoot's androids joined with Nab's cyborgs to fight off Hattonite assassins.

As Moniter started to make his move, his opponent leaned forward, bringing his face into the light.

"You!"

X

Joe Feegle wrote, "It was a two-person, zero-sum game. Stan Houseman had established that general strict determinateness held in all cases of special strict determinateness, and in other cases as well, but he had not excluded the possibility that the advance from special to general determinateness was no advance at all! Then he himself was an android, too!"

Joe was working on his novel, ANDROGYNOID, written under the pseudonym "H. K. (Kid) Cliplip." Joe suffered from the delusion that he himself was written, under a pseudonym.

XI

"You see," said the president of Eurafoot, "when Nexus Brill broke that window, he cut himself. He is now infected with a virus that will scourge our planet. It causes the feet to rot off, heh heh."

"I think Amos Honks will have something to say about that," said a voice from the dark doorway.

"The autistic child!"

"Wrong," said Stan Houseman. He fired the demoralizer beam once, and the odd president flopped, spineless, to the floor. It was the end of the universe, all agreed.

XII

Nexus Brill saw the great ruled line coming across the sky. He speeded up the autogyro and tried to take evasive action, but it was no use. The ruled line reached him and cut him, along with the earth and sky, clean in two.

XIV

"So it was Ed Pagon who gave birth to the new universe, eh?"

"Right. There weren't really any sides, since each company owned all the stock of the other, anyway. And since both were really owned by the Hattonites . . ."

"Then everyone was an android, really."

"Brill must have suspected as much. When he cut himself on that window, he failed to bleed."

He shook his head. "Brill *was* human, though bloodless."

She smiled. "Then . . . it's all over?"

"In a sense."

So saying, Stan and Karen Houseman walked barefoot with the other pilgrims, into the former shoestore.

One Damned Thing
After Another

A Co-ordainer's Myth

Floogy Flarl was a wipeout man
Cashed his cogs, that wipeout man
Nobody knew how it all began
But Floogy Flarl

The Co-ordainer's name was Hampton Syzygy of the planet Chicago, and he longed to go home. Even though he had to travel far beyond the Astcroid River of Mkaj, far beyond the Gaderene Galaxies and even to the edge of Edgeitself itself, his heart was turning ever homeward, toward the old Folkstad Ohm. But when his heart turned toward Folkstad Ohm it was full of bitterness and revenge, for Ohm was the ancient Lord of the Facility who had inherited Chicago, inherited it by killing former owner, the tyrant Stulk Hermanø. Ohm had ended Hermanø's reign of blood only to begin his own. There was a song about this, too:

Stulk was wrong, but he wronged the wrong
While Folkstad wronged the right.

Hampton would soon do something about Folkstad Ohm, just as he would later undergo seven trials on the seven planets of Smurr. He would do these things that the adventure books might be filled with stories. But the adventure books came later, and Hampton Syzygy knew

212

nothing of them, for he lived in the present. There was a song about this, too, but now is not for songs, but stories. And of all stories, the most strange and wonderful is the story of how Hampton Syzygy came home to Chicago, and why.

Hampton came back to Chicago by way of an other-folk planet, Marvin Jarvis. The people of Marvin Jarvis were all otherfolk, created from animals to serve the human race and the Lords of the Facility. Two guides met Hampton at the spaceport: a sly-looking couple named F'Red and F'Annie, with their little son, F'art.

"We're not completely human," F'Red said. "We're really cleverly mutated foxes. That is, I am a fox, and F'Annie is a vixen. I forget whether F'art is called a pup or a cub." After failing to sell Hampton a used car, the couple drifted away in the crowd of otherfolk.

There were all kinds here: B'Ernie, the beaverman who built dams; E'Laine, the elephantgirl with the phenomenal memory; P'Rick, the porcupineman, a deadly archer. Of course there were ostrichfolk hiding their heads in the sand; swanfolk who could break a human's arm with one stroke of a powerful wing; snakemen who hypnotized (though their chief victims were birdfolk); electric eelmen working at the power station and many more. Hampton strolled through the streets, nodding and smiling to animalfolk friends. B'Ill the batman was trying to entangle himself in a womanman's hair. B'Ill the bearman seemed hungry enough to eat a horseman. B'Ill the budgieman and W'Rita the wormgirl dropped their tasks and followed at Hampton's command.

It was here that Hampton met M'Arlene, who taught him subtle and peculiar ways. He would not be able to take M'Arlene with him when he left Marvin Jarvis planet. She knew that and accepted it, and yet she ached to go with him, along with W'Rita and B'Ill. But they could help Hampton Syzygy, and M'Arlene could not.

There was nothing on Chicago that a monkeywoman could do.

Before he reached Chicago, Hampton Syzygy had to spend a year being scent-cleared on the planet Kipling Glory. The police agents of Chicago were dog-robots, trained to detect the smell of any out-planet on a man, be it eleven months old. This was the only out-planet where a man could acquire a new, acceptable smell.

Kipling Glory was a skull, the skull of the ancient giant Jo-how, slaughtered, it was said, by the Montag brothers. They had made of his spine a great starship capable of "light-doubling" itself across the universe, and they had set out to find the Center of the Pattern. Living here on a giant skull reminded Hampton of what Folkstad Ohm had done to the Syzygy family, and his thoughts were cold-tinged with the feel of revenge.

The day for revenge must come, but now it was time for waiting and for watching, and for washing the dishes. Disguised in the body of an idiot dishwasher, Hampton waited and watched and worked. The dirty dishes came in to the steamy yellow kitchen. Hampton breathed upon them, reaching down inside each dish with his mind and making it *wish* to be clean, making it vibrate with the hope of cleanliness. Dish-wishing, he called it, and worked at it for eleven months and more, until it was time to throw off his disguise and come to Chicago.

On Chicago he first visited, almost without realizing where he was going, the Shrine of the Seventh Type of Ambiguity. It stood on a hill overlooking the Desert of Doris Deadlock, an old computer set in the ruins of what once had been the English department of a university, when men had studied English as a medical and legal language. This old computer had long been used by the otherfolk as an oracle.

"Why do we come to this place, O Human?" said W'Rita. "You do not believe in the power of the oracle."

"I do not disbelieve, either. Anyway, this place is sacred to my family. It was near here my father, Herman Syzygy, fought the Last Light-Swallower and killed it, and for that they made him a Protector of the Check."

W'Rita smiled, insofar as a worm can be said to smile. "That is true. What will you ask the oracle?"

But Hampton could not answer, for he would not allow himself to think of a question in advance. That way the computer's telepathic capabilities would become as nothing, and he might gain power over it.

The question he finally did ask, standing on the wind-swept bluff overlooking the Venn Diagram Lakes, was:

"What has one leg in the morning, four legs in the afternoon and three legs in the evening, and when is a door not a door?"

"Hmmm," said the old computer. "That's a toughy. Would it be Long John Silver with a three-legged parrot?"

"No."

"How about a leg of mutton magically transformed into a dog that pees on your doorstep at dusk?"

"No."

"Okay, I give. What is it?"

"A coffee table, made from a door!" Hampton explained how one began in the morning by putting one leg on, and then had all four in place by the afternoon, but one fell off in the evening. The old computer gave him a secret whereby he might ensnare the tyrant Ohm. W'Rita, the wormgirl who had been bred and created to tie packages up real pretty, now tied herself around Hampton's finger so he would not forget the secret. They descended and began to cross the Desert of Doris Deadlock.

They made the crossing at night, when the sand was cool and blue-gray, and the sagebrush silver in the moonlight. Now and then Hampton glimpsed the desert's owner, Doris herself, flitting behind a rock or bush. He knew it was truly Doris, for the moonlight gleamed on the padlock through her nose.

At dawn Hampton entered the capital city Vb and went straight to the palace of Folkstad Ohm. On the way, he explained to B'Ill the budgieman why he was needed.

"Like all budgiemen, you were bred and created to guard mirrors, and that is what you must do now. I want you to guard all mirrors at the palace against the false image of Folkstad Ohm; otherwise he may slip in among his false images and escape my revenge. Do you understand?"

"I understand and obey, O Human," said the budgieman, and seeing that the occasion was serious, he forbore adding the "Who's a pretty boy?" that was at the tip of his tongue. Hampton entered the palace the way M'Arlene had showed him, and made his way to the private chambers of the tyrant.

"I've been expecting you," said Ohm, looking up from his clairevoyance machine. Suddenly he made a dash at a mirror on the nearest wall, trying to slip into his false image, but B'Ill was there before him.

Now Folkstad Ohm turned craven. "What do you want of me, Syzygy? I can't bring your wife and children back to life, can I?"

Revenge clouded Hampton's mind, as he raised a death-weapon to spill the tyrant's blood. Ohm had done a terrible thing to Mrs. Syzygy and the children, by changing their spaceness. Hampton's wife had been shrunk to the size of a dust mote, and battered to death by the Brownian motion in a sunbeam. The oldest of his two children had been made to swell to such a size that gravity collapsed his bones. He was now the Ricky Syzygy mountain range. Little Lydia, the baby, had been neither shrunk nor grown, but made so heavy that she sank to the molten center of the planet and became one with it. Hampton thought of her every time he felt the tug of gravity. Revenge clouded his mind and he raised his weapon.

But then he saw W'Rita tied to his finger, and remembered the secret of the old computer. Reaching down inside the future, Hampton made some adjustments. This event became contingent upon that and the other, while another event vanished for good. As he worked, he spoke to Folkstad Ohm.

"Whatever you hurt, you will be. Whatever you hate will be you. All your daggers backwards turn. O-U-T spells out goes he, with a dirty dishrag on his knee."

Disbelieving in the spell, Ohm tried kicking a passing dog. In the instant before it felt the crushing pain of his iron boot against its ribs, the dog and Ohm exchanged consciousness. As a dog, he felt the ribs crack, and hot electric pain shot through him. He tried to bite the tyrant leg, and found himself back in his own body to be savaged by a pain-crazed animal. The sentence was eternal, and just.

Hampton Syzygy returned to his own home, where he lived in peace for many years, until he fell asleep and went to hunt with his ancestors. But high above the Venn Diagram Lakes, the old computer still chuckled to himself, for the sixty or seventy millionth time:

"A coffee table! Well I'll be damned!"

The Sublimation World

by J. G. B——

CHAPTER I: THE ETERNAL GROCER

Price looked across the lagoon, a dry sweep of land, at the mirage. The lagoon was sublimating, turning from liquid ice directly into crystalline air, and through its wavering layers he could make out a Giacometti statue that was probably one of King's men, grown thin. Fronds of zygote enwrapped the old supermarket now, smothering it in lianas and spermaceti, turning it into a fairly good Jackson Pollock painting, the one he always dreamed about. This, too, had a dreamlike mist about it, as did King's man, turning and turning, driven by a wind of solidity. Pterodactyls honked overhead.

CHAPTER II: THE HARPIES' BAZAAR

It had become more than a month between Price's visits to the kayak. Mona lay back in the kayak in her yellow empire gown, trailing one lavender glove in the water. Pterodactyls watched as she combed and brushed out her hair, using for a mirror a smoothed slab of the atmosphere. Price felt suddenly very tired—but then he had always been suddenly tired. He wanted to give it all up, to sublimate awhile with the world around him, to rise beating leathern wings into the hot purple sunset. But this could not be, not for the moment. He still felt a peculiar loyalty to the human species. There was still the scurvy to be cleared up, the report to write, the generator to be fixed. He lit his pipe and frowned through its azure smoke at King's elephant. It was marching about in a circle, waving a black flag.

CHAPTER III: MIRROR OF XANADU

He would write to the government, he thought, coming out of the dream. It was always the same—a hollow, hot, heavy jungle tree, bright green, growing right in the middle of a frozen desert amid yellow orange flames and bearing seven blue grapes. He picked them, one at a time, and crushed them between his toes. The juice ran like blood into the parched flank of earth. But the last grape he reserved, to crush against the roof of his mouth like a spy's poison capsule, before he died. In the dream he never died.

CHAPTER IV: DESERT OF GAS

Man has caused the sublimation. For years, decades, man had poured black, oily fumes into the atmosphere. Some of these fumes descended as solids, to soak into the earth once more, to polarize its proteins. Other matter had risen, faster during the warm days and slower at night, until it reached the sun, altering it slowly and subtly. For over a hundred years, the sun had been getting dirty; now its purplish glow turned the sensitive proteins of earth into iodine.

Price lived in a small, abandoned Abbey, sleeping on the altar and using the decaying harmonium for a cupboard. He kept in the cupboard a few time-fragments, relics of his own past: a bead belt he'd made in scouts; a rusted mouse; a stamped, self-addressed envelope; a bottle of hair-oil that he kept despite his baldness. It was *oil*, after all, sacred chrism, and things in the Jurassic past had died to create it . . .

A shot echoed across the iodine flats. One of Mona's kites fluttered like an angry angel's wing, flickered across his vision and fell. In the distance, Joe Olifant had wrapped himself in a black mantle. He drove madly about in his chariot, his whip flickering out like the tongue of a lizard. Price could hear the frightened screams of the horses and Joe's dark, Rasputin laugh.

CHAPTER V: THE PARSEE OF THE COBRA CASINO

King had in his great circus train more food and water and treasure than he and his assassins could hope to use up. It was foolish of Price to try holding out against them. They were the cruel life-force itself. Why should he drink dew? Why cook his last tins of food over a fire of pterodactyl guana? There was finally nothing left to eat but his beaded belt and the few peanuts that King's sharp-eyed elephant might overlook.

King had parked his train in a circle, broken only where the chip of blue lake lay soundless, mirroring nightly strange rites. By the light of gas torches, the tattooed woman was charming a cobra. King lay, in his red silk mandarin pajamas, on an enameled couch, fanning himself with one of Mona's kites. He was barely visible, a slash of red among the yellow balloons, like a wound. At his feet, the pet pterodactyl was busy, methodically ripping apart a peacock.

CHAPTER VI: AN OZYMANDIAN TANGRAM

There was no water anywhere. All the water had grown heavy and sunk out of sight beneath the earth, which was slowly turning to dry ice. At last Price hitched up the remains of his belt—so emaciated was he become that, though he had eaten half of it, the belt still fit him—and struck out for the purple flats. *I must look like a Giacometti,* he thought. The silver flats turned azure-gray at noon, while the heated air became dank and brown. He looked back and saw the galloping skeleton of the elephant, the howda swaying. King, or the ghost of King, was pursuing him, a ghost. They couldn't let him go off and die alone. They wanted to punish him for turning his back on them, for refusing, like some inverse Toby Tyler, to join their circus.

The elephant was dissolving, and King, sinking slowly

to the ground, was falling behind. He took up the electric megaphone and shouted: "Come back, Price. We need you at camp. Don't be a bloody fool, man!"

CHAPTER VII: THE BLOODY FOOL

He came upon the dead city at dusk. For awhile he was apprehensive that King might pursue him here, too, using the circus train. Then he saw that the railroad had long since vaporized, leaving only an ash of tracks. The station, too, was a ghost. He had reached the end of the line, the terminal terminal. The whole city was a gibbous dune, once a mercury refinery, now frozen into a single gaseous crystalline chrysalid, depended from what was once a flaming bloodfruit tree, now gone to iron, ironically.

The tree reminded him of something. He took out the blue grape to eat and found that it, too, was diminished, worn away by the invisible though solid wind that moved from past to future.

Fantasy Novels *from* POCKET BOOKS